WILL KEDRIGERN LEAVE THE DAMSELS SPELLBOUND?

Clearing his throat, he said, "Forgive my intrusion, toad, but are you weeping?"

"Yes, I am," came a tiny voice in reply. "And who would not weep at such a fate as mine? Oh, misery!"

"Come, now . . . is it really so bad being a toad?"

"It is when one was once the most beautiful princess in all the land," came the indignant reply.

"Oh, dear. Yes, in that case, I imagine it is. I'm terribly sorry, toad."

"Princess," the little voice corrected him.

"Yes, of course, Princess. My apologies."

"No need to apologize, good sir. Your sympathy does you credit. Alas, I need more than sympathy to escape my plight. I am the victim of wicked enchantment."

"Well, now, I may be able to help you, Princess. I don't suppose a kiss from me would do much good, but I know a reasonably handsome prince and he owes me a favor . . ."

JOHN MORRESSY
A VOICE FOR PRINCESS

ACE FANTASY BOOKS
NEW YORK

Portions of this book have appeared, in somewhat different
form, in *The Magazine of Fantasy and Science Fiction*.

This book is an Ace Fantasy
original edition, and has
never been previously published.

A VOICE FOR PRINCESS

An Ace Fantasy Book/published by arrangement with
the author

PRINTING HISTORY
Ace Fantasy edition/December 1986

ISBN: 0-441-84800-1

Ace Fantasy Books are published by The Berkley Publishing Group,
200 Madison Avenue, New York, New York 10016.
PRINTED IN THE UNITED STATES OF AMERICA

For James Oliver Brown

"...Mend your speech a little,
Lest it may mar your fortunes."

—SHAKESPEARE

⋯⋮ *One* ⋮⋯

a matter of principle

THE MEETING WENT on and on and on. And on. Everyone, it seemed, had a report to deliver, and was determined to deliver it in the lengthiest and most tedious manner possible.

Kedrigern heaved a desolate sigh, unfolded his arms, folded them again, shifted his weary bottom, and gazed forlornly out the small window at the glorious midsummer scene. Out there was where a man belonged on a morning like this. He should be smelling the flowers, counting the clouds, working small, helpful spells for jolly peasants—not sitting through a dismal business meeting. But here he sat, feeling as if he had been imprisoned in this room since the dawn of time, like a bubble in a stone.

Hithernils, treasurer of the guild, paused and put down the ledger from which he had been reciting dreary strings of figures. Kedrigern leaned forward. Deliverance at last, he thought. But his hopes were dashed when Hithernils took up another ledger, cleared his throat, and began a new litany of expenditures, or collections, or projections, or some such foolery.

Kedrigern made a soft throaty noise somewhere between a groan and a growl and abandoned his efforts at attention. This was all nonsense, he told himself, and he was foolish to go along with it. The very idea of a wizard's guild was preposterous. Wizards were solitary workers, like spiders. An occasional get-together for purely social purposes was very nice, but formal organization, and such things as officers, and meetings, and by-laws, and dues, and passwords, and secret handshakes, and lofty titles, were simply ridiculous. One would think that the disastrous example of the Brotherhood of Hermits would have taught people a lesson.

He blamed the alchemists for this notion of organizing. It was automatic with Kedrigern to blame the alchemists for anything that went wrong, even the weather, but in this case he had good cause.

Alchemy was fairly new to Kedrigern's part of the world, and it had caught on quickly. It was especially popular with the young, for reasons Kedrigern could only brood about with increasing disgust. Perhaps the attraction lay in the pompous titles, and the jargon, and the gaudy regalia, and the endless round of windy self-celebrating meetings, conferences, and workshops that filled the alchemical calendar; they were the sort of thing to appeal to infantile minds of all ages. And, too, alchemists were quick to speak of the immediate and lucrative employment opportunities in their field. No long, slow, rewarding struggle for them; they promised an immediate payoff, something attractive to far too many people. It took time, a lot of hard work, and a considerable risk to become a really first-class wizard. One could pick up a degree in alchemy in a few years, with no great effort, and at once haul in whopping great fees for the most egregious flimflammery.

No wonder the field attracted the worst and the dimmest, Kedrigern thought sourly. And they're welcome to them, to all the castoffs, washouts, and wimps who lack the stuff of a real wizard. He recalled Jaderal, a onetime apprentice of his, a weasely little scut who had spent his unobserved moments rooting about Kedrigern's workshop for professional secrets and whom Kedrigern had at last ejected bodily, with great pleasure, from his service. Now, there was a man born to alchemy: he was rotten to the core.

And yet the wretches were successful. Alchemists had quickly become serious competition for established practitioners of the subtle arts. Witches and wizards, warlocks and sorcerers, found old clients deserting them, fleeing to the faddish new alchemists, with their spacious laboratories and shiny equipment. It was all flash and glitter, of course. The alchemists never accomplished anything beyond a quick profit, and yet they somehow got away with it. And instead of taking direct and forceful action against the upstarts, his fellow wizards had reacted by forming a professional organization scarcely distinguishable from a typical alchemists' chapter. A craven and ultimately self-destructive reaction, he thought. Things were falling apart. It was all downhill from here.

While Kedrigern pondered the follies of his colleagues, Hithernils brought his report to an end. Amid restrained applause, Tristaver rose, smiling his bland habitual smile at everyone. Tristaver fancied himself a diplomat, an oiler of troubled waters. Kedrigern thought him too clever by half; a fair hand at shape-changing and simple straightforward love spells, but basically a shifty man. But if he was about to announce a recess, thought Kedrigern, Tristaver would be redeemed forever.

Tristaver beamed his smile at those assembled around the table and said, "My brothers and sisters, I have an announcement that I'm sure will gladden the heart of every wizard in this room. . . ."

Kedrigern smiled and hitched forward on the hard seat in anticipation of the blessed word *adjournment*.

". . . And all our absent friends, as well," Tristaver went on. Kedrigern's heart sank. No release after all. More gab.

"We have a surprise guest this morning, a professional gentleman of the highest standing in his field. While his chosen field is not our field—indeed, there has been regrettable ill feeling between our callings in recent times—we feel that the recognition of true accomplishment must take precedence over such petty rivalries . . . ," Tristaver continued.

There was a good deal more of this sort of talk, to which Kedrigern paid only marginal attention. His mind was on the import of Tristaver's babbling, not the babble itself. Surprise guest? Ill feeling between our callings? What on earth was Tris up to? And who was up to it with him? He glanced around the table; Hithernils looked smug and Tristaver looked unctuous, but there was nothing unusual in that. The others appeared to know no more than Kedrigern himself did. Conhoon scowled, Belsheer nodded sleepily, Axpad and his neighbors gazed dreamily into space, but no one looked like the bearer of a secret. It was puzzling.

The words "honorary membership" seized Kedrigern's attention, and he listened more carefully as Tristaver concluded. ". . . By the unanimous vote of the executive committee. And so, without further delay, I would like to present our special surprise guest, Professor-Doctor-Master Quintrindus, formerly of the University of Rottingen, presently Visiting Alchemist at—"

"Tris, are you crazy?" Kedrigern shouted.

"What? What?" Tristaver said, looking about in alarm. "Who said that? Who spoke?"

"I did," Kedrigern said, rising. With arms akimbo and jaw thrust forward, he looked coldly across the table at Tristaver and said, "If this is a joke, it's not funny. And if it's not a joke, then you're crazy. The whole executive committee is crazy."

"Brother Kedrigern, you're out of order," said the President.

"Me? Out of order? I'm not the one who invited an alchemist to become a member of the Wizards' Guild."

"It's entirely within our prerogative," said Tristaver primly.

"Prerogative, my foot! The man's an alchemist—a *notorious* alchemist! He's the enemy!" Kedrigern cried.

Tristaver had regained his poise. Smiling graciously on Kedrigern, he said, "But Brother Kedrigern, there's no need for Professor-Doctor-Master Quintrindus to remain our enemy. We've been having private meetings for quite some time—"

"Skulking around in back alleys," Kedrigern muttered.

"Really, Brother Kedrigern," said the President.

Tristaver ignored the interruption. "And we have discovered a very real community of interest between our disciplines. It occurred to us that if we were to cease belaboring each other and join forces, the mutual benefits would be considerable."

"Oh, I see," Kedrigern said scornfully. "We'll make them respectable, and maybe they'll send back a few of the clients they've stolen from us."

An angry murmur arose on all sides, and Kedrigern took heart. It was clear that his colleagues were as outraged by all this as he was. He turned to his fellow wizards and said, "Are we going to let—"

"Sit down, Keddie!" someone shouted.

"Yes, sit down and let's get on with the meeting," another voice said peevishly.

"Don't you realize what's going on? They want to make an alchemist a member of our guild. An *alchemist!*" cried Kedrigern, investing the term with all the loathing and revulsion he could muster.

"Quintrindus is a very influential man," said Hithernils, wagging a finger at him.

"He's a big name, Keddie," said old Belsheer gently. "Everyone knows Quintrindus."

"Everyone knows he's a fraud. They're all frauds. Alchemists don't *do* anything, they just natter on about turning lead into gold," Kedrigern said, looking from face to face. "Have you ever seen one of them do it?"

"No . . . but if they ever do, it would be good to have them on our side," Axpad pointed out.

Tristaver pounced on the remark. "Our thinking exactly, Brother Axpad! It will do us no harm to permit Quintrindus, and perhaps a few other carefully selected alchemists, to join our guild, and the benefits could be enormous. Now, if there's no further discussion . . ."

"I want a show of hands," said Kedrigern.

"Oh, really now," Hithernils sniffed, but Tristaver, smiling benignly, said, "I think we can accommodate Brother Kedrigern. Perhaps when he sees the will of the meeting, he'll decide to be more reasonable."

Kedrigern snorted.

"Will all those who support the committee's decision to admit Professor-Doctor-Master Quintrindus as an honorary member of the Wizards' Guild please raise their right hands?" Tristaver said. Hands went up all around. "Thank you, brothers and sisters. And those opposed . . . ?"

Kedrigern's hand rose in splendid solitude. Tristaver glanced around the room, chuckled, then said, "Now, perhaps Brother Kedrigern would like to withdraw his vote so we can go on record as unanimously approving of Professor-Doctor-Master Quintrindus's membership."

"I do not approve of that fraud or of any alchemist who ever lived, and I will not change my vote."

A groan arose from the assembled wizards, and Kedrigern heard several unflattering remarks. He held his tongue for a time, but then he could take no more. He glared from face to face around the table.

"Brothers and sisters, you've made your choice. You got Quintrindus, but you lost Kedrigern," he said. Turning and swirling his cloak about him with a dramatic sweep of his arm, he stalked from the room.

That evening, camped in a flowery meadow by a swift-running brook, he thought things over. He had no regrets about his resignation, and wished that he had never gotten involved with the guild in the first place. The invitation to become a charter member had appealed to his vanity and overridden his good sense.

One thing was certain: there would be no more organizations in his life. And there would be no more wandering, either. The time had come to settle down.

He had long possessed property on Silent Thunder Mountain. It was a very picturesque spot, abandoned and long unfrequented. Barbarians avoided the place because there was no one left there to kill, and nothing to steal. Alchemists, with their cravings for public attention and their greed for profit, tended to flock to the cities; and the nearest wizard was many days distant. All other people feared the ghosts known to haunt the approaches to the mountain.

Here Kedrigern would enjoy peace and solitude befitting a wizard. He would have no neighbors, no random visitors, no passers-by. He could pursue without interruption his study of counterspells and his experiments in temporal magic.

There was no question of running short of funds. He was already the best counterspell man for hundreds of leagues around, and everyone knew it. He would be semiretired, but still available for consultations—at a stiff fee. And not to alchemists, or their friends. Especially their friends in the Wizards' Guild.

Best of all, he would squander no more of his life on windy meetings, where the only thing anyone ever decided was that it was not time to make a decision unless it was a bad and stupid one. However things worked out, the only voice he would have to listen to in future was his own.

Kedrigern had never been a gregarious man, and the prospect of solitude appealed to him. If, in time, he grew lonely, there was always the possibility of seeking a wife; but he did not want to rush into marriage. The life of a wizard's wife was not for every woman. It was, in fact, for very few women. A wizard had to marry with great caution, not impetuosity. He was still young, for a wizard—little more than halfway through his second century—and still engaged in study. There would be plenty of time to think of marrying in another century or so.

He yawned and looked up from his little fire. The sky was dark now, and the night comfortably cool. He laid a simple warning spell around the perimeter of his campsite and settled down snugly under the stars. He went to sleep directly, and slept soundly until after midnight, when a low, reverberating rumble brought him awake.

There was no danger near, for the spell had not responded. What woke him was noise: a sound like a large wooden box, half-filled with stones, being tumbled end over end. It filled the air and made sleep impossible.

Kedrigern sat up, rubbing his eyes, muttering angrily, and looked about. He could see nothing. The noise seemed to come from the direction of the brook, and as he listened, Kedrigern perceived an undertone of sadness in it—as if a mountain were bemoaning some mishap. He groped inside his shirt and drew out the medallion that hung around his neck, the only useful thing he had gotten from the guild. Raising it to his eye, he peered through the tiny hole at its center, the Aperture of True Vision, and saw what was causing the commotion.

A lumpish figure stood at the edge of the stream, hunched over in a posture of desolation. It looked like an effigy made of wood and stone and dirt by inept, hasty hands which then concealed their handiwork by winding it in coarse rags. Its head was a hemisphere covered with warts and patchy hair, with a nose like a flabby conch shell protruding a good distance before it. It had no discernible chin. Under its thick arm was a bundle of rags. From its appearance Kedrigern knew that the thing was a troll; and from the pink ribbons binding up its tufted hair, he gathered that it was female.

The creature was wholly absorbed in her sorrowing. Kedrigern, with cautious step, approached to a few paces' distance and cleared his throat. When the troll did not respond, he cleared his throat again, louder, but was drowned out by a fresh lament. This time he could distinguish the words.

"Ah, woe and alas, what's to become of my darling, my dear, my beautiful one!" rolled around the meadow like the breaking of storm-driven surf against rocks.

"I beg your pardon, ma'am," Kedrigern shouted in as polite a tone as one can manage while shouting.

The troll-woman turned, slowly and ponderously, and fixed her tiny black eyes on the wizard. She stared at him for a moment, then rumbled, "And who do you be?"

"My name is Kedrigern," he replied, with a deep bow.

"Do you be Master Kedrigern, the great wizard?" she asked.

"I do. I am. Yes."

"Do you be truly able for making spells, and unmaking them if they go bad, and all?"

"Yes, I do. I can."

"Then that is good fortune to me, for I think that only a wizard can do help to me now."

A female in distress—even a female who resembled an overgrown midden—stirred Kedrigern's noblest instincts. If this poor creature needed his help she would have it.

"I am at your service, ma'am," he said, bowing once again, and adding a bit of a flourish of the hand.

"Oh, now, that do be nice," she said. "Always such a pleasure to meet a real gentleman."

"Thank you, ma'am. Now, if you'll just tell me your problem, I'll see what I can do."

"Well, it do be with my husband to start. Fine big troll he do be, name of Gnurtt. He be usually found under the Red Prince's Bridge, or thereabouts. Do you know my Gnurtt?"

"I don't believe I've ever..."

"Well, no matter. Gnurtt do be nothing but a big stone now, and no good to anyone." She paused and sniffled, and then broke out into a wail. "Oh, my darling, my pet, my beauty, what's to become of you now? Oh, cruel, cruel!"

"I beg your pardon," Kedrigern said gently. "Did you say that Gnurtt is now a stone?"

"He be that. A lovely big menhir, standing proud and alone in the middle of a field of daisies. He stayed out too late on Midsummer Night, and the sunrise caught him in the middle of his capering."

"And you'd like me to change him back?"

"Oh, no, Master Kedrigern, never that. I would not ask

you to tamper with nature. That's the way Gnurtt always hoped to go, and he do make a lovely stone. A beautiful shade of gray he do be now, with a nice rugged surface. Suits him perfectly, it do. Gnurtt never looked better."

"I see. Then do you want me to turn you into a matching menhir?"

"No need for that, though it do be kind of you to offer. Before dawn I will go up to the field where Gnurtt do stand, and wait there beside him for the sun to fall on me. And then there will be two fine big menhirs in the field, and lots of daisies around, and butterflies, and all. Lovely it will be, I'm sure."

Kedrigern nodded at the idyllic image. He waited a moment, scratched his chin, and said, "You seem to have it all worked out. I don't understand what you'd like me to do."

"Oh, it's the little fellow I do be worried for, Master Kedrigern. If you could give it a decent home . . ."

Kedrigern looked around. "What little fellow?"

She drew the bundle from under her arm and held it out for his inspection. It appeared to contain a miniature version of herself, sleeping peacefully. The troll-woman's huge lumpy face creased in a smile, and her tiny black eyes lit up with maternal pride. "Look at that, Master Kedrigern. Isn't it the dearest little thing you ever saw? Takes after my side of the family, it do," she said warmly.

"It has your nose," Kedrigern observed.

"Do you really think so?" she asked, pleased and flattered.

"Oh, absolutely."

"It do have Gnurtt's eyes, though. Gray as pebbles and so small you do hardly be able to see them."

"They certainly are tiny. And so very close together."

"And the ears. Lovely big ears."

"Lovely."

"Will you take the little fellow, then?" the troll-woman asked, placing the tiny bundle at Kedrigern's feet.

"Me?"

"No one better than a wizard for raising a troll-child proper and useful, Master Kedrigern. Ordinary folk be no good for that at all. Aside from their foolishness about wanting silly little things with big eyes and no noses at all, ordinary folk just don't last. They're all worn out and feeble of body and mind before a troll-child is half grown."

"But I'm not—"

"Your wizard, though, outlives everyone, even us trolls," she went on. "That's provided, of course, that he don't be caught in a moment of weakness with his magic down. But it's at times like those that a good strong young troll is handiest. Why, even the little fellow here, small as it is, could handle a pair of big strapping barbarians the way you'd flick pebbles with your finger."

"It could?"

"Oh, no doubt of it. And loyal, too. Your dog isn't in it for loyalty compared to a troll."

"Well, that's—"

"And better than any cat when it do come to keeping the mice away. And well behaved, too. Gentle as a breeze, most of the time, and if it do start to act up, all you have to do is slam it over the head with a good stout club, and it will understand. Raise a troll-child well, Master Kedrigern, and you do have a treasure that will last a wizard's lifetime," said the troll-woman, backing away.

"But is it housebroken?" Kedrigern cried desperately.

"That's a problem trolls don't have," she responded. Turning, she started off, calling back over her shoulder, "Now, if you'll excuse me, Master Kedrigern, I do be in a hurry to get to the field where my Gnurtt is waiting. Have to be in proper position by sunrise, you know. Wouldn't want to be caught on the way and turned into a foolish lonesome rock in the middle of the woods, no use to anyone and nobody to chat with."

As she moved off with slow, earth-shaking steps, Kedrigern called, "The name! Does it have a name?"

"Call it what you like, Master Kedrigern," she replied. "It's no matter. When the time do come, it will learn its proper name."

As the echoes of the rumbling voice faded, and the trembling of the ground subsided, Kedrigern looked down at the little figure. It was incredibly ugly. It began to wriggle, and kick away the rags that wrapped it, and the more he saw of the troll-child the more appalled he was. Mostly head, with huge hands and feet, it was warty and rough-skinned and spotty. He picked it up, gingerly, and tried to console it. It kept wriggling, and he set it down again. At once it began to crawl after its mother at great speed.

"None of that, now," Kedrigern said, grabbing it by one

stubby leg and lifting it off the ground. "Mother's going off to be turned to stone. We don't want that happening to you. First thing to do, I suppose, is find you a name. What about... how do you like Rover?" The troll-child emitted a scream that raised ripples in the brook and caused the bark to shrivel on the nearby trees. Kedrigern grimaced and quickly assured it, "All right, I won't call you Rover."

The little creature was still. Kedrigern put it down, and this time it remained at his side. "That's better," he said. He studied it thoughtfully and said, "Spot. How does that sound to you, little fellow?"

"Yah, yah!" the troll-child cried happily, and standing on tiptoe, it embraced Kedrigern's calf in a bruising grip and placed a noisy kiss on the wizard's knee.

Kedrigern, who had never had a troll of his own before, was touched by the gesture. He had a natural sympathy for abandoned children—even troll-children—anyway, and this one was turning out better than he had expected. "That's a good troll, Spot," he said, taking the creature up in one hand and its fallen rags in the other. "Now I have to get you all covered up before sunrise, or you'll turn into stone. We don't want that, do we?"

"Yah."

"Of course not. And once you're wrapped up, you're to stay wrapped, do you hear? No peeking."

"Yah."

"Good."

Once covered up, Spot went immediately to sleep. The creature was proving no trouble so far, but like all trolls it was rather heavy. That morning they covered scarcely a mile before Kedrigern was arm-weary. He stopped and arranged a sling that would enable him to carry Spot at his back, cushioned by his own small traveling pack, and proceeded much more comfortably.

They emerged from the forest and crossed the empty plain. Barbarians had passed this way not long ago, and laid waste all in their path. Farmsteads and hamlets were reduced to charred and tumbled ruins. Fields were trampled into muck. All the young trees had been hacked down, and the older ones turned into gallows for those who had not fled.

"These are bad times, Spot, and they seem to be getting worse. Between the barbarians and the alchemists..." Kedrigern shook his head ruefully.

"Yah," came in a faint muffled voice from behind him.

"It'll be nice on Silent Thunder Mountain, though. You'll see. Lots of sun and fresh air . . . room for you to run . . . I'll work a spell so you can stay out in the sunlight. You can plant a garden."

"Yah!" once again, sleepy but happy.

They traveled on, and came at last to the ruined, blasted tower where Kedrigern lived and worked. In the fading twilight it looked comfortably ominous, and he put down his burden with a sigh of relief. It was good to be home.

He unlocked the spell that held the tower secure against intruders, entered, and reset the spell. One could not be too careful these days.

What was a ruined tower when seen from the outside was a cozy, if somewhat cluttered, wizard's workshop inside. Kedrigern lit a fire in the big stone fireplace, and the flames quickly rose to illuminate the interior. An unmade cot stood near the hearth. A large and very messy work table occupied much of the central space. The walls were covered with shelves. About half the shelf space was taken up by books, the rest by various accouterments of the wizard's profession, some of them nasty to behold, some unrecognizable as anything in particular.

Kedrigern leaned forward and placed his palms on the table in a proprietary gesture. He lifted them at once and began brushing them together to remove the dust. It was amazing how quickly dust accumulated. The brazen head that served as his filing system was very much in need of a good dusting, but he decided to put it off until tomorrow, when he could start breaking in Spot. As he stood in thought, a large black spider with a hairy body about the size of an apple dropped silently from the rafters and dangled before his face.

"Hello, Manny," the wizard said, reaching out to scratch the spider's belly. "I trust you've looked after things in my absence."

The spider waved its two forelegs gaily in reassurance. Its jeweled eyes twinkled in the firelight.

"I have good news, Manny," Kedrigern announced. "I'm going to follow your example and build a house of my own."

Manny stopped waving. He dropped a bit lower and pendulated slowly before the wizard, observing him cautiously.

"You're welcome to come along, Manny. I'm going to put

in lots of lovely dark corners. There'll be plenty of places to build, and lots to eat."

As Manny drew himself up into the rafters, presumably to mull over the projected move, Kedrigern straightened, brushed the last traces of dust from his hands, and turned to where Spot sat. The little troll was yawning and rubbing its tiny eyes with huge clumsy hands. Blinking, it stood and looked around the chamber.

"Yah?" it asked softly.

"We'll be here for a little while, Spot. I have to pack everything for the move, and then summon up a poltergeist to do the actual moving. That's always a tricky business."

"Yah?"

"Well, if you don't work the spell exactly right, everything gets thrown about and smashed to bits. No need to think of that at the moment, though. Right now, I'd like a snack and a good night's sleep. Are you hungry, Spot?"

"Yah!"

"What do you generally eat?"

Spot glanced about, then darted off with astonishing speed into a dark corner beside the fireplace. It returned to Kedrigern bearing a limp rat in each hand.

"Oh," said the wizard, swallowing loudly. "I think it would be best if you took your meals outside, then. Keep close to the tower, and mind you're inside before sunrise."

"Yah!" cried Spot, careening off.

Kedrigern fixed himself a simple collation and stretched out on his cot with a sigh of sheer bliss. No more Wizards' Guild. No more torpid meetings. One last journey, to Silent Thunder Mountain, and then no more traveling. Time to study, to learn new spells and polish up the old ones. If anyone wanted his services, they could just come to Silent Thunder Mountain and ask. If they could find their way to his house, and if he felt like helping, he would. And if he didn't, he wouldn't, and they could go find another wizard, who wouldn't be half as good.

He adjusted the protective spell to permit Spot's re-entry, then drifted off to sleep, wearied by his long journey, and enjoyed pleasant dreams. An odd, constricted sensation came over him, and his dreaming grew uneasy. He dreamed of an insect hovering near, a nasty snickering thing with a pinched human face, and raised a hand to brush it away. The hand hit something cold and hard and sharp, and Kedrigern came wide awake on the instant.

He froze. A hairy, dirty, emotionless face looked down on him and a large sword was poised less than a finger's breadth above his chest. The reek of stale sweat, blood, smoke, and rancid grease assailed his nostrils. A barbarian was here, in his sanctuary, standing over his very cot.

This was impossible. A nightmare. No barbarian could penetrate the spell that guarded this tower. Kedrigern closed his eyes tight, then looked again. The barbarian was still there, looking and smelling as barbaric as ever. Impossible it might be, but it was very real.

Another figure appeared at the opposite side of the cot. Kedrigern did not recognize him at first in the dim light, but when he heard soft, rasping laughter, he knew.

"I penetrated your spell, Master Kedrigern. Remember me? Remember Jaderal, whom you once threw bodily out of this tower?"

"I—"

"Don't try to speak or move!" Jaderal cried. "I know the spells you can work with a single word. If you try anything, Krogg will kill you. Just be still, and listen to me. You said I'd never be a wizard. You were right, for a time. No wizard would receive me once you cast me out. But the alchemists welcomed me, and took me in, and taught me. I'm an alchemist now, but I never forsook my wizardly studies, and now I'm about to become more powerful than any of you. I'm going to learn all your counterspells." Jaderal laughed again, a low unpleasant rasp of sound. "Everyone knows that Master Kedrigern is the great authority on counterspells. But soon Jaderal will be the authority, and no one will be safe behind a spell if I choose to undo it. With Krogg and his band to attend to the necessary physical details, I will rule all the land one day. And I will rule with a heavy hand, I promise you. They will all pay dearly for neglecting me."

"Kill wizard now?" said the barbarian.

"Not yet, Krogg. We want the master to answer a question or two." Jaderal laughed once more, and bent to say confidentially, "If Krogg asks a question, you will answer, Master Kedrigern. Krogg knows tricks that would make a statue talk."

"Wizard talk, he try make spell. Kill wizard now," said Krogg.

Jaderal paused in his gloating to stare thoughtfully at the shaggy swordsman. His gaze flickered from Krogg to Kedrigern, lingered on the wizard, and returned to the barbarian. "You may be right, Krogg," he said. "Perhaps it would be wiser to—"

Suddenly Krogg jerked upward, as if he had grown a foot taller in an instant. He gave a startled grunt, and then he flew across the chamber to slam full force into the stone chimney with a noise like a felled ox landing on a bundle of dry twigs. He adhered to the stone for a moment, then slowly peeled off and dropped to the floor.

With a word and a gesture, Kedrigern froze Jaderal into immobility. It was only a short-term spell, but sufficient for his purposes. The first thing he had to do was find out who, or what, had so effectively removed Krogg from the picture. As he glanced about the chamber, Spot hopped onto the cot and bounced merrily up and down.

"Yah! Yah!" it cried triumphantly.

"You?"

"Yah!"

"Well, I thank you, Spot. Very good work."

"Yah," said the little troll proudly.

"Now we'll see what remains to be done," Kedrigern said, turning to Jaderal. "I'm going to let you speak so you can answer my questions. If you try any tricks, of any kind, I'll turn you into a fly. A nice fat sluggish fly," he said, and as he spoke, Manny descended and hung by his shoulder, hopeful. Jaderal's eyes glazed with terror.

"How many men are with Krogg?" Kedrigern demanded.

"Eight."

"Anyone else out there?"

"Twenty-two captives. A wagon to hold supplies and loot. Nothing more, I swear," Jaderal said.

Kedrigern nodded and scratched his chin reflectively. He laid a hand on Spot's warty head and asked, "Do you think you could handle eight more?"

The troll's tiny eyes grew round. "Yah," it said in a chastened voice.

"It's all right, Spot. I was just asking. There's no sense

using magic to do what one can have done with muscle." He
thought for a time, then asked, "Could you free the prisoners
without making any noise, or letting the barbarians know?"

"Yah!" Spot cried happily, bouncing on the cot.

"Then do it. We can leave the rest to——"

A prolonged scream of pain came from outside, followed
by a chorus of hard laughter. Voices muttered low, and someone shouted angrily. Another agonized outcry followed.

"What are they doing?" Kedrigern demanded of Jaderal.

"They're only playing. It wasn't my idea. That's how they
treat prisoners," Jaderal whined.

Kedrigern glared at him murderously. A scream cut
through the night, and he turned and strode outside.

Two of the barbarians were feeding a fire, while two more
held a slumping figure whose ragged clothes were smoking.
The other barbarians were sprawled nearby, watching, while
the prisoners huddled by the wagon.

Kedrigern cried out in an unfamiliar tongue and raised his
hands high. The barbarians were alert in an instant, and as
they turned to face him, their swords drawn and ready, he
leveled his hands at them and spoke a guttural phrase. There
was a flash of green light, and eight shaggy mongrels stood
stunned before him. Kedrigern stooped, took up a heavy stick,
and sailed into the pack, flailing to his left and right with
pleasure and great vigor. Yelping and howling, the dogs took
to flight.

As he stood looking after the last of them, he saw Jaderal,
the spell worn off, slip from the tower and skulk off after the
barbarian dogs. Kedrigern pointed and spoke the phrase of
transformation, and a bony yellow cur went yapping after the
rest of the pack.

The captives were dumbstruck by their sudden reversal of
fortune. They looked on in terrified silence as Spot snapped
their chains, and submitted meekly to Kedrigern's ministrations. Only when they had been fed and had their injuries
cleaned and bandaged, and looked upon the abandoned
weapons of their captors, and seen the mushy remains of
Krogg, did they fully realize what had befallen. And then they
began a great outpouring of thanks and praise.

Kedrigern accepted it all very humbly and graciously, and
insisted on sharing the credit for their liberation equally with

Spot. Several of the freed prisoners timidly patted Spot on the head, but most of them preferred to address their gratitude to the wizard.

"There's no way to thank you proper, Master Kedrigern, and that's the plain truth," said their spokesman, a burly, neckless, bald-headed man named Mat. "You saved us all from a terrible fate, you did, surely."

"I'm happy to be of service, Mat. Decent folk have to help one another out whenever they can," said Kedrigern, smiling placidly.

"True enough, Master Kedrigern, but all the same we'd like to repay you. Not that we're wealthy men, but we're none of us beggars, either. We're honest working men, and good at our work, every one of us."

Kedrigern waved off these protestations with a good-natured smile. "I did what any true wizard would have done. No need to talk of rewards."

"Must be *some* way we could show our appreciation, Master," said one of the others.

"Just knowing that you're back at your honest toil is sufficient reward. What exactly do you do?"

"Myself, I'm a stonemason," said Mat. "Tib and Burt and Gully are carpenters. Ham and Vill are thatchers, best in these parts. Most of the others are good all-around handymen. They can fell trees for lumber, and dress stone, and dig a good well or a foundation; anything that needs doing in the building line. And Robey's a kind of architect. He hasn't built anything yet, but he has some grand ideas."

Kedrigern listened thoughtfully. In the first glow of false dawn he could see the silhouette of the wagon and the two shaggy ponies. It occurred to him that the wagon was just the right size to hold his household goods. And horses, though slower than poltergeists, were much more dependable.

"So like I say, Master Kedrigern," Mat went on, "we're not rich men, but we want to show our gratitude."

"I'm deeply touched, Mat. But of course a wizard could never accept money for doing what I've done."

Mat frowned in perplexity and rubbed his shiny pate. "Is there nothing we can do then, Master Kedrigern?" he asked plaintively. "Some service, maybe . . .?"

"No, I'm afraid . . . well, wait a minute, now. There may

be something," said the wizard slowly. He reflected for a moment, then shook his head. "No. No, I'm afraid it's too much to ask."

"Too much? You've saved our lives. Just say what you'd like us to do, Master Kedrigern."

"Are you sure?"

"We'd consider it an honor," Mat replied, and all around him, the men nodded their heads in agreement.

"In that case . . . do you and your men know the way to Silent Thunder Mountain? I have some land there, and I've been hoping to build a little place. Nothing elaborate, you understand, just a workshop and a kitchen, and a spare room or two, and some good storage space, and a terrace where I can sit in the sun, and plenty of fireplaces, and good chimneys that don't smoke up the rooms," Kedrigern said, putting his arm amicably around Mat's burly shoulder. "Perhaps we should talk to Robey. He could do a few sketches, just rough ideas for us to discuss. And did you say that one of the men was a gardener? I'd love to have a nice herb garden, and a place to grow fresh vegetables."

"Well, I think maybe Goff knows a bit—"

"Good. That's fine. We'll talk to him, too. And while we're doing that, the others can be loading my household goods. No sense hanging about wasting time," said Kedrigern, steering Mat to where the others sat. "I had planned on doing all this myself, with magic, but since it means so much to you I've decided to put the whole thing in your hands."

"The whole thing," Mat repeated in a subdued voice.

"Oh, and a breakfast nook. I've always wanted a nice sunny breakfast nook. And shelf space. Lots of shelf space."

"Shelf space," Mat repeated dazedly.

"No such thing as too much shelf space for a wizard. And if one of the men is a glass blower," said Kedrigern enthusiastically, "well, that would be altogether too . . . but we can talk about all that later. This was a wonderful idea, Mat. I do appreciate it."

Mat nodded slowly. The rest of the men looked at him and at one another, and one murmured, "It's an honor, Master Kedrigern."

"You're too kind, really," said the wizard. "I thank you. Spot thanks you." He rubbed his hands together briskly and added, "And now let's get moving."

···⟡ *Two* ⟡···

the wizard's home companions

MAT AND HIS men were speedy, skillful workers. Their speed was whetted by eagerness to complete the job and return to their homes, and their skill was such that even haste could not diminish the quality of their work. Kedrigern, feeling pangs of conscience, assisted them with spells for the heavy work and the small finishing touches, and refrained from anything that might be construed as criticism. Before the summer was out, a neat little cottage stood overlooking the great meadow halfway up Silent Thunder Mountain, facing south, out over the valley.

Off to the east rose the mountain's peak, gleaming white. Behind the house, and curving around to the west, was an arbor of shade trees dominated by an aged oak. Sunlight flooded the dooryard, where greens flourished in the kitchen garden, and a sheltered terrace provided an ideal site for afternoon naps in all but the most extreme weathers. Kedrigern stood at the far slope of the meadow, gazing up fondly at the house, hands clasped behind him, immensely pleased with everything. Mat was at his side.

"It's splendid, Mat. Just absolutely splendid. It's exactly the place I've always wanted. You and your men did a wonderful job," the wizard said warmly.

"Your magic was a great help to us, Master Kedrigern. We wouldn't be halfway along if you hadn't cleared the ground and dug the foundation and cut and cured all the lumber for us."

With a smile and a little self-deprecating gesture, Kedrigern said, "Not much point in being a wizard if you can't make things easier for your friends. Those earth-moving spells aren't all that demanding, anyway."

"Still and all, you spared us the hardest work. It's a pleasure to see you so satisfied."

"Far more than merely satisfied, Mat. It was generous of you and your men to make the offer. I fear I took some advantage of your good nature."

"No advantage at all, Master Kedrigern. Building a house is little enough to do for the one who saved our lives."

Both men were silent for a time, embarrassed by the exchange of praise and gratitude. Kedrigern shielded his eyes and looked up, scanning the skies for an imaginary bird. Mat looked down and dug at the ground with the scuffed toe of his boot. The sound of voices drifted to them, and an outburst of laughter.

"I expect you and the men will be leaving soon," the wizard said, still intent on the vacant blue above.

"We will, Master Kedrigern. It's three years since some of us have seen our homes. We're all anxious to get back to our families."

"Of course you are. Thanks again, Mat," Kedrigern said, extending his hand. Mat clasped it in a firm grip, and before he could speak, the wizard went on, "I'll just say good-bye to the others, and you can be on your way home before midday."

They walked side by side up the long slope to where the men were gathered. Under Kedrigern's close supervision, Spot had prepared little packets of cold meat and bread, and filled water jars from the spring. Their job done, the workmen were packed and ready to be moving on. Kedrigern shook their hands, thanking each man individually and wishing him a safe journey, pressing a gold piece into each hand. He guided them through the maze of twisting, branching paths that protected him from chance intruders, shielded them on the way from the things that lurked in the shadows, and when they reached the foot of the mountain he stood careful watch until the last man was lost to view.

That evening, alone save for Spot, he wandered through his new home. It was a roomy house, and seemed even roomier for being so scantily furnished. A few of the rooms were completely empty; the rest held no more than a battered, unsteady stool or chair, or a teetering table, a creaking bed, or a chest. This did not trouble Kedrigern. A satisfied and generous client had bestowed upon him a castle filled to bursting with magnificent furniture and the best of furnishings—fine crystal and plate, heavy tapestries for the walls and rich draperies, cushions and pillows of marvelous softness. He had only to collect them; but until now, he had had no room for such things, and little desire for them. Even now, with lovely spacious rooms and a grand network of tunnels and niches and grottoes running in all directions under the house, he felt no need to clutter his life with such commonplace items as tables and chairs. Surely these nice rooms could be put to better use.

Now, if he were married it would be different, he thought as he walked through the echoing spaces and his eye lit on the great dark carven chest that was sole occupant of one sizeable chamber. It was a gift from Ulurel, a charming sorceress whom he had once assisted with a timely counterspell. Ulurel had smiled in her inscrutable way and said only that the chest held a wardrobe fit for a princess and was her gift to Kedrigern's bride, not to be opened until the appropriate moment. Wanting no trouble, Kedrigern had never peeked.

He did not expect to view the contents of the chest soon, and would not have been surprised to learn that Ulurel had been speaking metaphorically, or in jest, and that he was to remain forever single. Wizards did not, as a rule, marry. Most of them were clubby types, fond of masculine surroundings and disorderly digs, keeping irregular hours and feeling comfortable amid the kind of clutter and stink that no wife has ever been known to tolerate. When their work was done, wizards generally preferred a friendly drink with colleagues, grousing about how spells don't work the way they used to, or telling the latest alchemist joke, to being sweetly dangerous among the ladies. There were, of course, the occasional passionate relationships—wizards were only human, after all—but they seldom turned out well. Merlin's disastrous affair with Vivien served as both scandal and exemplum on the subject.

Kedrigern, however, had no objection at all to marriage, provided it came at the proper time. He felt that he was still a bit too young to make a commitment. A wizard in his early hundred-and-sixties had centuries ahead of him, ample time to settle down. Now was the time for work and study and professional growth. One had to be sensible about these things, and he was being very sensible.

He knew, of course, that if the right woman came along all his sensible plans would go out the window like flung dishwater. But the likelihood of the right woman—or the wrong woman, or any other woman—ever finding her way to his cottage was so small that he felt in reasonable control of his own destiny, at least where marriage was concerned. And so the rooms of his fine new house were not filled with furniture and rugs, neatly-made beds and gleaming tableware. Instead, as the months passed and he settled in, they slowly filled with a mixture of dust and trash and unidentifiable objects collected at random during his fitful experiments in temporal magic. He had no idea what these oddly-shaped things plucked from the future might be, or what they were meant to do, but on the chance that he might one day find out, he kept them all. From time to time he would have Spot haul the bulkier ones down to subterranean storage so that he could move about the house more freely, but he discarded nothing. A wife would not have permitted this, he was certain.

A wife would also have had something to say about Spot. At this early stage in its training, Spot could be very exasperating. One had to think carefully before issuing the simplest instructions, and check minutely afterwards. Kedrigern vividly recalled the time he had bagged a bulky object from the future, a shiny white box with a glass door and dangling entrails. Uncertain whether it was alive or mechanical, he had said irritably, "Get this out of here, Spot," and turned just in time to see the little house-troll making ready to hurl it through the wall. Neither could he forget what had appeared on his plate in response to his casual, "Throw together something for dinner, Spot," though he would have preferred to obliterate it from his memory entirely. His experiences taught him the importance of communicating with Spot in only the simplest and most direct language. Loose, inaccurate, or figurative speech was out.

Whatever its limitations, Spot was living, moving com-

pany. It could carry on conversations—not very abstruse in
nature, since its vocabulary consisted of a single expletive, but
at least it responded verbally to Kedrigern's own speech—and
it was roughly human in general configuration. When trained,
it would be useful.

Kedrigern had given some thought to acquiring a pet, but
could think of nothing satisfactory. A dog would not do at all.
A large one would go for Spot at once, and a small one would
be too tempting a morsel for the little house-troll to resist. A
cat, the traditional domestic companion of people in Kedrigern's field, would constantly be competing with Spot for
mice, causing rivalry and ill will. A bird, like a small dog,
would quickly become an item of Spot's diet.

For a time he toyed with the notion of something more
exotic. A wyvern could be a pleasant little pet if raised from
the egg and kept small by a spell. For that matter, a miniature
dragon would do nicely, and would have the additional advantage of being useful for starting fires. But he came to the sober
realization that such pets were meant more for display than for
companionship or utility, and since he expected no chance
visitors, he would have no opportunity to display them. The
only callers he expected to see in the next few months were
the representatives of the guild, come with profound and grov-
eling apologies and belated acknowledgment of his superior
judgment regarding alchemists.

But they did not come. He waited patiently, a full year
passed, and no one from the guild came to apologize and beg
him to return and give them the benefit of his sagacity. Kedrigern was adamant. He counted up all the demands on his time
and attention and told himself that he was the most fortunate
of wizards to be so far removed from the intrusions of the
world.

By the end of the first year on Silent Thunder Mountain his
magic was back to full strength. During the construction of the
cottage, and in the early days of getting all the details just
right, he had been profligate with his power, moving trees and
boulders, clearing pathways, stocking up for his first winter. It
had taken most of the fall and winter, and a good part of the
spring, to rebuild his resources. Plenty of rest, good food, and
regular study had left him feeling fit and ready to take on the
occasional commission.

Still no word came from the guild, and no colleague

dropped by for a casual visit and a chat about old times. On occasions when he craved the sound of a human voice, Kedrigern conjured up Eleanor of the Brazen Head, who served as his filing system. Her conversation was not much more scintillating than Spot's, but her vocabulary was considerably larger.

It occurred to him one quiet evening to test the extent of Eleanor's power. He was well aware of her retentive memory and made good use of it, but he had never inquired about her other talents. After dinner, leaving Spot to clean the kitchen, he went to his workroom and stood before the brass head at the end of the cluttered table.

It was a head ample of chin and jowl, tidy of coiffure, prim of expression. Behind tiny round rimless spectacles, its eyes were serenely shut. Raising his hand, Kedrigern solemnly intoned, "Eleanor of the Brazen Head, I conjure you to speak."

Eleanor blinked, yawned, and turned to fix her gaze on him. "Come to give me a nice dusting and polishing, Keddie? My, that's sweet of you. I knew that if I just waited, and waited, and sat up here all alone in the dark, sooner or later you'd think of me," she said, sighing patiently.

"No polishing right now, Eleanor. I'll have Spot do it later on, as soon as it's finished the kitchen."

"I'd rather have you do it, Keddie. I like to have a nice chat with whoever polishes me, and it's hard to chat with Spot."

"I know," said the wizard. "But I don't have the time this evening. I really have a lot to do."

Eleanor sighed once again. "Well, I suppose I'll just have to wait. I must remember, I'm not with Friar Bacon anymore, where a brazen head was treated with respect. I'm just an index now."

"Ah, but you needn't be just an index," Kedrigern said brightly. "That's what I want to talk to you about, as a matter of fact. Have you the power to observe distant people and places?"

"Well, I don't know. I'm sure I could do it very nicely if I was all dusted off and polished," she replied.

"You'll be dusted, Eleanor. I promise. This very night."

"And polished?"

"Yes."

"By you?"

"By Spot!" the wizard snapped. Closing his eyes and breathing deeply to calm himself, he said after a time, "I'm sorry, Eleanor. I have something on my mind and you can resolve it for me. I really want this information. Now."

"Why, of course, Keddie, of course," she said in a soothing tone, as one speaks to a petulant child. "You just tell Eleanor what you want to know, and she'll have a look."

"I want to know how Quintrindus is getting along in the Wizards' Guild. Have they seen through him yet? Has he been sent packing?"

Eleanor closed her eyes. Her mouth tightened; a double furrow appeared between her brows. She was silent and motionless for sufficient time to make him wonder whether his conjuration had worn off, then she said loudly, "No."

"What do you see? Can you tell me?"

In a hushed oracular voice, Eleanor said, "I see the alchemist Quintrindus at a table with . . . with three members of the Wizards' Guild. The wizards are laughing merrily. One of them pats Quintrindus on the back. The alchemist smiles. He looks very happy, content, fulfilled. Everyone drinks ale. They all look happy. One of the wizards summons two . . . no, three colleagues to the table. They all shake the hand of Quintrindus warmly, affectionately. One of them puts his arm around the alchemist's shoulder. The wizards raise their mugs in a toast. . . ."

"That's enough, Eleanor," Kedrigern broke in.

"Don't you want to hear the toast? It's very touching."

"I don't care to listen to a lot of grown wizards making fools of themselves over a shifty fraudulent sneaking dirty rotten alchemist."

"Is this Quintrindus fellow so bad? He looked like a pleasant man," Eleanor said mildly.

Icily, Kedrigern replied, "He may look like a seraph, but he has the greed of a shrew and the morals of a graveyard rat. I'm not sure what he has in mind, but I know the guild is going to lament the hour they first heard his name."

"He's very popular now. He even has a little yellow dog following him around and wagging his tail."

"Oh, he can be ingratiating. That's the first thing an alchemist learns. It may be the *only* thing they learn, but they learn it well. Quintrindus could probably charm a dragon off its gold-hoard. He's already swindled a small kingdom and two principalities out of their treasuries. I can't figure out what he expects to get from the guild, though."

"Respectability?" Eleanor suggested.

Kedrigern laughed unpleasantly. "People who befriend alchemists forfeit their respectability among respectable people. And it can't be money. The guild treasury isn't big enough to interest a swindler."

"All the same, Keddie, maybe you ought to warn them."

"Warn them?" he cried. "I tried, Eleanor. I was calm, and logical, and perfectly reasonable, and they flew into hysterics! Shouting, threatening . . . they were like a bunch of barbarians. It was a disgrace. I had to resign. No, let them learn for themselves," he said, setting his face like flint.

After a pause, Eleanor said, "Well, if that's all you wanted, Keddie, would you send Spot up to polish me?"

"At once, Eleanor. Thank you for the information."

"That's what I'm here for, Keddie," she said, smiling and closing her eyes.

So Kedrigern, having examined the alternatives, opted to bide his time and keep his arrangements, both domestic and professional, as they were. He spent the days as he pleased. He worked until he felt like stopping, dined when he was hungry, and slept until he was in the mood to get up. Now and then a messenger would arrive, sent by an old client in sudden need, and the wizard would hear just enough news of the world to make him reaffirm his decision to keep it at a comfortable distance. He made it his practice to have messengers wait until he had finished the necessary counterspell, so they might carry it back with them. In this way he avoided travel. Only one case, a counterspell for the unfortunate daughter of Morgosh the Indulgent, required too much work to make this practicable, so he sent the messenger on his way and put Morgosh's request on his list of things to be done at his earliest convenience.

The seasons passed quickly. All in all, privacy was wonderful and solitude was sweet, but as the end of his second year of defiant isolation drew near, he began to feel undeniable pangs of loneliness. He craved companionship.

On a brilliant beautiful morning in spring, when the air rang with birdsong and the smells of the newborn earth lay heavy on each breeze, Kedrigern could control his feelings no longer. He closed with a decisive, dust-scattering *thoomp* the great book of spells before him. Reading about spells was all very well; one had to keep up; but how much more enjoyable to sit in the shade of an ancient oak with a pitcher of cold ale and two frosty tankards, discussing the subtleties of spells with a fellow wizard. Better yet, with two or three fellow wizards and a few attractive sorceresses. But that was not to be, not for a long long time, certainly, and maybe never again.

He sighed, and rose, and stood by his cluttered worktable for a time, fingering the medallion that he still wore around his neck and thinking of his guild brothers. Vain, fidgeting Hithernils, and crusty old Conhoon, and all too clever Tristaver. He missed them all. Of course, even now, he need only apologize, and everything would be forgiven. . . .

No! he thought angrily, banging his fist down on the table-top, raising a small dust cloud and knocking a little silver bell from its place on the edge, to fall with a bright tinkle. Eleanor of the Brazen Head rocked a bit, but not having been properly summoned, did not speak or open her eyes. "No!" said Kedrigern aloud. "Never!" If *they* apologized, everything would be forgiven. He was prepared to be generous, would hold no grudges, wipe clean the slate, but principles are principles. They were wrong, he was right, and that was that. But he was still lonely.

Spot came bounding into the chamber, its huge ears flapping, eyes rolling, tongue lolling. "Yah, yah!" it cried, bouncing eagerly up and down.

Kedrigern was puzzled for a moment by his house-troll's presence, and then he noticed the fallen bell. "I didn't mean to ring, Spot, but as long as you're here, I'll have lunch. Just a slice of bread and some of the soft cheese. And a mug of ale. Bring it out under the oak," he said.

Spot whirled from the chamber, and the flapping of its huge feet dwindled down the hallway. Kedrigern followed the little troll out, carefully closing the door behind him, and started for the front yard.

Spot was useful, no question about it, but Spot was not company. It was an ideal servant: loyal, energetic, eager, versatile, and untiring. But not a chum. They could not even sit down to a nice game of chess on a dark and stormy evening. Spot got excited and ate the chessmen.

Outside, in the shade of the great oak, the air was cool.

Kedrigern finished his bread and cheese, licked his fingertips clean, sipped his ale, and evaluated his situation coolly and calmly.

His work in temporal magic was cluttering up the house and accomplishing nothing. Getting things from other ages was no problem at all, and some of the things were fascinating to examine, but he was not yet certain where most of it was coming from or what it was. Further study was required. That meant a thorough search of his library, and that, in turn, practically necessitated the cataloguing ordeal that he had been putting off for so long. The counterspell for the daughter of Morgosh the Indulgent was completed, and need only be delivered. No other work was at hand, and if something did not turn up soon, he would have no choice but to get to work on the cataloguing, a lonely, dusty job with a Sisyphean potential for frustration.

Kedrigern thought of Morgosh, and his daughter Metalura, and tapped his fingertips together briskly. In conscience, he ought to delay no longer. It was the kind of counterspell that he had to work himself, not something that could be trusted to some local practitioner. Delivery and execution would require him to leave the little cottage on Silent Thunder Mountain for the first time, and that was bad; but it would also give him a few days at Morgosh's castle, where the accommodations were excellent and the cuisine incomparable, and that was good. Spot's menus were beginning to pall. Morgosh was known for prompt and generous payment, and that, too, was good, but it was not really a concern that Kedrigern took seriously. A wizard seldom had trouble collecting payment. Kedrigern was thinking not about Morgosh's treasury but about his greatest treasure, his only child, Metalura.

The unfortunate girl had been a statue for nearly a year now. That was ample time for her to meditate on the need for good manners when dealing with witches. Good manners were about the only thing Metalura lacked, if rumor were to be believed. She was said to be a fine-looking woman, intelligent and clever; but her tongue was like a flaying knife. Even the generous dowry offered by Morgosh could not bring suitors to his castle, and Metalura was no longer in the first blush of youth. She must be at least twenty, he reckoned. Now, if her ordeal had added civility and a gracious demeanor to her other attributes, she would be . . .

Kedrigern set his mug down and pondered just what Metalura would be. His thoughtful frown became a smile. His eyes brightened. A beautiful woman with a lively wit and a discerning eye, civil, gracious, and highly dowered; a grateful doting father who would grant any reward to the one who freed her from her spell; and a lonely wizard. The ingredients were perfect. Rubbing his hands together in anticipation, grinning as he had not grinned in a long time, he rose and summoned Spot.

"There is packing to be done, Spot," he announced when the little creature arrived. "I'm going away for a few days, and I'm leaving you in charge. Mind you keep the place tidy —I may return with a wife." Humming to himself, he patted Spot on the top of its warty head and entered the house with an unaccustomed bounce in his step.

···᪥ Three ᪥···

wizard goes a-courtin'

THE JOURNEY TO Mon Désespoir, the castle of Morgosh the
Indulgent, was as bad as Kedrigern had expected it to be,
but—to his small relief—no worse. Travel was not one of
life's pleasures for Kedrigern. In his personal menagerie of
bêtes noires it ranked between simple fractures and the company of drunken alchemists. Travel, to Kedrigern, was nothing more than a long series of self-inflicted discomforts,
hardships, and dangers that brought one to a place where it
was not necessary to go, in which one slouched about, homesick, in squalid surroundings, until it was time to repeat the
whole foolish process in reverse. The fact that there were several extenuating circumstances to this trip—his presence
really was required, and there was nothing squalid about Morgosh's treatment of his guests—did not elevate his mood.
Travel was travel, and it was all bad.

One could, of course, travel from place to place instanta-
neously by means of a spell, but transporting spells consumed
enormous amounts of magic. One arrived at one's destination
with one's resources dangerously depleted. The advantages of
a flashy entrance were more than offset by the fact that having
arrived promptly and dramatically, one could barely levitate a
napkin. It took days to get back to full strength. One might as

well spend those days in travel, and preserve one's image.

At times like this, he envied witches. A broomstick was fast, serviceable transportation, easily acquired, and used scarcely any magic at all. But a wizard seen on a broomstick would never live it down.

He took a little-used footpath through the woods to Morgosh's lands. There were no inns along the way, and few inhabitants of any sort, but Kedrigern did not mind the lack. He preferred solitude in which to think pleasant thoughts about his triumphal return, a beautiful bride at his side, a dowry in his possession, and an escort of Morgosh's sturdiest guardsmen before and behind, spurs a-jingle and armor gleaming.

He arrived at Mon Désespoir in the afternoon of the eighth day on the road, having traveled by foot, mule, horse, cart, and wagon, as the opportunity offered. He was very dusty, and it was almost as uncomfortable to sit as to stand. But Morgosh the Indulgent received him at once, with all the enthusiasm he was capable of showing.

When they were alone in his state chamber, Morgosh sighed, gazed at the floor, and said, "Tell me the bad news at once, wizard. Your efforts have failed, and my Metalura is lost to me forever."

"Not so. A counterspell exists."

"Indeed?" Morgosh cried, starting up from his throne. But he sank back down, and his face fell. "Ah, but you have come to tell me that the counterspell lies in a chest in a cave at the bottom of the sea, guarded by Leviathan. Or buried under a mountain, in the care of a fire-breathing dragon."

Kedrigern shook his head. "No, my lord."

"No? Then tell me, how long must my dear daughter remain locked in stone?"

"No longer than you wish, my lord Morgosh."

"Do not taunt me, wizard. If it were up to me, my dear Metalura would be freed from her spell this very day."

"So she shall, then," said Kedrigern triumphantly, pulling a packet from his tunic and raising it aloft dramatically. "Behold the remedy!"

"Can it be true?" Morgosh cried.

"Absolutely."

"Then let us go at once to the chamber where my poor Metalura stands! She will dine with us this very evening!" said Morgosh exultantly.

"Your lordship, if I might have a few moments. . . . I have traveled long and far. I'm covered with dust, and weary. If you would permit—"

"When my dear daughter moves and speaks once more, you will bathe in asses' milk and go in silks and velvets, my honest Kedrigern," said Morgosh, seizing the wizard by the arm and dragging him to a heavy tapestry, which he drew aside to reveal a door. "But first, Metalura."

Morgosh pointed to a candlestick. Kedrigern took it up as Morgosh unlocked the door, locking it again once they were on the other side. They proceeded down a passage, side by side, to a narrow flight of stairs. Morgosh took the light and led the way upward, to another locked door. Once inside, he returned the candlestick to Kedrigern.

"Light the torches," he said.

The wizard did so, and as torch after torch blazed up, and the room filled with light, he had his first clear look at the statue that rested on a pedestal at the center of the little chamber that in happier days had housed the family's ancestral treasures.

It was Metalura in gray stone. She stood in an attitude of alarm, her left hand at her breast, her right extended as if to ward off an impending danger. Her eyes were wide, her lips parted, her head tilted slightly backward, away from the unseen threat. The stone folds of her robe clung to a mature but slender and perfectly formed figure. She was exquisitely beautiful.

"Here she stands, Kedrigern. She's been like this for almost a year, my poor darling," said Morgosh with a quaver in his voice.

"If you would refresh my memory, my lord—exactly how did it come about?"

"It was malice, Kedrigern, sheer malice. Someone put them up to it."

"Them?"

"The Drissmall sisters. Do you know them?"

"Ah, yes. Yes, I've heard of them. They're well known for plagues and rashes, but I've never heard of them in connection with petrifaction."

"There's no question but that it was a conspiracy," said Morgosh. "I had invited them here on business. While we were in conference, Metalura entered the chamber. I had no secrets from my dear daughter, and she had free run of the castle. I introduced my guests, and Metalura made an observation about the nose of one of the Drissmalls. When one of the sisters objected to the comment, Metalura made unfavorable reference as well to the warts on *her* chin. You must understand, Kedrigern, that the Drissmall sisters are extremely unsightly individuals. My dear girl was saying no more than the plain truth."

"I understand."

"Well, to put it briefly, they turned her into stone. As you see."

Kedrigern nodded, stroked his chin, and studied the ossified maid. "Do you remember what they said? It's very important, and your messenger was unable to help me on that point."

"Oh, they mumbled something. Typical witch talk. Hard to understand them, though. They haven't a single tooth among them. Their diction is terrible."

"They speak well enough to cast a first-class spell," Kedrigern said appreciatively. "I know something about petrifaction spells, and it's difficult enough just turning someone into a lump of stone. This is a beautiful piece of magic."

"You're not here to admire what they did, you're here to undo it!"

"Of course, my lord Morgosh, " Kedrigern said in a soothing tone. "But I must know all the circumstances. Did they say anything?"

"Some sort of jingle," Morgosh muttered.

"Do you remember it?"

Reluctantly, Morgosh recited, "'Lovely lady, stand in stone, Till you speak in milder tone.' Those were their exact words."

"Anything more?"

"Not another word. They said that, and they vanished into thin air before I could summon the guard."

"Mmm . . . That's a very straightforward spell. If I counter it, and free your daughter, she'll go right back to being a statue the first time she makes an unkind remark about anyone. It might be safer if I could get the Drissmalls to lift the spell."

"I can't wait any longer. My little girl was never unkind to a living soul, Kedrigern," said Morgosh, gazing with moist eyes on the figure that stood before them. "She was clever, and she never minced words. Had a great dedication to plain blunt speaking, Metalura did, but she never insulted anyone who didn't deserve it. Go ahead and unspell her. She'll be fine."

Kedrigern was beginning to feel serious misgivings. Surely her imprisonment in stone must have gentled Metalura's manners. But old ways die hard. A single relapse on her part might lose Kedrigern the entire reward and gain him the enmity of Morgosh. And probably the Drissmall sisters, as well. He felt himself on very shifty ground.

"Well, when can you start?" Morgosh demanded.

"I'll get to work right now. But I must warn you, with this kind of spell—"

"Yes, yes, I know, Kedrigern. Have no fear. My little girl will never say another word that even the most sensitive soul could take amiss. Now get to it."

Kedrigern got to it. Waving Morgosh back, he untied the packet containing the materials of the counterspell, and laid out two small pouches and a tiny leaden vial, tightly stoppered. He opened one pouch, which contained a red powder, and made a circuit of the room, stopping at each torch to toss a pinch of the powder into the flame. As a sharp scent began to permeate the air of the chamber, he returned to his place before the statue, opened the second pouch, and mixing a pinch of the green powder in it with the red, dropped the mixture on the candleflame.

Billows of rich purple-blue smoke coiled forth from the tiny flame, and rolled like sluggish serpents about the floor of the room. Kedrigern walked once around the statue, repeating an incantation, forming figures in the air with the thick ropy smoke. Setting down the candlestick, he opened the vial, and covering it with his finger he upended it. He touched his moistened fingertip to the statue's lips, eyelids, and wrists, then stepped back and quickly restoppered the vial.

At first, one might have thought it a trick of the smoke-filled air. But in a very little time, the flush of Metalura's cheek and the coral of her lips was unmistakable. Her hair turned from stony gray to white, to pale yellow, and at last to a rich gold. Her breast rose and fell with a deep breath. She blinked, and moved, and at last she spoke.

"What did they do to me, Daddy?" she said in a voice like

soft music, sleepily rubbing her hazel eyes.

"You were placed under a spell, dear girl. The Drissmall sisters turned you into a statue," Morgosh explained, looking adoringly upon her.

"You should have told me they were witches, Daddy," she said, pouting.

"There wasn't time, my treasure. It all happened very quickly."

"It certainly did. I should've guessed they were witches, I suppose. The nose on that fat one was—"

"Stop!" Kedrigern cried in a mighty voice, flinging his arms wide. "Speak no more, lady!"

"And who is this?" Metalura asked coolly.

"I am Kedrigern, the wizard of Silent Thunder Mountain," said he with a bow and a flourish that shook loose the dust of the road that still lay heavily in the folds of his cloak.

"You're a very pushy wizard. What do you mean, coming into my presence dressed like that? You look—"

"Stop, my dearest child!" cried Morgosh with a cautionary gesture. "You must not say another word!"

"To *him?*" Metalura said scornfully. "He looks like something you put up to keep the pigeons off my shoulders. I never saw such—"

A sharp *clingg* resounded through the chamber, and Metalura stood in pale unweathered stone, hands on hips, head atilt, looking gorgeously down in unfavorable judgment on all the world.

"What have you done?" Morgosh howled.

Indignantly, Kedrigern replied, "I restored your daughter to normal. She managed to turn herself back into a statue. Don't blame me."

"You're all alike! You're all in on this!" Morgosh cried, in a rising rage. He dashed to the wall and wrenched free a large, very spiky morningstar once used by a warlike ancestor against invading barbarians. Raising it high overhead, he charged at Kedrigern.

With no time for a protective spell and no place to hide, Kedrigern cast an instantaneous oblivion on the angry noble. Morgosh slowed, staggered, and then, gazing blankly at the wizard, dropped the morningstar. He tottered in place for a moment, sagged, slumped to the floor on his knees, and then stretched out prone on the flagstones.

The spell was a stopgap, and Kedrigern had to think fast. At Morgosh's first recovering groan, the wizard rushed to his side, loosened the collar of his tunic, and began to fan his face, inquiring with the greatest solicitude, "Is your lordship well? How does your lordship?"

Morgosh groaned again, heaved a deep sigh, and came wide awake. Sitting up, he exclaimed, "What happened? Something came over me . . . a seizure . . . a fit . . ."

"Understandable, in view of the terrible disappointment your lordship must have felt. But one must be brave at times like these. One must set an example for one's people," Kedrigern said with great earnestness, clasping Morgosh's forearm in a firm manly gesture of support.

"What times? What disappointment?"

"To have your beloved Metalura back, and then to give her up so generously! So nobly!" Kedrigern wiped his eyes and added, in a choked voice, "Forgive me, your lordship. One seldom sees such a display as I have seen in this chamber."

"What did I do?" Morgosh asked wildly.

"When I freed Metalura from the spell—"

"Freed her? She's still a statue!"

"Observe her attitude. It's not what it was."

Climbing unsteadily to his feet and shaking off Kedrigern's assistance, Morgosh approached closer to the statue and studied it, muttering, "No. No, it's not. Her hands were different . . . and her expression. . . . Tell me, Kedrigern, what's become of my precious child?"

"Once restored to common life, she began to weep piteously. Surely you remember, my lord."

"I remember nothing! It's all blank!"

"She had found great peace and happiness in her enchanted state, it seems, and she begged to return to it for a time, until her enlightenment is complete. Your lordship acceded to her entreaties, but the shock to your system was great. You . . . you fell in a swoon," Kedrigern explained, averting his eyes.

Morgosh studied the statue's expression. "She doesn't look as though she was imploring," he said dubiously.

"Well, I didn't mean to suggest that she groveled. A woman of her breeding, after all . . ."

Morgosh grunted. He lowered his gaze, and noticed the morningstar. "What's this doing here?" he demanded.

Kedrigern looked away. Awkwardly, he said, "Your lordship was . . . reluctant to comply with her request. But the reluctance quickly passed."

"Reluctant? Do you mean that I . . ."

"You very nearly did."

With a horrified cry, Morgosh took a step backward and flung an arm before his face. "My darling treasure—I might have chipped her! Smashed her to gravel!"

"Your lordship might—had I not prevented it."

Morgosh turned to Kedrigern, and the look in his eyes was that of a lost and freezing man seeing the lights of a distant cabin. He stumbled to the wizard's side and threw his arms around him. "How can I thank you, Kedrigern? How can I reward you as you deserve?" he blubbered.

"Your lordship will think of something," said Kedrigern.

He stayed at Mon Désespoir for two nights, and left on the gray morning of the third day. His accommodations were luxurious, he was waited on hand and foot, and the food and drink were superb, but Morgosh's interminable encomiums for his daughter eroded all patience. Not a crumb of bread, not a sip of wine could pass the lips without a tearful reminiscence of the lapidified Metalura. Kedrigern found it insufferable, and was happy to put it all behind him.

He had lost his opportunity to wed a clever, well-born beauty, but there were compensations. Life with Metalura would have been a life of constant warfare, he was certain of that. And a woman of her standing would not be happy in his simple cottage, with only a troll to wait on her. There would have to be extensive remodeling, and troops of people everywhere, and Morgosh coming for long visits and bringing a small army of retainers, and spoiling his daughter worse than ever. It might even have become necessary to relocate entirely, and take a larger house down on the plain, where there were people coming and going in all seasons, no peace, and precious little privacy. The very thought of such a life made Kedrigern's stomach churn.

He told himself that it had all been an idle fancy, and he was lucky to have come out of it as well as he did. His marrying a nobleman's daughter was a preposterous notion. But now the idea of marriage was in his head, and it was not easily dislodged.

Morgosh had rewarded him generously. There was no

need for him to consider the dowry when choosing a wife; he could marry anyone he liked. He could have a partner, not a despot.

He weighed the question carefully before coming to a decision. A strong, sensible woman with some experience of life as it really is: that was the kind of wife for a wizard. She need not be of noble blood. What, after all, was birth? Go back a few generations, and every noble name had its roots in brigandage. Nor need she be clever, or witty; he was not seeking a match with a jester. She need not be a legendary beauty, either. Of course, she could not be some slack-jawed dull-eyed cow who conversed in grunts. A comely lass with a clear mind and a sweet temper, that was the wife for him. Though he had yet to meet the woman, and had no idea how to begin his search, he was confident that their life together would be sublimely happy.

Along with two pouches of gold and a rather gaudy ruby ring, Morgosh had given Kedrigern a donkey, to facilitate his return home. Kedrigern took the high road back, camping in the forest for the first two nights, guarding his small encampment with a simple spell against predators of all kinds. On the third afternoon of travel, he came to an inn. It looked clean, and the aromas that drifted forth promised good dining. After two nights of sleeping on hard ground and eating dry bread and cheese, he was ready for something more civilized. He stabled his donkey and entered the inn at an eager pace. A girl was scrubbing the flagstones of the entry, and Kedrigern nearly fell over her. She looked up at him timidly, and he saw bright blue eyes and delightful freckles and a long tumble of hair the color of fresh-scraped carrots and a charming snub nose and, as she rose and pulled her tattered skirts close around her, soft white arms and a neat slender ankle.

"I'm terribly sorry to give you a start, miss," Kedrigern said with a slight bow. "It was clumsy of me."

"It were my fault, sir, all my fault. I be in the way, as I mustn't be," she said, with rustic intonations that lent charm to her simple speech. She curtsied repeatedly and looked up at him with wide, frightened eyes.

"Here, now, what you be up to, Rasanta?" said a gruff voice from within. "You be warned about your carelessness, girl, and you pay no heed, and if I have to—" A large red-faced man with scraggly brown hair and a thick brown beard came into view, scowling menacingly and shaking his fist. At the sight of Kedrigern he stopped short, turned his fist-shaking into a clumsy wave of welcome, and smiled brightly at the wizard.

"Welcome to Stiggman's Inn, traveler, where weary wanderers find the finest food and the bonniest beds this side of the mountains," he said jovially. To the girl, he snapped, "Be off, slut, and take your mop and your slop-bucket with you," and then returning his attention to Kedrigern, he gestured to the main room, where a fire burned brightly. "Have a nice bit of warm, traveler, and I be bringing you a mug of my best ale to make up for this clumsy chit," he said, aiming a backhand swat at the red-haired girl.

She ducked the blow, glared at him, gave one appealing glance to Kedrigern, and fled. He could not help noticing that she had a fine figure. A very fine figure.

"More trouble than she be worth, that slut," Stiggman grumbled as he arranged a footstool before the fire for Kedrigern's greater comfort. "Wife have to pound her like bread dough to get a lick of work out of her. And a surly trollop, too, she is."

"She seemed rather well-mannered, I thought."

"Oh, she know well enough how to please the men. They come flocking here to see the flirting and the flouncing and the jiggling of her. She be good at bringing the young men here to gawk and gape, though she be good for nought else," Stiggman said. He quickly added, "It be going no further than the gawking and the gaping, though, sir. Stiggman's Inn be no house of bawdry, I tell you."

"Clearly not," said Kedrigern righteously.

The ale was very good, and very cold, and very refreshing. The food was hot, and delicious, and in generous portion. As the evening wore on, young men began to fill the room, and as Stiggman had predicted, their eyes remained hungrily fixed on Rasanta as she hurried back and forth bearing mugs of ale. She was a very attractive girl, and even her ragged, dirty clothes could not detract from the beauty of her face and the perfection of her form. Kedrigern looked on every bit as appreciatively as any man in the room, though his admiration was more detached than theirs. They were burly, noisy bumpkins whose small eyes glimmered with uncomplicated lust; Kedrigern was a man who knew beauty, and he savored the sight of Rasanta's fluid motion as he would the splendor of a fine sunset, or a difficult spell well wrought.

He could feel the glimmer rising in his own eyes when Rasanta stopped at his table to bring a fresh mug of ale, and he smelt the sweet fragrance of her hair and was warmed by the brightness of her smile. But of course anything more than detached admiration on his part was out of the question. She was hardly more than a child, and having passed his hundred-and-sixtieth birthday Kedrigern accepted the fact that he was no longer a stripling. A light-hearted roll in the hay was out of the question, and a more serious relationship was impossible. Respected master wizards simply did not marry kitchen slaveys. Not even young, beautiful slaveys with figures that grow more incredibly perfect as one observes them. No. He shook his head, drained his ale, and slipped up the stairs to his chamber.

It was a small room, and he was fortunate to have to share it with no one. Unfortunately, it was directly over the great room of the inn, and the customers had by this time grown very noisy. For silence, and for the security of his two bags of gold, he placed a small enclosing spell upon the chamber, to endure until he woke. Tugging off his boots and pulling his tunic over his head, he fell on the bed and went at once into a sound sleep.

Next morning, as Kedrigern breakfasted on bread and butter and cold cider, Stiggman slipped up beside his table and in a confidential voice inquired, "And did you be having a good night, sir?"

"Yes, I did. I fell asleep as soon as my head hit the pillow, and didn't wake until after daybreak."

Leering, Stiggman said, "Ah, I understand, sir, I understand." Winking and nodding and leering, he sidled out of the room.

That was odd behavior for an innkeeper, but Kedrigern paid it no heed. Nor did he trouble himself over the pouting glance Rasanta gave him from the doorway, nor the imperious toss of her head as she turned her back on him. He finished his breakfast, paid his bill, and made ready to leave.

It was a fine crisp morning for traveling. Kedrigern started down the forest road at an easy pace, and just as he passed from sight of the inn, Rasanta dashed from the roadside and clutched at his boot, sobbing piteously. He halted the donkey and dismounted.

"What's wrong, you poor child?" he asked.

"Oh, sir, take me away. Take me with you, please!" she implored, throwing herself at his feet, clinging desperately to his boots. "They treats me awful here. Take me back to my father, and he be rewarding you generous."

"Just relax, Rasanta," said the wizard, lifting her to her feet. "I'll help you if I can. Now, tell me what's wrong."

"I want to go back to my father, sir, and they be never letting me go. They keeps me here for to bring the young men to the inn. I hates it, sir, I hates it awful, but they forces me to smile, and lure the poor lads to drink."

"You seemed to be enjoying yourself last night."

"Oh, they beats me fierce if I don't look happy, sir. Look at this," she said, hiking up her skirt to reveal a set of purple fingermarks high on her thigh. "And this here," she added, pulling her blouse down to show a similar mark on her breast.

"Oh dear me. . . . Well, who is your father, Rasanta? And where can I find him?"

"He be a great merchant, sir, in the islands over the western sea. I was stole from him by pirates when I was a baby, and he be seeking me ever since. A traveler told me, sir. My father, he be ever so rich, sir, and he says he be giving my weight in gold to the man who brings me home. And his blessing on our marriage," she added, shyly lowering her eyes, "if the man do want me."

This new configuration of circumstances was very pleasant, and Kedrigern took a moment to allow it to sink in. A wealthy merchant's daughter in distress. A girl as lovely as Metalura, younger, and far sweeter tempered. A chance to do a fine, noble deed, and reap a charming reward. He took Rasanta by her slender waist and swung her up into the saddle.

"Up you go, my dear. I'm taking you home," he said.

"Oh, thank you, sir. I know the way. We have to take a little side trail not far from here."

"Lead on, then," Kedrigern said with a flourish. He felt a hundred and twenty again.

They proceeded down the road for a short distance, then Rasanta swung the donkey onto a narrow trail leading off to the right. At first Kedrigern walked by her side, but as the forest closed in, he was forced to take the lead. He glanced back from time to time, and each glance was rewarded by an adoring look. Rasanta looked happier than he had ever seen her before.

The trail ended in a circular clearing. Kedrigern, puzzled, turned just in time to see Rasanta spring lightly from the donkey's back. She stuck two fingers in her mouth and gave a piercing whistle. A large man stepped from the woods; then another; then two more. They spread out in a line before him. Their expressions were serious, and they carried clubs.

"He do have a good bag of coins in each boot," Rasanta said.

"Rasanta, my dear girl, you disappoint me," said Kedrigern sadly.

She smiled, shrugged her pretty shoulders, and stepped back to allow the four ruffians room for their work. As they hefted their clubs, Kedrigern raised a hand and said, "Before you do anything we'll all regret, I must warn you that I am a wizard. If you attack, I will defend myself in ways you're sure to find unpleasant."

One of the ruffians laughed scornfully. "You be no wizard. I did see wizard once. I knows wizard."

Kedrigern sighed and nodded wearily. "I suppose your wizard had a long white beard, and wore a pointy hat."

"Aye, he did."

"And he also wore a long black robe, covered with mysterious symbols."

"Aye, that, too. A real wizard, he were," said the ruffian. His companions looked on, envious of his wide acquaintance.

"Alas, the poverty of your experience leads you to false conclusions. Despite my plain attire, I am a wizard. My anger will be hazardous to your well-being."

"He be no wizard, you bunch of ninnies!" Rasanta cried.

"I have a feeling that all you lads have been as badly used as I have at one time or another. I have no wish to embarrass you further, or to harm you. Just go away, and take the lady with you, and no one need suffer."

The four burly ruffians hesitated at his calm words. They looked uncertainly at one another, each of them clearly wanting to get out of this perplexing situation but unwilling to be the first to suggest it. Then Rasanta's furious voice cut the tense silence.

"Fine lot of babies you be! Four of you, with clubs, and you be shaking in your boots for fear of one skinny little geezer!" she cried. "Hop to it!"

That set things in motion. The four lurched forward, raising their clubs. Kedrigern, his eyes blazing, swept his hands wide and spat out a short, hissing phrase. In an instant, he was surrounded by five astonished cats: four big striped toms, and a fluffy, carrot-colored little female.

"Work it out among yourselves," he said coldly, and turned to where the donkey was placidly grazing.

He had not gone far down the trail when a great yowling and screeching broke out behind him. He smiled a grim smile and rode on. The spell would be of brief duration, but he was confident that the memory of the experience would linger. Travelers would be safe in these woods for a long time to come.

For the rest of the way home, Kedrigern took the low road, through the heart of the Dismal Bog. It was a gloomy place at any time of year, and he knew that it would suit his mood. He felt foolish, and ashamed of himself. A mature, respected wizard, a man of stature and reputation in the wizardly community—not a geezer, by any means, but certainly someone old enough to know better—should not go panting after scullions, however buxom and bright-eyed they be. Nor should he dream of wedding the pampered daughter of a foolish nobleman because her dowry is more generous than her mind. As well dream of marrying a princess, he told himself.

Greed and lechery. That's the way of the world, he reflected, and it nearly won me over and did me in. I was right to turn my back on it all. I belong on Silent Thunder Mountain. Just me, and faithful Spot, and good old Eleanor.

Kedrigern had given up on the world some years ago, and was ashamed of himself for having wavered in his resolution. The world, to him, was a noisy, busy place, overcrowded with people he did not wish to meet—brutes, thieves, liars, viragoes; alchemists trying to turn everything into gold, and barbarians trying to turn everything into ashes. The rare souls who worked hard and lived decent lives generally died at an early age, victims of the brutes and blackguards. No, the world was no place for a conscientious wizard.

He felt all this, and truly believed it, but he was lonely still, and the company of a brass head that always wanted polishing and a knee-high troll with a one-word vocabulary was not a cheering prospect. With a deep, heartfelt sigh, he reined in the donkey and dismounted. He wanted to sit on a rock and gaze into the gloom and feel sorry for himself, and this was just the place for it.

It was the quiet time of early afternoon, and his sighs were much too loud against the profound stillness of the bog. The infrequent *bideep* of a restless peeper, or the *brereep* of a toad, or the surly *grugump* of a bullfrog only heightened the quietude. He soon fell silent, and then there was only the soft brush of the wind and now and then a distant splash as life and sudden death went on in the far reaches.

He became aware of the faint, small sound of a woman crying. She was weeping bitterly, with deep heart-rending sobs that brought the moisture to Kedrigern's own eyes. The sound was faraway, as if diminished by distance, yet it seemed to come from nearby—as if a tiny woman were weeping her heart out almost within reach of his hand. And there was not a living creature near but himself, the donkey, and a scattering of toads seated on lily pads, a few so close he could reach out and touch them.

"Oh, woe! Woe and alas, to be a toad," said the small, sad voice.

This was enchantment, no doubt of it. Some unfortunate woman had gotten herself turned into a toad, and now she was wailing away, hoping to arouse passers-by to pity. Pity, indeed, thought Kedrigern indignantly, hardening his heart. She needn't look to me to solve her problem. Did she think he was going to go sloshing about in these chilly waters, kissing every toad in sight? Weep away, madam, he muttered under his breath. You probably deserve your fate. If I turn you back into a woman you'll only insult witches, or lure travelers off to some isolated spot to have their heads bashed in. Twice fooled is enough, thank you.

The sound of weeping came again, very near. Kedrigern noticed, for the first time, a tiny green toad on a lily pad, so close he could make out every detail. For a toad, it was rather an attractive little creature. It had a certain dignity one does not expect of a toad. On its head, between the two big bulging eyes, was a tiny circlet of gold. Clearly, this was no ordinary toad. He began to relent a bit.

Clearing his throat, he said, "Forgive my intrusion, toad, but are you weeping?"

"Yes, I am," came a tiny voice in reply. "And who would not weep at such a fate as mine? Oh, misery!"

"Come, now . . . is it really so bad being a toad?"

"It is when one was once the most beautiful princess in all the land," came the indignant reply.

"Oh, dear. Yes, in that case, I imagine it is. I'm terribly sorry, toad."

"Princess," the little voice corrected him.

"Yes, of course, Princess. My apologies."

"No need to apologize, good sir. Your sympathy does you credit. Alas, I need more than sympathy to escape my plight. I am the victim of wicked enchantment."

"Well, now, I may be able to help you, Princess. I don't suppose a kiss from me would do much good, but I know a reasonably handsome prince, and he owes me a favor. If you don't mind waiting, I'm sure he'd be willing—"

"It wouldn't help. I appreciate your kind offer, but a prince is useless in my case. I require a wizard. A very special wizard."

"Indeed?"

"In all the world, only one wizard can help me—the great master of counterspells, Kedrigern of Silent Thunder Mountain. But alas, he remains aloof in his retreat, and never sets foot in the world below."

"Never? Are you positive?"

"So I am told. Oh, sir, I've thought so long and deeply on Kedrigern that I feel as if I know him . . . and knowing him, I love him."

"Do you know anything about this Kedrigern?"

"Only what is in my heart," the wee voice said sweetly. "I know he must be handsome, and wise, and kind, and good."

"He is," Kedrigern assured her.

"And if he heard my tragic tale, he would assist me."

"He will. You can count on it. Tell me, Princess: who placed this enchantment on you?"

"It was Bertha the Bog-fairy, kind sir."

Kedrigern gave an involuntary groan, and was silent for a

moment. Bog-fairies were a mean, tricky lot, and Bertha was one of the meanest and trickiest. Any spell of hers would carry a full freight of hidden traps for the unwary. Unless, of course, it had been cast impromptu.

"One thing more, Princess: was this enchantment the result of an outburst of pique on Bertha's part, or was it premeditated?" he asked hopefully.

"It was very premeditated. The invitations to my christening were garbled somehow, and Bertha was overlooked. She took offense, and placed the spell. On my eighteenth birthday . . . just as I blew out the candles. . . ." The little voice broke in a sob.

This complicated matters. Bertha, with time to plot and plan, had probably interlarded her basic enchantment with all sorts of traps and pitfalls to be triggered by any attempted counterspell. This unfortunate little toad might find herself transformed into a beautiful princess with an insatiable appetite for flies, or an uncontrollable desire to hunker down on a lily pad for the night.

Kedrigern had confidence in his powers. But he had been in his profession long enough to know the danger of overconfidence. Magic was a slippery business; even a few centuries' experience was no guarantee against unpleasant surprises. In the midst of his ruminations came the tiny voice of Princess.

"Please, kind sir, help me if you can. Bring Kedrigern to me, or me to Kedrigern. I can go on no longer. Set me free," she said piteously.

That resolved the issue for the wizard. Rising, he said solemnly, "It will be dangerous, Princess. Are you willing to take the risk?"

"Oh, yes!"

"Then hop up here, onto dry ground," said Kedrigern, pointing to a little knoll that rose between the ground and the bog's edge. The toad did as instructed, and he said, "Good. Now stay very still. This won't hurt a bit."

"What are you going to do, sir?" she asked, and in her tiny voice was a note of apprehension.

"A counterspell. You're about to become a princess, Princess. Now, not another word."

Kedrigern drew a pouch from inside his shirt. He shook out five small black stones, each a perfect hemisphere about the size of his little fingernail, and set them in a pentacle around the motionless toad. From another pouch, he trickled a thin stream of sparkling silvery powder to form a runic figure. He walked three times around the knoll, muttering under his breath, then reversed himself and walked nine times around in the opposite direction.

This done, he took a pin from his tunic and pricked his finger—it was the part of the spell he disliked—and squeezed a single drop of blood into each of the interstices between the black stones. Now all was ready.

He stepped back, sucking his finger, to make a last-minute check. Then he raised his hands and began to speak in a soft, liquid language that rose and fell melodiously. He brought his hands together suddenly; a great thunderclap rolled over the silent bog, and a flicker of darkness like the swirl of a cloak passed over them.

On the knoll stood a woman in a gown of pale yellow and green, with a cloak of deeper green over her shoulders. Her blue eyes were wide with astonishment. Glistening jet-black hair tumbled in waves to her hips, restrained only by a simple golden circlet on her brow. She was the most beautiful woman Kedrigern had ever seen, or hoped to see, or imagined he ever would see, and all his heart went out to her at first sight.

He stepped forward, took her hand, and raised it to his lips. "Forgive me my deception, Princess. I am Kedrigern, the wizard of Silent Thunder Mountain, and when you spoke my name, I knew that some kind fate had brought me here. I was destined to free you from your enchantment. And now that you see me, tell me, are you disappointed? Am I all you hoped I'd be? Speak to me, Princess!"

She looked up at him with eyes the color of cornflowers. Her perfect features softened in a tender smile, and she opened her arms to him. "*Brereep*," she said.

···❧ *Four* ❧···

when the spirit moves you

KEDRIGERN COULD NOT help peeking back over his shoulder
every few minutes to reassure himself that this was all real,
and not a deception placed upon him by some rival. Each time
he looked, Princess was still there. She had not turned back
into a toad, or metamorphosed into a bundle of rags or a
hideous old crone. If anything, she was more beautiful than
ever. And she—this vision of loveliness, this radiance—was
Kedrigern's bride.

He thought fondly of the hermit Goode, who lived his
pious life in the wood bordering the Dismal Bog. Goode was a
kindly, considerate, compassionate soul, not some prying
snoop smouldering with unhealthy curiosity. It was not
Goode's way to ask for explanations of people's little idiosyncrasies. He had been quite content to allow Princess to partake
in the marriage ritual by means of written word and manual
gesture, without insisting on oral response, thus sparing em-
barrassment and avoiding lengthy explanations. A good man,
Goode.

Ahead of them, the road rose, curved to the right, and
disappeared into the dense forest on the slope of the mountain.
Kedrigern fell back to the side of the little donkey upon which

Princess rode, and taking his wife's hand, said, "That's Silent Thunder Mountain just ahead, my dear. We'll be home within the hour."

"*Brereep*," she said sweetly.

"Once we're settled in, I'll get right to work on finding a counterspell. We'll have you talking again in no time."

"*Brereep*," she said, squeezing his hand gently.

"I'm sure you'll like the place. It's practically brand new. I had it built to my specifications by the best workmen in three kingdoms. It's beautifully landscaped. Lovely little garden. Magnificent views."

"*Brereep?*"

"Well, yes, there are a few things still to be done. A bachelor wizard living alone—practically alone—falls into fairly rough and ready ways. Now that there's a lady of the house, we'll need some furniture...dishes and goblets... silverware...draperies...rugs...linens...a lot of little things that a man living by himself overlooks."

"*Brereep*," she murmured uneasily.

"Oh, there'll be no problem obtaining everything we need, my dear, no problem at all. I once did a small spell for Wuxul the Well Provided, and he rewarded me with a castle filled with the most sumptuous furnishings. Wuxul's part of the kingdom is no fit place to live—the climate is filthy and the woods are crawling with alchemists and barbarians—so I've never taken advantage of the stuff, but we can have the best pieces brought up here."

Princess smiled with obvious relief. Kedrigern kissed her hand, returned her radiant smile, and stepped out to lead the way up the narrow road. A guide was an absolute necessity; the road turned and branched and forked in a most confusing way, purposefully designed to discourage the idle wanderer and confound anyone bent on mischief. In the night, ghosts and hideous apparitions stalked the labyrinthine ways. Only the most determined traveler, with a lion's courage, a migrating swallow's sense of direction, and an excellent map, could hope to find the way to the house of Kedrigern without the aid of magic.

In less than an hour's time they emerged from the shadowed cool of the overhanging trees into an upland meadow. At the far edge of the meadow, on the fringe of the forest, stood a trim little house with a large, well-tended garden. A sunny dooryard faced the south, and shade trees stood to the west.

Princess said nothing as they drew near the garden gate, but the look of pleasure in her blue eyes warmed Kedrigern's heart. This was a cozy place. All it had ever lacked was a woman's warming presence, and now, with Princess as its chatelaine, it would be a perfect home.

He helped her dismount, and looked on proudly as she sniffed a flower, plucked a peapod, and with a slim hand shading her eyes, admired the prospect from the sunny dooryard. She turned to him, eyes bright with joy, lips parted, and then she suddenly gave a cry of horror and flew to his arms, where she buried her head in his shoulder and clung to him, trembling.

"What is it, my love?" he asked, bewildered.

"*Brereep*," she said in a voice faint with terror.

"Oh, that," he said, relieved, glancing at the doorway, where a grotesque little creature stood gesticulating wildly in greeting. "That's only Spot, my dear. The house-troll. A handy thing to have around, believe me. It won't hurt you."

Spot had grown a bit. It was almost all head now, and a very ugly head, too, with its tiny eyes and bulging brows and scarcity of forehead; with its great hook of nose, like a drinking horn covered with warts; with its ledge of chin and hairy ears like wide-flung shutters. Two great dirty feet splayed at the ends of the creature's tiny legs, and hands like butter paddles jutted from its sides. The top of its mottled, warty, scurfy head reached just to the height of Kedrigern's knee.

"*Brereep*," said Princess, her voice muffled.

"Don't be hasty. It's almost impossible to get good help around here."

"*Brereep!*"

"Spot is very strong. It can cook—if you give very clear directions. It cleans boots, tends the garden, dusts. . . . It's a dependable all-around servant. And a good mouser."

Princess stopped shaking. She moved her head slowly around to take a second look at the house-troll. Spot was bouncing up and down on the doorstep now, crying out "Yah! Yah!" in jubilant welcome, waving its enormous hands and flapping its ears. It was an extremely ugly creature.

"See? It likes you," Kedrigern said reassuringly.

"*Brereep*," she murmured.

"No, really. Spot can be very friendly. I should have

warned you about its appearance, though. I'm sorry you had such a start. I've become so accustomed to Spot that I scarcely notice it anymore." Turning to the exultant troll, Kedrigern said, "Bring us a bottle of the best wine, Spot. And the silver goblets. And bring a slab of cheese, and some bread, too."

"Yah!" the troll cried, and disappeared inside.

"Would you like to eat out here, my dear, and enjoy the sunset, or would you prefer to go inside?"

"*Brereep*," said Princess, starting for the doorway.

She stepped inside, and halted. When her eyes had adjusted to the interior gloom, she gave a soft groan.

In the pursuit of his profession, Kedrigern was correct to the point of punctiliousness. Every ingredient of a spell was told out exactly, every syllable pronounced with precision; he tolerated no makeshifts, accepted no substitutes, permitted no stopgap measures. This was not a question of conscience or temperament, it was a matter of survival. Magic was an iffy business even when practiced with care. One botched ingredient in a spell, and there was no predicting the outcome.

But in the nonprofessional area of his life, Kedrigern was casual to the point of anarchy. It mattered little to him whether clothing lay heaped on a chair or footstool, or in a corner, until the passing of the seasons recalled it to active use. Dust, unsteady tables, stains and spills did not trouble him, as long as they were confined to the living area. Making a bed seemed to him an enterprise of consummate futility, on a par with ostentatious use of tableware. A single plate, cup, and utensil were enough for anyone, he believed; and by a careful choice of food, one might even dispense with the utensil.

From the look of dismay on her face, he could see that Princess followed a different school of domestic economy. She looked like one who has been promised a scepter, and handed a shovel.

"Bit of tidying up to do," he said cheerfully. Princess turned and glared at him, and he explained, "I've been away for a while. Things get messy."

She said "*Brereep*" under her breath, and slowly scanned the room, shaking her head.

"I'll have Spot get to work on it at once."

She did not reply, merely shook her head in mute censure. The furniture—what little there was of it, and such of that as was visible under heaped garments—looked as if it had been hurled into the room from a great height and then trodden upon by giants. The floor was thickly covered with rugs which, in turn, were thickly covered with dust, dirt, and a variety of unidentifiable objects. Small bright eyes peered at her from the corners, then disappeared into trembling webs of heroic size. Here and there, on shelves and under tables, things moved.

"Not bothered by the occasional spider, are you, my dear? They're practically part of the family. Quiet little chaps."

"*Brereep?*"

"They're Manny's descendents, every one. Manny was with me for a long time. He stayed on in my old place when I moved here. Just couldn't bring himself to leave it. I imagine it's all one big web by now." Kedrigern sighed nostalgically and gazed at Manny's progeny in fond reminiscence. Taking Princess's hand, he said, "Why don't we have our wine and cheese out under the trees, my dear? Spot can clean up in here while I show you the grounds."

"*Brereep,*" she said noncommittally.

"Before we go out, I'd like you to see something," said Kedrigern, leading her to another room where a massive carven chest stood against one wall, covering most of it. "It may be some time before we can locate a sempstress, and meanwhile you might find a few things here."

He raised the heavy lid and propped it in place. She looked at the contents of the chest and gave a little gasp of astonishment and pleasure. Rich silks and samite and satins, gleaming damask and glittering brocades, smooth linens and glossy lampas shone in the beam of fading light from the far window. Gold and precious stones winked in the recesses of the chest as Kedrigern raised a lantern to assist her inspection.

"*Brereep?*"

"They were given me by Ulurel, a very kindly sorceress I once assisted," Kedrigern explained. "She knew your measurements. She could read the future."

He took her arm, and they withdrew to the shade of the trees, where Spot had laid out a light collation. The goblets were slightly tarnished; otherwise, everything was just right. The evening was pleasantly cool, the food was tasty, the wine superb. In the gentle twilight, Princess saw her surroundings at their most beautiful, and her mood began to soften. Noises suggesting the migration of entire nations came from within, and when they returned to the house, Princess found the great room emptied of furniture, dust, and cobwebs. She smiled at Kedrigern, and gave Spot a gingerly pat on its warty head.

The bed chamber had been cleaned and aired out, and the musty bedclothes replaced with fresh linen, sweetly scented with herbs. Spot had wrestled the chest of garments into the room and placed a mirror beside it. At Kedrigern's urging, Princess tried on her wardrobe, and found each new item more becoming than the one before. As promised, they fit her slender figure to perfection.

With the garments and jewelry draped over chest, chairs, and bed, the room glowed with warm color. Princess looked around the bed chamber with obvious pleasure, then turned and threw her arms around Kedrigern and kissed him most tenderly.

"*Brereep*," she whispered.

"*Brereep*," he replied, snuffing out the candles.

The next morning, immediately after breakfast, Kedrigern went to his study. He had a busy day planned, and wanted to make an early start.

His worktable contained a few extraordinary objects, but most of its surface was covered with books, opened and piled one atop another in precarious towers nine or ten deep. Books stood in stacks about the room, and were crammed in no discernible order on the shelves that ascended from floor to ceiling. Kedrigern's library needed proper cataloguing, but he had not yet found time to get around to it. Fortunately, he had a filing system, or index, or whatever one chose to call it, that was reliable most of the time, though it required patience to operate, since it kept trying to turn the subject to how nice it was to be polished at regular intervals.

Kedrigern stood before the brass head at the end of the table, raised his hands, and in a solemn voice intoned, "Eleanor of the Brazen Head, I conjure you to speak!"

The eyes opened, blinked once, then fixed on him. In a warm motherly voice, the head said sweetly, "Oh, mercy me, Keddie, is it time for a dust-off and a nice polishing already? Just fancy that! It seems like only four or five months ago . . . no, more like seven or eight. . . . Well, I'm all ready."

"I have come for knowledge."

"Not to polish me?"

"No polishing today, Eleanor."

"You *never* polish me. You never even dust me off anymore, Keddie. Look at this dust. Now, I ask you. . . ."

"I'll send Spot, when it can spare the time."

"Spot is too rough. It uses abrasives. You do a nice polish, Keddie. Can't you spare a few minutes for Eleanor?" the brazen head said in a querulous voice.

"I'm very busy."

"So busy you'll let me tarnish? Don't you care? I remember everything for you, and look at me, all discolored and covered with dust. It's squalid, that's what it is. This whole house is squalid."

"Well, that's why I'm here, Eleanor," Kedrigern said. "I'm married now. There's a lady of the house. Things are going to be different. Neat. No more squalor. Everything polished. We're doing a thorough cleaning, and moving in all new things, and I need to call up a poltergeist to do the moving."

"I don't much like poltergeists," said the brazen head, pouting. "All noise and carelessness, that's what poltergeists are, when they're not downright nasty and wicked. Throwing things around, and knocking things over, and breaking everything in sight. Why, when I was in Friar Bacon's house, he conjured up a poltergeist that nearly dented my—"

"There's no need to worry, Eleanor," Kedrigern said in his most soothing manner. "I want you to find me a book that contains spells for summoning up spirits to assist with the transportation of material objects. It's a small book. I think it has a green cover."

The brazen eyes clicked shut, and the head was silent for a time, then Eleanor announced, "Third pile to the left of the stool, second from the bottom."

"Very good. I'll also be wanting Isbashoori's *Guide To Countering Complex Curses, Subtle Spells, And Multiple Maledictions*. I'm not sure what this one looks like. Thick, I imagine."

After a slight pause, Eleanor said, "It's on the table. Fourth one down in the stack next to the Sphere of Luminosity."

"Thank you, Eleanor."

"Now do I get polished? Dusted, at least? For your *wife's* sake, if not for mine? Maybe *she* has some pride."

Kedrigern blew away the outermost layer of dust and gave the brazen head a few quick swipes with his sleeve. He straightened it in position, then stepped back, smiling.

"Is that all?" she asked.

"I'm very busy. I have to bring a lot of furniture here in a hurry, and I want to be careful about the kind of help I get. I want a nice quiet poltergeist who knows how to handle valuable furniture."

"There's no such thing," Eleanor snapped.

Kedrigern sighed and began to leaf through the green book. He came at last to the spell he was seeking—a surprisingly simple one, he thought—and frowned at the sight of the admonitory rubric in bold letters immediately beneath: *Employ with extreme caution. This spell may be hazardous to property and is liable to cause serious bodily injury.*

Here was a complication. Kedrigern pushed aside some of the clutter on the worktable and sat down to peruse the book more carefully in hope of finding a spell that did not come equipped with its own caveat. He found none. Leafing back, he reread the disconcerting passage, and remained for a time deep in thought.

All spells were tricky. When one was singled out, and specific warning given in red letters, it was the sort of magic one avoids unless one is very rash. Kedrigern was not rash.

But Princess was looking forward to the arrival of the furniture. To go after it in the customary way, with wagon, and oxen, and hauling and lifting and packing, and a long bumpy dusty drive home, and then more hauling and lifting, and then unpacking, was too dreadful to contemplate, even with Spot to do the heavy work. Time would be wasted. Things would be scratched, dented, broken. Needless anxiety would be generated. Tempers would be strained. Kedrigern did not like to travel, even on a brief trip, lightly and swiftly. A long expedition, heavily encumbered, was a dreadful prospect. A poltergeist could avoid a lot of unpleasantness.

On the other hand, one should not use a spell to do what could be done in other ways merely because one is disinclined to exert oneself or put up with a bit of inconvenience. Magic was not something to be squandered or used lightly.

But on the third hand, Princess was here, now, and growing impatient. She deserved comfort after all those years in a bog, and Kedrigern wanted her to feel happy and at home. The more relaxed she was, the more likely his counterspell would be to work properly and restore her speech. And what good was being a wizard if one could not use a bit of magic now and then to make one's wife happy? It was either use the poltergeist spell or disappoint Princess.

Kedrigern swallowed, set his jaw bravely, and began to intone the spell, pronouncing each word distinctly. It was a harder spell than it appeared, full of difficult words, in a language not ordinarily spoken by human beings, and he took a long time to finish. When he came to the end, he was perspiring freely, his throat was sore, and the muscles of his jaw ached from the effort of enunciation. The room was very still.

"Put me down!" Eleanor howled.

Kedrigern watched her brazen head rise slowly from the table, tilting slightly. The features scrunched up in obvious distaste, and the loud smacking sound of a sloppy kiss broke the ensuing silence. Eleanor's head descended and came to rest gently on the table.

"Disgusting creature! You have no manners at all!" she said furiously.

A low, rustling chuckle filled the room. A stack of books rose in the air, teetering precariously, suddenly turned top to bottom, and dropped noisily to the floor. A chair began to move in slow circles.

"Hold, spirit!" Kedrigern commanded.

The chair stopped for an instant. Then, in a flurry of movement, Eleanor shot into the air while the chair hopped to the table directly under her, and then the brazen head, with astonished expression, settled on the seat while the pages of the topmost book on every pile riffled as in a high wind and all the other books flew from stack to stack, exchanging places. The chuckling grew louder.

"By Fleen and Higibil, and by the Six Doorts, I order you to cease at once!" Kedrigern commanded.

Chuckling and riffling stopped immediately. A hollow, mournful voice said, "I was only having a bit of fun, honored sir. No harm done, no hurt feelings, no offense meant and none taken, that's how I see it. A friendly prank or two is no cause for good gentlemen to get upset and start calling upon powers that mean no good to a decent poltergeist."

"That was a little too lively to be classified as a friendly prank," said Kedrigern.

"It was vulgar and disgusting, that's what it was. He hasn't changed a bit, not Rupert. He's as bold as ever. Why you want to conjure up the likes of *him*, I don't know," Eleanor started in. "But then, *I'm* not a wizard. *I'm* not expected to understand things. All I do is keep track of everything, and not even the flick of a dustcloth to—"

"Do you know this poltergeist?" Kedrigern broke in.

Before Eleanor could resume her plaint, the hollow voice, sounding somewhat more cheerful, said, "Oh, yes, sir, Ellie and me, we go back ever so far, don't we, Ellie? Ever so far, sir. Been a while since I've had the pleasure of her company, though, isn't that so, old girl? Last time we had a quiet moment to ourselves was at Friar Bacon's house, sir, and that must be . . . let me see. . . ."

"Quiet moment? *Quiet moment?!*" Eleanor shrilled. "There's no such thing as a quiet moment when Rupert is around! He hasn't known a quiet moment in his life!"

"That was cruel, old girl. My whole life was as quiet as a church at midnight. It's only since I've been a poltergeist that I've been able to cut up now and then. Not all my doing, either, sir. As you must know, a certain amount of prankishness goes with the profession. It's expected. Let a poltergeist once get a name for behaving in a refined and dignified manner, and he'll soon hear about it from them as can make him listen, if you follow my meaning, sir."

"I think I do," Kedrigern said.

"Then you're a man of some understanding, sir, and you must realize the pain it gives me to have aspersions cast on my past life and my present profession all in a single breath by someone for whom I have always entertained the most tender feelings," the poltergeist went on, his voice now practically honeyed.

"I'm amazed you don't choke on your words, Rupert," Eleanor said. "Do you dare tell this wizard how you treated me in our last 'quiet moment'? Can you speak your shame?"

"Ah, now, Ellie, it was not all my fault. I admit my hand was just a trifle unsteady, but that Friar Bacon, he worked us something fierce. Had me to Cathay and back twice that morning, and to Ind later in the day. No wonder I wasn't at my best."

"You dropped me!" Eleanor cried in a chilling metallic keen.

"Not very far, old girl."

"Far enough to dent me! Far enough to leave me dazed and

stunned just at the moment of my greatest opportunity! I, who
was formed to unfold strange doubts and gnomic sayings, to
read a lecture in philosophy, and there I was, groggy as a
drunken student, mumbling 'Time is,' and 'Time was,' and
'Time is past.' Friar Bacon was furious. He would have ham-
mered me into a salver."

"And who was it saved you, old girl? Who whisked you
out of harm's way before the hammer fell, and substituted a
battered old cuspidor to·fool poor nearsighted Bacon? It was
Rupert done it, old girl, that's who."

"It was the least you could do," said Eleanor.

"But I did it. I saved you, old girl."

Eleanor ignored the remark and went on, "I could have
been somebody. Uttered strange and uncouth aphorisms, and
girt fair England with a wall of brass. And that would only
have been the beginning. Scholars and seers, pyromancers and
wizards, all the wisest men in the world would have come to
listen to my speech. But that's all over now," she said, sighing. "Look at me, Rupert. I'm nothing but a catalogue, dusty
and tarnished, buried in obscurity."

"Now, just a minute, Eleanor," Kedrigern said irritably.

"Nothing personal, Keddie. Let's face it, you're not Roger
Bacon, and I'm all washed up, anyway. Just an old brass head
with a dent in it," she replied dully.

"Well, what about me? Look at me, old girl, moving furniture and running errands halfway across the world on a moment's notice. I used to be a man of some prominence in my
village, I'll have you know."

"What does it matter? I'm a fallen woman. Abuse me,
mistreat me, neglect me. It doesn't matter anymore."

"I tell you what, old girl, you'll feel different after a good
buffing up. If the honored sir here will just give me his permission—"

"I will do no such thing," said Kedrigern. "This is not a
lovers' tryst, Rupert. You're here on business. I have valuable
property to be moved, speedily and with great care. Not a dish
is to be chipped, not one chair or table nicked, or Fleen and
Higibil will hear of it. Curtains, rugs, and draperies are to be
folded neatly, and everything delivered according to a plan
which I have sketched out. Do you understand?"

"Yes, sir. Absolutely, sir. Of course, being a poltergeist,
I'm not authorized to guarantee the condition of the goods

upon arrival, sir. All I can promise is speed. A nick here, a
chip there . . . that sort of thing is just about unavoidable, sir."

"But you will avoid it, won't you, Rupert?" said Kedrigern
sternly.

"I'll do all I can, sir, but like I say, I can't make any
promises."

In a weary voice, Eleanor said, "Don't try to reason with
him, Rupert. He doesn't care about the likes of us. Look at the
condition he's let me lapse into. Our problems don't matter to
him. Just do as he says, and hope that he only neglects you, as
he does me." She ended with a deep, prolonged sigh.

"That's very unfair of you, Eleanor," said Kedrigern. "You
refuse to let Spot polish you. That hardly gives you the right
to complain about neglect."

"Spot is too rough. Spot would rub me smooth as a platter
in no time."

"Now, I'm very good at that sort of thing, sir," Rupert
interjected. "I could have the old girl gleaming like the king's
punch bowl in no time at all. Just you say the word and I'll be
about it. It'll do wonders for her, sir."

Kedrigern folded his arms and looked hard at the brazen
head. "Is that what you want, Eleanor?" he asked.

"He'd have to promise not to drop me."

"It's a promise, old girl. Have no fear, sir, she'll be as safe
as houses," Rupert hurriedly assured them.

"I thought you couldn't make any promises," Kedrigern
said.

"Ah . . . well . . . with a single item, sir . . . and not moving
it over great distances . . . a different situation entirely, sir."

"I see," said Kedrigern, nodding judiciously. "Then consider this, Rupert. If my goods arrive here no later than this
afternoon, undamaged, you have my permission to give
Eleanor a careful polishing. Agreed?"

"You're a true wizard, sir. Friar Bacon never dealt as fairly
with a spirit in his life as you're dealing with me this minute,
sir. If I may have the directions and any special instructions . . . ?"

Kedrigern held out a map to Wuxul's castle and an item-
ized list of furniture and household goods, together with a
diagram indicating the desired placement of the articles in his
house. Map and list rose, unfolding in their ascent, and hovered just above his head; either Rupert was an exceptionally

tall spirit, or he was floating in midair. Then, without a word
of farewell, there was a great whoosh of wind, and Kedrigern
knew that the poltergeist was gone.

As the sun touched the far mountaintops, Princess stood
before the fireplace, hands on hips, looking pleased. Kedrigern's little cottage had not been transformed into a palace,
but at least it no longer resembled the den of careless bachelor
ogres. It was a fit and cozy home for a princess. Light winked
on polished oak and cherry, silver and crystal. Bright tapestries hung on the walls, rugs lay on the floor, draperies covered the windows. All was of the finest quality, and all had
made the long passage from Wuxul's castle unharmed. Not a
chip, not a nick, not a dent was to be seen.

Kedrigern poured wine from a many-faceted crystal de-
canter into two delicate silver chalices and handed one to
Princess. "Is everything satisfactory, my dear?" he asked.

"*Brereep*," she said brightly.

"Delighted to hear it. Let us drink to our comfortable
home. And to Wuxul. And to Rupert, who turned out to be a
remarkably solicitous poltergeist."

"*Brereep*," said Princess, raising her vessel.

They sipped the very good wine, and Kedrigern looked
over his transformed room with a calm proprietary air. "It's all
in the way you handle them," he said sagely.

"*Brereep?*"

"Poltergeists, my dear. Some wizards would sooner traffic
with devils than call up a poltergeist. But if you treat them
with the right combination of firmness and fairness, they can
be very helpful."

"*Brereep.*"

"Yes. And tomorrow, I think I'll have Eleanor and Rupert
work together on my library. She can locate the books, and he
can shelve them. Once my books are in order, I can look up
all the ones called for in the *Guide*, and get to work on a spell
for you. In a few days, you'll be—what was *that?!*" Kedrigern cried as the house shook and a loud thump echoed
through the newly furnished rooms.

A louder thump followed, and then a crash. With an inarticulate growl, the wizard thrust his drinking vessel into Princess's hand and set off at a run for his study. As he reached the
door he heard another crash, followed by a scraping, scratch-

ing noise, with hollow laughter and a metallic giggle in the
background.

He flung open the door, and cried out in rage at the sight of
the chaos within. Amid a blizzard of flying books and objects
of the wizard's trade, his worktable floated knee-high off the
floor, swaying like an unpracticed skater on slick ice.
Eleanor's head, gleaming brightly, hovered over the mael-
strom, transfigured with merriment at the sight of a chair and
joint-stool dancing like drunken peasants at a wedding.
Through the flurry of airborne articles, Kedrigern saw her expression change to dismay at his entrance.

"What's the meaning of this?" he roared.

His worktable crashed to the floor. Chair and joint-stool
stopped in mid-caper. Books began to mount guiltily in unsteady heaps. Globes, jars, coffers and cabinets, phials and
flaskets crawled into corners, where they huddled in untidy
mounds.

In a low, menacing voice, Kedrigern said, "Rupert . . ."

"Just having a bit of a frolic, sir, me and Ellie. 'When the
work is done, it's time for fun,' as they say. No harm done,
I'm sure. Look how nice she polished up. Does your heart
good to see her shine, don't it, sir?"

"I'm looking at my study, Rupert."

"Ah, well. Couldn't help myself, sir. I held myself back
something painful when I was moving all those lovely things.
Not a nick in the lot. It near destroyed me, sir. I'm a poltergeist, and that sort of thing goes against my nature. I need
noise, and crashing about, and thumping, if you know what I
mean, sir."

"You'll get thumping, Rupert. I'll see to it that you get
such a thumping as never—"

"Don't threaten my Rupert!" Eleanor burst in. "I don't care
what you do to me—dent me, scratch me, hammer me into
foil—I'll never remember another thing for you if you mistreat my Rupert!"

"Eleanor, get hold of yourself."

"Well said, old girl," said Rupert in a stage whisper.

Encouraged, Eleanor cried, "You'll never part us! Never!"

"If that's what you want, Eleanor, then that's what you'll
get," said the wizard in a fury, raising his arms and flinging
out his hands in a forceful gesture as he intoned, "Begone,
spirit and brazen head, and never return to me!"

As he stared in silent dejection, surveying the tumbled aftermath of their frolic, he heard a light footstep and turned to see Princess. She peered into the room and looked at him, wide-eyed.

"Things are a little messy, I'm afraid. Rupert needed more firmness and less fairness."

"*Brereep?*"

"Yes, both of them. Utterly banished from our ken. We'll not be seeing them again," he said. She laid a consolatory hand on his forearm, and he went on, "Just as well, I suppose. I'll have Spot clean up in here, and when he's done, I'll get to work on the counterspell for you. I just have to find . . . Oh, dear," he murmured. "Oh, dear me. I need . . . I have to locate . . ." He turned to Princess and placed his hands on her shoulders. "My dear, the spell upon you is a very complicated one. In order to undo it, I must first do considerable research. I'll need all the resources of my library." As one, they turned to gaze upon the higgledy-piggledy disorder of the study. "Eleanor was my filing system. She knew where every book is. Without her, it may take . . ."

"*Brereep?*"

"Longer, I'm afraid. Oh, my dear, can you ever forgive me?" he asked with a deep and desolate sigh.

"*Brereep,*" she said.

...⚜ *Five* ⚜...

a hedge against alchemy

KEDRIGERN TOOK PRINCESS'S needs and his wizardly pursuits seriously, but he was a sensible man withal. On a beautiful morning in early summer, he saw greater wisdom in sitting comfortably in his dooryard, soaking up the sun and letting his mind wander idly, than in conning ancient lore in his study. The secret to successful wizardry, he reflected comfortably, was knowing when and how to relax. One must never strain at a spell; especially when one's working area is an unholy mess and one's library is all a jumble.

He sprawled back in pillowed comfort, feet up on a cushion, and rang with languid gesture a little silver bell. From within came the sound of rapid motion, and soon the slapping of huge flat feet approached Kedrigern's side, and there stopped. Spot stood trembling with eagerness to serve its master.

"Ah, there you are," said the wizard.

Spot wagged its monstrous head, spraying saliva about in generous quantity, and said, "Yah, Yah!"

"Good fellow, Spot. Listen carefully, now."

"Yah! Yah!" said Spot, bouncing up and down excitedly.

"I will have a small mug of cold ale. Bring a pitcher, just

to be sure. And bring with it a morsel of cheese just of a size to cover the mouth of the pitcher, and a loaf of bread. And ask Princess if she'd care to join me."

"Yah! Yah!" said Spot, and windmilled off about its duties.

Kedrigern looked after it affectionately. Trolls were a troublesome lot, it was true, but if you got them young and trained them properly, they could be devoted servants. They never did acquire manners, but one could not have everything. One could not, he reflected, have much at all unless one was very lucky, and he considered himself lucky to have Spot.

And so lucky to have Princess that it did not bear thinking about.

He settled back into the cushions, closed his eyes, and sighed with quiet pleasure. This was the life for a sensible man, he thought smugly. Let the others fret and stew and struggle in the squalid world down there; he would stay on Silent Thunder Mountain with Princess, where life was good.

He frowned, thinking how very much better life would be if only he had found the counterspell to bring back Princess's voice before Rupert had made such a mess of things. A long, hard, frustrating search lay ahead of him, and a long wait for Princess, poor girl. The proper counterspell was there among his books, he was certain, but locating it was going to be like finding one particular leaf in a windswept forest.

There was only one possible alternative, and that was so remote that it seemed a foolish waste of time even to mention it to Princess; so he did not. The great Cymric bards were famous throughout the civilized world for their spells bestowing eloquence and sweet speech. One of them could probably solve her problem in a matter of minutes. But their land was far away, and they were a temperamental lot, and the price of their services was high. To find one, and bring him here—for their spells and charms could be worked only by them, and by no others—would require more time and patience than the most painstaking search through his scattered library. It would also require a large amount of gold, to be paid on the spot. Still, it was something to keep in the back of the mind; a last resort.

Now, if he were on speaking terms with the guild, he could ask his fellow wizards for advice and assistance; but that was out of the question. They had chosen to embrace Quintrindus, that fraud, that alchemist, and forced him to resign from the

Wizards' Guild for the sake of his honor and integrity. So much for his erstwhile colleagues.

He simply could not understand their unhealthy fascination with alchemy. After two years, he still had not come to terms with it. Wizards, of all people, should know better than to involve themselves with a pseudo-profession that was nothing more than a lot of smoke and stink and horrible messiness and pompous jargon about things no one understood but everyone felt obliged to discuss. Yet it seemed to be catching on. Clever young people were not interested in becoming wizards anymore. It was alchemy or nothing for them.

Young people, at least, had the excuse of their youth. His fellow wizards had no excuse at all, and ought to be ashamed of themselves. They would learn the error of their ways soon enough, he reflected, and he would cheerfully point out— when they came to him on their knees to apologize—that he had told them so.

It was just one more sign of the times, he believed, and bad times they were. Barbarians sweeping in from the east and burning the churchmen; churchmen issuing anathemas and burning one another; alchemists burning everything they could get their hands on, wild to turn lead into gold. Smoke and shouting and destruction, that's all anyone cared for these days.

Except for Kedrigern, who had Princess, and his work, and was happy with both. He was learning more and more about temporal magic and becoming rather good at it. He had reached into the future several times, even managed to pluck curious artifacts from that unformed age and retain them for study. There was much yet to learn, of course . . . much to learn. . . .

He fell into a light doze, awakening with a frown when a shadow fell upon him. He opened his eyes and saw a great hulk standing before him, blocking out the sun.

It took his eyes a moment to adjust to the light, and his wits another moment to reconvene in the here-and-now, and then Kedrigern saw that the creature before him was a man of a kind he had hoped never again to encounter—certainly not in his own dooryard.

He was half again the wizard's height and twice his bulk. Bare arms like the trunks of aged hornbeams hung from his beetling shoulders. Torso and thick legs were encased in coarse furs. A tiny head was centered between the bulging shoulders with no sign of a connecting neck. About him hung an effluvium of rancid animal fat and human perspiration. He was a barbarian, no doubt, and barbarians were not the friends of wizards. Or of anyone else, for that matter; not even of other barbarians. A thoroughly bad lot.

"This road to Silent Thunder Peak?" the barbarian asked. His voice was like a fall of stone deep in a cave.

"Yes, it is," Kedrigern replied, smiling brightly. He pointed to his left. "Just follow the uphill track. If you hurry, you can reach the peak by sunset. Marvelous view, on a day like this. I'd offer you a drop of some cool refreshment, but I'm—"

"You wizard?" the barbarian asked.

That was the sort of question one did not rush to answer. Far too many people were wandering about these days with the notion that slaying a wizard was somehow a deed of great benefit to the commonweal.

"Wizard?" he repeated, squinting up. "Do I understand you properly? Are you inquiring about the whereabouts of a wizard?"

"You wizard?" the barbarian asked, exactly as before.

An uneasiness came over Kedrigern. It was not at the barbarian's great size and ugliness, nor his noisomeness, nor even at his appearance here, in this isolated retreat, where one did not turn up by chance. It was intangible; a sense of presence. He had the eerie sensation that a member of his brotherhood was near, and that was manifestly absurd. This creature was no wizard.

"Interesting that you should ask," said Kedrigern thoughtfully. "It suggests an open-mindedness not immediately evident in your manner and your appearance." As he spoke, he slipped his hand behind him to work the figures necessary to a spell for the deflection of edged weapons. "Most people expect a wizard to go about in a long robe covered with cabalistic symbols, and wear a conical cap, and have a long white beard flapping down around his knees. I, as you can see, am plainly dressed in good homespun tunic and trousers, wear no headgear of any sort, and am clean-shaven. Consequently, a casual passer-by seeking directions, or the whereabouts of a world-famous wizard, might easily assume that I am some honest tradesman or artisan who for personal reasons has chosen to live apart . . . when I am, in fact, an adept in the rare and gentle arts."

With the spell completed, he hoped earnestly that this great brute would not decide to smash him flat with a club before he could proceed to a further, more comprehensive, protective spell. Even with the aid of magic, it was difficult to be ready for all contingencies.

The barbarian's tiny black eyes, set closely on either side of a shapeless little smudge of nose, peered at Kedrigern from behind a fringe of lank greasy hair. In them shone no glimmer of reason.

"You wizard?" he repeated.

"Me wizard," Kedrigern said resignedly. "Who you?"

"Me, Buroc," said the barbarian, thumping his chest loudly.

"Oh, dear me," Kedrigern whispered.

Buroc was the consummate barbarian, the barbarian's barbarian. Compared to Buroc, Krogg was a playful tyke. Buroc was known throughout the land as Buroc the Depraved, and had added to his name such epithets as Flayer of God's Earth, Fist of Satan, and Torch of Judgment, as well as other terms emblematic of mayhem and savagery. It was said of Buroc that he divided the human race into two parts: enemies and victims. Enemies he slew at once. Victims he slew when he had no further use for them. He recognized no third category.

Looking into that flat expressionless face, crisscrossed with pale scars, Kedrigern believed all he had ever heard of Buroc. The barbarian's face reminded him of a cheap clay cup shattered to bits and hastily glued together.

"You come with Buroc," said the barbarian.

"Well, now that's an offer that raises some unusual possibilities, but I'm afraid murder, rape, and pillage aren't my line of work, Buroc. I'm more the bookish sort. And I'm not as nimble as I used to be. Thoughtful of you to ask, though. Now, perhaps you'd best be running along," Kedrigern said, hurrying to the end of a backup spell against indeterminate violence. With that done, he felt secure against Buroc's displeasure.

"Buroc find golden mountain. Need magic."

"Oh?" Kedrigern was puzzled. Seekers of golden mountains often required the assistance of magic. Finders of golden mountains, as a rule, did not.

"Mountain all gold. Spell hide mountain. You break spell. Split forty-forty," said Buroc in an outburst of eloquence.

"Fifty-fifty," Kedrigern quickly corrected him.

Buroc's eyes glazed, and for a moment he stood immobilized. Then he nodded his tiny head and repeated, "Fifty-fifty."

"Where is this golden mountain, Buroc?" Kedrigern asked, spacing his words and enunciating carefully.

Again the barbarian's eyes glazed over, and Kedrigern realized that this was the outward manifestation of a reasoning process going on in the recesses of that little head. "You come. Buroc show," the barbarian replied.

"I have to have some idea of how far it is, so I'll know what to pack. Is it very far? Many days from here?"

After a time, Buroc said, "Sun. Sun. Golden mountain."

"Three days from here, I take it. Not bad. Not bad at all," said Kedrigern, his interest growing by the minute.

This was an opportunity indeed. It would set the alchemists on their ears and put them in their proper place once and for all. Let them stink up the countryside with their furnaces and fill the silence with their babble of Philosopher's Egg and Emerald Table and suchlike pseudo-magical rot in their feeble attempts to manufacture a pinch of third-rate gold dust. Using only his magic, Kedrigern would possess a golden mountain. Well, half a golden mountain. And with such resources, he could recruit his own choir of Cymric bards to come to Silent Thunder Mountain double quick and unspell Princess. Whatever the risks, magical or physical, Buroc's offer was too good to pass up.

"You're not the ideal client, Buroc, nor are you my first choice as a business partner. And I'm sure that somewhere in that miniature head of yours lurks an inchoate notion of mincing me small once we've achieved our goal. But I can't resist your offer," said the wizard.

"You come?"

"I come. And Buroc, may I inquire whether you saw any ghosts on your way up the mountain?"

"Ghosts?"

"Ghosts. Spirits. Sheeted fiends, squeaking and gibbering. Pallid wraiths and ghastly apparitions. Any or all of the foregoing."

"No ghosts."

Kedrigern nodded ruefully. It was as he had feared. In banishing Rupert, he had not only lost the services of Eleanor, he had also inadvertently released all the horrifying spirits that guarded his solitude. One must always be very precise in casting spells, even when angry. Now anyone, even a barbarian, could grope his way through the twisting paths and burst in on Kedrigern and Princess practically at will. Something would have to be done about that.

At this moment Princess made her appearance, entering on delicate and silent feet. She bore a silver tray on which stood a frosty pitcher, two gleaming silver goblets, a fist-sized chunk of golden cheese, and a loaf of pale brown bread. She halted abruptly at the sight of Buroc.

Princess was somehow even more spectacularly beautiful than usual this day. A tumble of glistening raven hair cascaded to her hips; her eyes were the color of a midday August sky; her features were sculpture perfect. A silken dress of emerald green clung to her slender form, and a circlet of gold ringed her brow. Buroc's little eyes gleamed at the sight of her. She moved close to Kedrigern and glanced at him, wide-eyed, in frightened appeal.

"No need to be nervous, my dear. This fellow and I are discussing business," he said, rising and taking the tray from her, setting it on the little table.

"*Brereep*," she replied softly.

"Lady talk funny," Buroc observed.

"That's my Buroc, always the gentleman. A connoisseur of linguistic elegance. Depend upon Buroc for the *mot juste*," said Kedrigern amiably, taking Princess's hand in his and raising it to his lips. His irony was lost on the barbarian.

"Lady talk like frog," Buroc said.

Princess glared at the hulking malodorous figure. Kedrigern squeezed her hand and said, "This lovely lady is my wife, Buroc, and we manage to communicate quite effectively. Don't we, my dear?"

She touched his cheek gently and murmured, "*Brereep*."

"Sweet of you to say so," he responded. Turning to the barbarian, he said, "Now, do you have horses for us?"

"Lady come?"

Kedrigern weighed that for a moment. He could leave Princess here, protected by a spell. But if anything befell him, she would be alone, and long unaware of her plight. And with the terrifying spirits banished from the mountainside, even a powerful spell could not provide the protection he wished for her. Much as he disliked subjecting her to Buroc's hungry eyes, he felt that the best course was to bring her along. "The lady comes," he said.

Buroc's eyes again glazed over in deep thought, then he lifted one columnar arm and pointed down the road. "Horses there."

"We'll pack some food and be with you shortly," Kedrigern said. His glance lighted on the tray Princess had brought. "Meanwhile, be my guest. Eat. Drink," he said, presenting the tray.

Impressed by the speed with which bread, cheese, and ale vanished, Kedrigern decided to use Buroc in an experiment. Leaving Princess to pack their food for the journey, he filled a sack with objects captured in one of his blind gropings into the future. They were small cylindrical things of bright metal, wound in bands of colored paper marked with symbols and pictures. At first he had assumed that they were talismans of some unintelligible magic, but he had learned, by dint of much exertion, that they were actually foodstuffs protected by a nearly impenetrable shell of metal. He could not imagine how they had been gotten into their shells in the first place, or why, or who or what might eat such things, or how they went about it. If Buroc could do anything to answer any of these questions, it would be a great help.

He glanced about his study. It was cluttered with paraphernalia, much of it from that remote future age whence came the cylinders. He had learned very little about the period so far, aside from the fact that it contained a great variety of mysterious objects, most of them shiny. But his investigations were still in their infancy.

Outside, he pulled a cylinder from the bag and tossed it to Buroc. "Food, Buroc. Good. Eat," he said rubbing his stomach.

Buroc bit down on the cylinder, frowned, and took it from his mouth. After staring at it for some time, he laid it on a stump, drew a huge, heavy dagger, and brought the dagger down hard, splitting the object in two. He picked up one half, sucked at it, tossed it aside, and did the same with the other half. "More," he said.

Kedrigern tossed him the sack, and Buroc treated himself

to a dozen more, leaving the dooryard littered with glinting metal. "Skin tough. Meat good," the barbarian said.

So that was how one enjoyed the contents of those metal cylinders. A dark thought came to Kedrigern. This remote age into which his magic had extended might be peopled by barbarians like Buroc. He pictured a landscape littered with shards of scrapped metal trodden by huge barbarian feet, and shuddered. Perhaps it was a sign that the alchemists would triumph in the end; it was the kind of world to gladden their hearts.

Buroc led them to where two shaggy horses stood tethered, grazing complacently. He mounted the larger one, leaving the smaller one for the wizard and the lady. Kedrigern mounted, and reached down to swing Princess up before him.

They traveled in silence for some time. Kedrigern was absorbed in his troubled speculations, Princess was fascinated by the unfamiliar sights, and Buroc was completely occupied with keeping to the trail. The way led through pleasant open countryside, across meadows full of wild flowers and down a fragrant woodland track, then through a valley to the outskirts of a little market town. Kedrigern, still deep in thought, grunted in surprise as Princess squeezed him tightly and clung to him in fear.

The town was a grisly sight. Smoke hung in the air, only now beginning to dissipate on a gentle breeze. Doorways and windows gaped, and the village church was open to the skies. Above whirled flights of crows, and Kedrigern saw a wolf start from their path. When they came upon the first bodies, he raised his hand to caress Princess's head, buried in his shoulder, and worked a small concealing magic to hide the desolation from her. He could feel her shivering.

"It's all right now, my dear," he whispered.

"*Brereep,*" she said faintly, not moving her head.

Buroc reined his mount to a halt and made a sweeping gesture. "Buroc do this," he announced.

"Why?"

The barbarian turned his little eyes on the wizard, held his gaze for a moment, then pointed to the ruins of the church. "Me burn." Swinging his hand to indicate a heap of sprawled corpses, he said, "Me kill." Jerking his horse's head aside, he rode on, erect and proud in the saddle.

At the sound of Buroc's voice, Princess gave a little shudder and clung more tightly to Kedrigern.

"Odd, isn't it, my dear, how barbarians seem to have no knowledge whatsoever of the nominative singular pronoun?" he said by way of creating a distraction.

"*Brereep*," Princess said softly.

"Yes, it's always 'me' this and 'me' that with barbarians, particularly when they're feeling boastful. Their grasp of proper grammatical usage is at about the lowest possible level compatible with spoken communication." After a brief silence, he added, "I sometimes wonder if it's just an affectation."

"*Brereep?*"

"No, I really do." Kedrigern fell silent again. They rode on for a time, then he laughed softly and furtively and whispered to her, "I sometimes picture them off by themselves, sitting around the fire all hairy and rank, far from the eyes of non-barbarians, dropping the pretense and cutting loose with long compound-complex sentences and sophisticated constructions in the subjunctive. Can't you see it?"

She laughed at the suggestion, and Kedrigern went on to spin it out ever more elaborately, happy to see her cheerful again. From time to time, as they proceeded, she glanced at Buroc, then at Kedrigern, and the two of them smothered laughter as children do at a solemn ceremony.

For the most part, though, Kedrigern was thoughtful. He had traveled very little in recent years, and the world he now saw was a far worse world than the one he had left. Nature was as lovely as ever, but where the hand of man had fallen all was blight, and ruination, and death. The barbarians were overrunning everything; what little they left, the alchemists pounded, and boiled, and burned in their insatiable hunger for gold.

He felt a great foreboding that however he might struggle against the tide, the alchemists were going to win in the end. They would persist until they had turned every bit of base metal into gold, and their work would precipitate an age of chaos. The future world that Kedrigern had touched with his magic was sure to be a place of horrors, if he read the indications correctly. It was a troubling prospect, and he sank into gloom.

Their journey was relatively quiet. They passed through three villages which lay in ruins and skirted two more, and at each one, Buroc stopped to point out the more gruesome scenes of carnage and destruction and claim credit for them loudly and ungrammatically. He evidenced a growing attentiveness to the reaction shown by Princess, and that disturbed Kedrigern. But at night, when they camped, the barbarian behaved himself. All the same, Kedrigern cast a precautionary spell around the tent which he and Princess shared.

They came on the third day to a sunless valley where nothing grew. Carrion birds watched with interest from the twisted limbs of dead trees as the riders picked their way across this place of muck and stone toward a low hill that rose in its center. Only as they approached the last barren ground around the base of the hill did Kedrigern determine that the bristling outline of the mound before them was caused not by the remains of a forest but by bare poles thrust into the ground at disturbing angles. He felt the tingling of magic in the air, and reined in his horse, calling sharply to Buroc.

"No farther! That place is protected."

Buroc jerked his horse to a halt and turned to face the wizard. On his flat face was the faint hint of a smile, making him appear even less pleasant than usual. He pointed to the hill. "Golden mountain," he said.

Kedrigern was annoyed with himself. He should have known. There were few better ways to keep people far distant than giving a place the appearance of a barrow-mound of the Old Race. He dismounted, and cautioning Princess to stay behind with the restless horse, he walked closer. The sensation of enchantment grew.

He reached into his tunic and drew out his medallion. He raised it to his eye and sighted through the tiny aperture at its center.

Before him rose a mound of gold. It was not a mountain; not even a fair-sized hill. But it would do. It was pure, glittering gold, flooding the gloomy valley with its light.

Kedrigern tucked the medallion inside his tunic and rubbed his eyes wearily; using the Aperture of True Vision to penetrate a concealing spell was always a strain. When he looked again, the mound rose as before, like the trodden corpse of a giant hedgehog. He turned in time to see a flash of silver in Buroc's hand, which the barbarian quickly removed from before his eye and dropped inside his furs. Kedrigern recognized the silver object, and a chill went through him. A lot of things that had puzzled him were suddenly clear.

"How did you learn about the golden mountain, Buroc?" he demanded.

"Man tell Buroc."

"Freely and cheerfully, I'm sure. And you went at once to find a wizard who could lead you there, didn't you? Well, didn't you, Buroc?"

The barbarian looked at him, his smile gone. "Do magic. Buroc share gold," he said.

"No hurry, Buroc. I'm curious about this other wizard. Did you take something from him?"

"Do magic," Buroc said, and his voice was cold.

"Right now I'm not interested in the golden mountain, I'm interested in the silver medallion that's hanging around your filthy neck. You took it from a brother wizard."

The barbarian reached inside his fur tunic. He hesitated, then he drew out an empty hand. "Wizard give to Buroc. Mine."

"No wizard would give away his medallion. You came upon a brother wizard when his magic was low, and you killed him. That's how you found the golden mountain. But you don't know how to break the enchantment, and you never will." Kedrigern folded his arms and looked coolly and scornfully up at the mounted barbarian. "So, you great greasy heap of ignorant brutality, you can look until your greedy heart consumes itself, but you can never possess."

With a snarl of anger, Buroc sprang to the ground, drawing his long curving sword with smooth and practiced swiftness and charging at Kedrigern. The wizard stood his ground; the blade hummed down, then rebounded with the sharp crack of splintering crystal. Fragments of glinting steel spun through the air, and Buroc howled in pain and wrung his hands.

Kedrigern moved his lips silently, extending his hand before him. With a shout, he flung a shriveling bolt of magic at the raging barbarian. It struck, and dissipated in a shower of light, and it was Kedrigern's turn to cry out and nurse his hand. But worse than the pain of rebounded magic was the shock of realization—the power that protected him, protected Buroc. The medallion knew no loyalty but to its wearer. It betokened fellowship in the company of wizards, and it protected each wizard—while he wore it—from the magic of his fellows.

They faced one another, Kedrigern standing his ground, Buroc circling warily, each eager to strike but cautious from the first shock. Buroc, growling like a hungry dog, wrenched a jagged stone the size of a cauldron from the muddy ground. Raising it high overhead, he flung it squarely at the wizard's chest. It shattered into gravel in midflight and fell like hard rain around them.

"No use, Buroc. You can't hurt me."

The barbarian, panting with anger as much as with exertion, glared at him, motionless, eyes glazing in a furious attempt at thought. After a time, a malicious grin cut across his face.

"Buroc no hurt wizard. Wizard no hurt Buroc."

"I'll think of something."

"Wizard no hurt Buroc!" the barbarian repeated triumphantly.

"Don't gloat. You're only making it worse for yourself."

With unnerving speed, Buroc turned and raced to Princess's side. He seized her wrist in one huge hand, clutched her hair with the other, and roared, "Buroc hurt lady! Wizard try hurt Buroc, Buroc hurt lady!"

Kedrigern felt his stomach flutter at the thought of Princess in Buroc's power. In desperation, he aimed a spell at the barbarian's tiny head. The recoiling force staggered him, and he heard Buroc's laughter through a haze of pain. Princess's shriek brought him to his senses.

"I can't reach him, Princess!" he cried. "The medallion protects him, just as it protects me. I'm helpless!"

She writhed, and turned her frightened eyes on him. Buroc forced her closer, grinning with pleasure at this turn of events.

Only one recourse remained to Kedrigern. His magic was useless against the barbarian, but it would work on Princess. It was dangerous for anyone to be subjected a second time to shape-changing enchantment, but anything was better than mauling and ravishment at Buroc's hands. As a bird, Princess could escape; as a woman, she was lost.

"Be brave, my dear. There's still something I can do," he said. And shaking his head to clear it, Kedrigern began to recite the necessary words, spurred by the sight of Princess's struggles.

Buroc pulled her to him. She clawed at his face, and he struck her hands aside. She tore at his tunic, while he laughed and lifted her off her feet to shake her violently. Still she clawed at him. Then, with a bright flash, the medallion flew through the air.

Kedrigern abandoned his enchantment to catch the silver disk in flight. He dangled it by its chain and laughed aloud. Buroc flung Princess aside and hurled himself at the wizard, groping wildly for the medallion. Kedrigern raised his other hand, and Buroc froze in midair, then crashed to the ground with a loud *splap* and a spattering of mud. He was rigid as stone.

Kedrigern rushed to Princess's side and took her in his arms, holding her tight, stroking her hair, until she had stopped trembling. He led her, half carrying her, to the horse, and drew from his saddlebag a heavy cloak, which he threw over her shoulders.

"You're very brave, Princess. And quicker with your wits than I am," he said.

"Brereep?" she asked weakly.

He glanced at Buroc. Already, the clarity of his outline was fading and crumbling as the petrifaction spell did its work. Soon the Flayer of God's Earth would be no more than a curiously formed pile of gray stone. The general barbarity would, no doubt, continue; but Buroc's special contribution would be missing.

"Quick and painless, Princess. Better than he deserved, but under the circumstances I wanted something instantaneous. Anything more appropriate would have required more time than either of us could spare." A glint of gold caught his eye. He stooped and took up the golden circlet, wiping it free of mud before replacing it gently on her brow. "We'll leave with no more gold than we brought, if you have no objection, my dear."

"Brereep," she said decisively.

"I didn't think you would." He gestured vaguely toward the bristling barrow. "We know how to get back, and I doubt that anyone will stumble upon this and carry it off in the meantime. This valley is not a popular place. We've got time to work out our plans," he said, swinging her up into the saddle.

He mounted Buroc's horse, and side by side they started back. He was silent for a time, deeply preoccupied, his expression serious. When he became aware of Princess's curious gaze, he explained himself.

"I may as well tell you now, my dear," he said, sighing, "that pile of gold may well be more trouble than it's worth. For one thing, it will take me a long time—you know the state of my library—just to locate the proper spell to disenchant it so we can actually pick it up and take it away. And then there's the transporting. I'm certainly not going to work with a poltergeist again, so that means negotiating with movers, and guards, and all sorts of other people. And then we'll have to worry about storing it properly. And then there'll be all that travel. . . . I think we'll be better off if I just concentrate on finding the counterspell for you myself. Besides, the way things are going . . ." He sighed again and shook his head sadly.

"*Brereep?*" she asked, laying a consoling hand on his. He smiled a wan smile, but said nothing, During the day he frequently murmured under his breath, and at night he cried out in his sleep, "Blasted alchemists! They'll turn all the lead in the world into gold!" and gnashed his teeth.

But at the very foot of Silent Thunder Mountain, Kedrigern raised his eyes from the dust and let out a soft cry of joy. "I think I've got it, Princess! The golden mountain . . . I've figured out . . ." He clapped his hands and laughed aloud. Princess, unable to resist the display of gaiety, laughed along with him but looked upon him with open curiosity.

"Once I've found the counterspell to help you, my dear— that's the very first priority—we'll beat those alchemists at their own game."

"*Brereep?*"

"Simple. When they've turned all the lead in the world into gold, what will be the rare and precious metal? *Lead!* So we'll outsmart them all. We'll spell the golden mountain into lead! Isn't that a brilliant idea, my love?"

"*Brereep,*" she said.

···} *Six* }···

the gifts of conhoon

TO THE UNTRAINED eye, the medallions were indistinguishable one from the other. Even Kedrigern could not say with certainty which of the two had hung around his neck since the day he joined the guild, and which had belonged to one of his fellow wizards, nor could he guess which of his former colleagues had been so rudely parted from the powerful talisman. Foul play was a certainty; the victim's identity remained a mystery.

At times like this Kedrigern sorely missed Eleanor of the Brazen Head, but there was no sense in crying over cast spells. Eleanor was gone, leaving him with no quick and easy avenue to hidden knowledge. If a colleague—or the entire guild—were in trouble, he might be long in finding out the truth. And considering the way they had treated him, it would serve them right, he thought.

But this was no time for pettiness or thoughts of revenge. He had a problem on his hands.

The medallions lay side by side on his worktable. They were round, of a size to cover a man's palm, about the thickness of a small fingernail's breadth but as light as a dried leaf. One side was as smooth and slick as the peeled white of a hard-boiled egg. Around the rim of the other side ran a band of quaint and curious symbols cleanly and deeply incised into the metal. At the bottom was a geometric figure of crossing broken lines. At the upper edge, bounded by the rings to which the silver chain was attached, were two notches: the larger, the Cleft of Clemency; the smaller, the Kerf of Judgment. In the exact center was a tiny hole, the Aperture of True Vision.

Kedrigern hefted the medallions in his hands and laid them gently in the pans of his balance. They came to rest on a perfect horizontal. He placed them back to back. They fitted so smoothly that he could scarce discern the crack of their junction. He turned them this way and that, squinted and peered and scrutinized, and at last came to the conclusion that they were indeed identical. Sighing, he replaced one medallion around his neck, laid the other on the table, and rang the dainty silver bell that stood close by his hand.

Moments later, Spot careened into the chamber on great slapping feet, announcing its arrival with cries of "Yah! Yah!"

"You're getting faster, Spot. That's very good," said Kedrigern with an approving smile.

"Yah! Yah!" Spot responded proudly.

"Fetch me a nice cold mug of ale, Spot. One of the larger mugs."

"Yah?"

"No, just the ale. Be quick about it, but mind you don't spill any."

"Yah! Yah!" Spot cried with great enthusiasm, and reeled out of the chamber like a top-heavy galleon under full sail.

Kedrigern pulled up a chair, settled down comfortably, and licked his lips in anticipation. Even here, in the shadowed cool of his study, the warmth of the summer afternoon was beginning to penetrate. He looked again at the medallion, lying in a patch of sunlight on the table, and on an impulse, he snatched it up and hung it around his neck.

An instant later, with a cry of dismay, he tore it off and dropped it back on the table. It had weighed around him like an anchor, and the slender chain had been like a toothed garrote against his flesh. No more of *that*, he told himself, rubbing his nape gingerly. Clearly, wearing the medallion along with his own was not the solution to his dilemma.

What, then, was? A medallion of the guild was meant to be

worn by a wizard, and Kedrigern was the only wizard for leagues around. It was not meant to be buried, or hidden away. It could not be destroyed. Most certainly, it was not to be left lying about where anyone might chance upon it. The medallion had great virtue, and conferred a certain amount of power even on the uninitiated. If Buroc had been just a bit smarter . . . Kedrigern shook his head to drive away the dark thought.

It was a problem, and right now he had a much more pressing problem, that of restoring Princess's proper speech. He wished that the second medallion had never come into his possession.

Spot came flapping in with a frost-coated stone mug of cold ale on a wooden salver, and wheeled off again to be about its household duties. Kedrigern took a deep draft of the ale, sighed with comfortable satisfaction, and cocking his feet up on the edge of the table, he tipped his chair back and stared with aimless gaze into the cobwebby corner of the room.

Dust was thick everywhere. Since Rupert's depredations it had settled deeply on the mess left behind, on the books hastily reshelved and on the freestanding heaps and mounds about the room. Spot had done little to clear it away.

That was the trouble with Spot. Anything within the troll's reach was kept relentlessly scrubbed and dusted, but its range was limited. The upper shelves were blanketed with thick gray dust, like beds of dead ash, and the corners were all rounded by the cobwebs of Manny's numerous and sizeable progeny.

Kedrigern pondered the jumble for a time, then, taking another pull at the mug, he rose to inspect his shelves more closely. They were very dusty indeed. It was shameful. As his eyes darted back and forth over the disorder, they fell on a small black book, passed it, returned, and held. A glow of triumph lit the wizard's face. He had found his solution.

Plucking down the book and blowing the dust from its upper surfaces, he leafed methodically through its pages until he came to the desired rubric: "To Summon Up An Unidentified Essence, Either Dead, Distant, Or Sleeping, For Informational Purposes." With a quiet little chuckle of pleasure, he withdrew to his table, pausing on his way to bolt the study door.

A few hours later, just at sundown, all was in readiness. The ring was drawn, the candles placed and lit, the medallion in proper position. Kedrigern cleared his throat—it was dry, but there was no time to remedy that now—and began to recite the spell.

For a time, nothing happened. But when Kedrigern intoned a certain phrase, the candles wavered, and then steadied and burned evenly once more. He came to the end of the spell, and waited in silence. In the center of the ring, hovering over the medallion, was a shimmering wisp of smoke, no greater than the dying breath of a snuffed candle. It moved, and it grew, and as Kedrigern looked on it filled out to the shadowy likeness of a bald old man, white-bearded, untidily dressed, with an expression of puzzlement on his vague and insubstantial features and an ugly gash in his naked scalp.

"Who are you who wore the medallion?" Kedrigern asked with solemn intonation.

"Devil a bit I know about that," said the apparition in a far, hollow voice.

"Has your identity been taken from you by enchantment?"

"Hard to say, that is."

"What befell you, then?"

"All that is known to me is a bloody great bash on the head that has left me with the mother and father of all headaches and set me to blowing about the between-worlds like a puff of smoke."

"A ghost cannot have a headache."

"Easy for you to say, Mister Flesh-and-Bones," said the apparition peevishly. "For all your cocksureness, I have a head on me throbbing like the Black Drum of Dun na Gall when it summoned home at evening the nine thousand and six red cows that were the wealth and glory of Robtach of the Silver Elbows, Robtach who dwelt in the high hall of—"

"Conhoon!" Kedrigern cried happily.

"He did not dwell in Conhoon, that much I know, and I would appreciate your keeping your bloody voice to a whisper."

Lowering his voice, Kedrigern said, "*You're* Conhoon. Conhoon of the Three Gifts. Conhoon the wizard."

"That may be," said the other cautiously.

"It very definitely is. You belonged to a guild of wizards. I'm Kedrigern. I used to be a member, too, until . . . until I resigned. Each of us wore a silver medallion like the one I have around my neck. You seem to have lost yours, and it's come into my possession. Do you remember anything about it?"

"I do not."

"Do you remember any of our brothers and sisters in the guild? Perhaps you recall Axpad, or Tristaver."

"I do not."

"Or Krillicane? Or Belsheer?"

"Not one."

"Surely you remember Hithernils. He was the treasurer. Everyone met Hithernils at one time or another."

"I do not remember your Hithernils or any of the others, and for the love of God, will you shut your gob and give me a cold cloth to put on my head before I faint with the pain? Cruel enough you are to drag me here from the blessed quiet of between-worlds, but to torture me with questions is inhuman."

"Ghosts do not have headaches."

"This ghost could kick the eyes out of your head if he ever got loose from his spell, and we would see about headaches then," said the apparition grimly.

Kedrigern bit back his instinctive angry response and said mildly, "Conhoon, don't you remember anything? Don't you remember your three gifts?"

"The only gifts I require now are a cold cloth for my head, wool to plug my ears, and a stone the size of a healthy baby to throw at you."

"Your first gift was sweetness of the tongue." Kedrigern paused for a moment, then went on. "The second gift was keenness of memory." He paused again, longer, and his expression grew thoughtful. "I cannot now recall the third gift of Conhoon, but I begin to wonder whether you are really he."

"Do you say so now? Well, Mister Flesh-and-Bones, you will be pleased to know that your nagging has given a push to my memory, and I now recall—"

A knock came at the door. Kedrigern turned, and in the moment of his distraction, the apparition in the circle began to fade. It dwindled quickly, like smoke blowing through a crack, as Kedrigern looked helplessly on. The spell was completely shattered now, and there was no short way to mend it. Muttering angrily, he went to the door, unbolted it, and pulled it wide.

"Well?" he snapped.

"*Brereep?*" came a voice, gently, from the shadows.

At once his manner softened. "Ah, Princess, I'm sorry. I was working, and I forgot dinner completely. I hope it isn't spoiled."

"*Brereep,*" she assured him.

"Good. I'd feel terrible if it were. Come inside. I'll just put a few things away, and we'll go to dinner directly," Kedrigern said, waving her into his sanctum.

The soft candleglow struck highlights from Princess's ebony hair and the golden coronet on her brow. Kedrigern gazed at her lovingly—she was wearing the dark green gown, one of his favorites—and squeezed her hand before turning to his cluttered table.

"*Brereep?*" she asked, looking curiously at the circle on the floor.

"Nothing much, really. Just a small magic to find out who owned the medallion we took from Buroc." He turned to join her. Wetting his thumb, he rubbed a break in the circle to neutralize it. This done, he removed the candles to the table and then took up the medallion. "It belonged to Conhoon of the Three Gifts, I think. He was one of our Irish members. Kept pretty much to himself."

"*Brereep.*"

"No, you wouldn't. He was a surly fellow. And it was all a waste of good magic, anyway. I still don't know what to do with this thing." He held it up, and it turned slowly, flashing mirrorlike in the multiple candlelight. Princess looked at it admiringly and reached out to touch it. He placed it in her hand.

"Lovely thing, isn't it? It would look magnificent against that dress. I always thought that silver looked best on dark-haired women. Something about the way the light . . ."

Their eyes met. She held the medallion against her dress and with a faint smile said, "*Brereep?*"

"Oh, no. That's only supposed to be worn by a wizard, and you . . . well . . ." He faltered, and paused to weigh the possibilities. The consequences of magic were never predictable, even to a wizard. Unauthorized wearing of the medallion might cause Princess to turn back into a toad, or into something worse. Still, Buroc had not been harmed. And Princess had already been enchanted once, and was related by marriage to a guild member; she might qualify, however marginally, as a wizard.

He looked at her, beautiful in the soft candleglow, and thought how nice it would be if she had her full power of human speech. They communicated fairly well now, but there were times when he longed to hear a soft voice whisper his name. A croak did tend to undermine romantic moods. The sound of sweet song would be a welcome addition to the household... conversations by the fireside on cold winter nights... reading aloud from the fine old tales... And then it came to him that Conhoon's first gift was sweetness of the tongue. Clearly, the gift did not reside in Conhoon's person; it might be in the working of the medallion; if so, it might be transmissable to a suitable wearer.

Kedrigern took the medallion from Princess's hands and held it up before her. "There'll be a bit of a risk, my dear. Perhaps a big risk," he said.

"*Brereep*," she replied staunchly.

"Brave girl! Here goes, then."

He placed the silver chain around her neck, and she reached back to draw her hair free. She took a deep breath, swallowed, and looked at him, wide-eyed but not fearful.

"How do you feel? Different? Better? Sick?"

She wet her lips, and in a low and mournful voice she said, "It is odd that I feel, and in three ways do I feel it, and it does me small good in body, mind, or heart to feel as I do, and less good to know that there is devil a thing you or I or anyone can do about it. First, I feel like the grain of sand in the eye of Ciallglind that caused him to run mad and screaming in pain stark naked the length and breadth of Ireland for twelve years, day and night, regardless of the weather. Second, I feel like the splinter of pine in the ball of the thumb of Goiste that festered and grew red and pus-filled and caused his arm to swell up to the thickness of Kathleen MacRossa's leg, and him sworn to do battle singlehanded against the sons of Nish at break of day. Third, I feel like the flea in the ear of Seisclend that caused him to forget wife and children and home, and forsake the gift of honeyed song and the making of golden sound on the harp, and live for sixteen years filthy grunting ragged and stinking among the pigs of his own yard. And that is how I feel, and not pleasant is it, my husband, to feel this way."

"I should think not," said Kedrigern.

"There is more to say, and say it I will in good time, but now a hunger is on me greater than the hunger of the sons of Eogan after doing battle four days and nights, without stopping once for breath or refreshment, against the followers of Goll Black-Tooth to save the honor of the fair Fithir. Lead me to dinner," said Princess.

"By all means, my dear," said Kedrigern, taking her arm.

She spoke not a word during the meal. Kedrigern observed her closely, but could see no side effects brought on by her wearing of the medallion. As far as he could tell, it had given her back her speech, and nothing more.

Of course, it had given her back a considerably greater amount of speech than she might reasonably be expected to have lost. Kedrigern was fairly certain that Princess, before her enchantment, had not gone on like a superannuated Hibernian chronicler. But this spate of talk, he assured himself, was probably a natural reaction to a long period during which she was unable to do anything but croak, and the manner of speech was the aftereffect of Conhoon's long possession of the medallion. Things would surely improve.

"A delightful dinner," he said, patting his lips with his napkin.

"Grand it was, and great is my satisfaction thereat," said Princess. Kedrigern smiled and nodded politely, and she went on, "I am pleased and comforted by this meal in five distinct ways, and I shall now expatiate upon my satisfaction under these five headings at length, in prose of an incantatory nature."

"Oh, there's no need——" Kedrigern began, but she spoke on.

"The first way I am pleased is in my eyes, by the sight of the clean napery and the shining silver, and the gleaming of candlelight on the wine glasses and the pleasant view of the deepening twilight on the hills that rise like the hills of Musheele beyond the farther window, and especially pleased am I because there have many a time been greasy fingermarks on my dish and I unable to articulate my displeasure thereat. These cleanly sights are as pleasing to me as the sight of the

small white foot of Saraid of the Three Twins was to King
Rory the Much-bathed."

"Well, I'm glad to hear—"

"And the second way I am pleased is in my nostrils, by the
smell of the roasted duck and the tang of the wine and the
clean scent of these fine wax candles. As pleasing to me are
these mingled aromas as the fragrance of his stable was to
Tuatha of the Black Bull. And the third way I am pleased is in
my ears, by—"

"You must excuse me, my dear," said Kedrigern, starting
up. "I just remembered that I left a candle burning in my
study, and if—"

"You did not," she said. "Sit down and listen in full to my
account of my satisfaction if you are any kind of a gentleman."

Kedrigern returned to his seat. He remained seated, fidgeting discreetly, while Princess went on to explain, with the help
of illustrative examples, how the dinner had given her pleasure, satisfaction, and delight of the ears, taste buds, and
fingertips. Having exhausted her sensory inventory, she
paused for a breath and concluded, "And that is how I am
satisfied by this lovely dinner."

"I'm glad," said Kedrigern warily, fearful that any words
might bring on another monologue but too polite to remain
churlishly silent.

Princess smiled, but spoke no more. For the rest of the
evening she sat at her loom, and for a time, she sang softly, to
herself, in a low sweet voice that Kedrigern found utterly en-
trancing. He could not distinguish the words, but the melody
was of a beauty that needed no adornment and he could not
bring himself to interrupt her. He listened, eyes closed, while
the evening breeze cooled his brow, and he relished his good
fortune. Here was a pleasant domesticity unknown to his fellow wizards. He was a fortunate man indeed, and if Princess
chose to ramble on now and then, well, he could put up with it
in exchange for moments like this. She had listened to him
often enough; now she could talk and he would listen. Nothing so terrible about that, he thought.

The next day, he began to doubt his power of endurance.
Before breakfast, Princess spoke for the better part of an hour
on the nine joys of a good night's sleep and the sixteen beauties of the dawn. He spent the morning in his study, but at

lunchtime she was ready with an extended recitation on the four goodnesses of bread in which a woman named Dairne of the Plump Hands figured repeatedly in a way that never became clear to him. He returned quickly to his study, his stomach protesting the haste with which he had dined, and emerged for dinner with great, and justifiable, trepidation. Dinner was eaten in blessed silence, but was preceded and followed by a two-part soliloquy on the thirty-three proper seasonings for a midsummer repast. Kedrigern heavily oversalted his meat, drank an inordinate amount of wine to assuage his thirst, and fell asleep grumpily just after sundown, to the strains of an elegiac song.

The next day he spent in the wood, stocking up on necessaries of the profession. He left early and returned late, well past dinner time, and thus was audience only to a long lament concerning the tribulations of one Barach of the Tiny Foot, which consumed the entire evening. It was sufficient to give him a mild headache. He noticed that Spot had taken to tucking in its ears and entering rooms cautiously, lest it blunder into Princess and be forced to hear out one of her monologues. Trolls, he recalled, were noted for their powers of endurance.

For the next three days it rained, hard. Confined to the house, unable to remain long in his study, where the humidity was practically subaqueous, Kedrigern was talked at all day, each day. He longed for the sound of a sweet "*brereep*." He began to have thoughts of counterenchantments to neutralize Princess's medallion; even of outright stealing it, as she slept. But these were dangerous courses, both to himself and to her. He had placed the medallion around her neck, and that was a deed not lightly undone. To complicate matters, she seemed quite content with her newfound multiloquence, and Kedrigern knew that he could not, in the end, bring himself to deprive her of her evident pleasure. Talky she might be, but she was Princess, and he loved her.

On the first dry morning he awoke early, to blessed quiet. For a time, not even a bird peeped. Kedrigern drank in the sweet silence, knowing that it would end all too soon.

He raised himself slowly, stealthily, and leaning on one elbow he looked down on Princess. Her dark hair lay like a pool of night around her fair face. Her coral lips were barely parted, and her breath was slow and regular. She was absolutely silent. Princess looked especially lovely this morning, and Kedrigern, forgetful of all else, reached out to take her in his arms.

But he hesitated, his fingertips a scant handbreadth from her shoulder. He wanted to embrace her, to make love with no more speech than was necessary or fitting, as they had always done before—and he feared that instead of the sweet sighs of past days he would hear still another tale of mighty-thewed heroes and long-suffering damsels, reckless oaths and base treachery, related in a manner more suited to a maundering old sagaman than to the fair lips of Princess.

As he held his hand poised over her shoulder, she stirred, opened her eyes, and looked directly at him. Startled, he drew back his hand.

"Troubled were my dreams last night, Kedrigern my husband, and troubled my sleep as the sleep of Draigen of the Bloodshot Eyes in the Black Bed of Goome," she said. She yawned and went on, "For ten distinct dreams did I have, and all of them filled with omens that would make the hairs of your head to stand up like thorns and your blood to run as cold as the brook of Kilfillin in the springtime, when the melting snows run down the stony flanks of the hills of Musheele. And tremble I did, and cry out, and try to flee, but my voice was taken from me and my feet as still as the Stone Dog of Moycashel."

"Probably something you ate, my dear," said Kedrigern, slipping from the bed. "I noticed an odd tang to the gravy last night. Perhaps Spot—"

"It is not gravy that filled my sleep with the horrors of Hell, and I would think the better of you if you did not flee like the hinds of Sliabh Luachra at the sight of Finn Quick-Spear every time I open my mouth to speak," Princess broke in coldly.

Kedrigern bit his lip and said nothing. Princess looked at him darkly and disapprovingly for a time, then drew a deep breath preparatory to resuming her account of the night's dreams. At that moment a loud knock at the front door echoed through the house.

"It's probably for me," said Kedrigern, grabbing for his clothes.

"You will sit and hear me, husband. Spot it is who answers the door in this house."

The knock resounded again, accompanied by indistinct but

angry-sounding words from below, just under the window.

"I will go. There are some pretty undesirable types around, my dear, and with the ghosts gone from the wood, they're liable to turn up on our doorstep anytime. Remember Buroc. That was not a friendly knock," said Kedrigern as he tugged on his boot.

Working a quick temporary spell against bodily injury, he stalked to the door, threw the bolts, and flung it wide. At the sight of a familiar figure, he gasped and started back. Before him stood a bald old man covered with the dust of the road, white-bearded, untidily dressed, a dirty blood-stained rag binding his pate and an expression of great anger on his face.

"Conhoon! You're alive!" Kedrigern cried.

"I am, and I want my medallion," said the visitor, brandishing his staff in a menacing gesture.

"Ah, yes, your medallion. Come in, Conhoon. We were just about to have breakfast. My house-troll makes wonderful pancakes. Why don't you—"

"I want my medallion, and no bloody foolishness from anyone in this house."

"Of course you do. Come in, and we'll break bread, and talk about the guild. I'd love to have a good long chat about the guild. We'll discuss the whole question of the medallion and come to an amicable solution."

"To hell with an amicable solution! I want my medallion!" howled Conhoon.

At that moment, Princess appeared. She wore a gown of deep dark green. Her hair hung loose around her shoulders, and the medallion glistened like a star on her breast. When he saw it, Conhoon's eyes widened and he began to sputter. Kedrigern quickly made introductions.

"My dear, this is Conhoon of the Three Gifts. Conhoon, this is my wife, Princess. Conhoon is a colleague of mine, my dear, and we—"

"And would you leave the dear man standing out in the morning chill, and him with a bandage to his head and no food at all in his poor stomach? Come in, my fine Conhoon, come in to a chair and a good dish of porridge."

"I thank you, lady, but it's for the medallion I come, and if you'll just be giving it to me, I'll be on my way," said Conhoon, his tone subdued but still firm.

"It is a fine medallion," said Princess thoughtfully.

"It is, and sorry I am to be without it."

"How did you come to lose it?" Kedrigern inquired.

"Devil a thing I know about that. One minute I'm dozing off in my garden, weak and exhausted from a spell to rid three counties of mice and moles, and the next thing I know I have a gash in my scalp and a headache to make the eyes hop around in my skull and my house is all torn to pieces and my medallion gone. Lucky I am to be Conhoon of the Three Gifts, and my three gifts sweetness of the tongue, keenness of the memory, and hardness of the head. And if I find the evil bugger who laid me out, he will need a harder head than mine or we will hear no more from him," Conhoon replied.

"He already has a harder head. I turned him to stone."

"That was good of you," said Conhoon, almost graciously. "And now I will take my medallion and go."

"Fond have I grown of this medallion," said Princess softly, touching the smooth silver disk with her fingertips. "And I think that if I wished to keep it, my brave Kedrigern would come to my aid against any sorcerer or wizard or fellowship thereof. . . ."

"Oh dear me," said Kedrigern under his breath.

". . . But I would not cause such bitter conflict in his soul," Princess went on. "My Kedrigern, my beautiful one, my beloved," she crooned. "Fair he was in his youth, by the look of him. Fair the hair and the brows of him, and smooth the skin of him, and long and slender the hands of him and clean the fingers and the fingernails thereof. Like blood on the breast of the white dove was the redness of his lips. Like red gold after the burnishing was his hair, and like cornflowers the blue of his eyes. Straight the shins of him, and long the legs, and round and hard the knees of him as two wave-washed seashells."

"Very nice of you to say so, my dear," Kedrigern said, smiling and much relieved at this new turn to her speech.

"But the years are quickly passing, and heavy will be their burden on my Kedrigern, the wise, the kindly, the once-fair. Gray as the dust bunnies under our sagging bed will soon be the hair of him, and the lines in his face as deep as the furrowed gullies in the hillsides of Musheele after the torrents of spring have dropped from the skies. Around his eyes the tiny lines are already as numerous as the hairs on the heads of all the warriors who faced—"

"You needn't go on, my dear. Conhoon has the idea."

"I will go on," said Princess implacably. "The warriors who faced—"

"For the love of God, woman, will you give me my medallion?!" cried Conhoon in an agony of impatient longing.

Princess paused. She looked fondly at Kedrigern, then she took the medallion in both hands. "Loath am I to lose this lovely and useful ornament and the rich abundance of speech it has bestowed upon me, and saddened by the thought of once more being forced to croak like a toad in response to intelligent and subtle questions. And I am saddened in nineteen distinct ways. But I will keep them to myself." And lifting the gleaming silver disk from around her neck, she placed it in Conhoon's outstretched hands.

That evening, Princess and Kedrigern dined in the shade of the great oak. When Spot had cleared away, Kedrigern reached over and took Princess's hand.

"That was a fine and decent thing you did this morning, my dear. And a wise thing, too. A battle of wizards can be a terrible ordeal. Devastate the landscape, and do all sorts of odd things to innocent bystanders. It was good of you to avoid bringing one about," he said.

She smiled at him. He squeezed her hand and went on, "I promise you, from this moment on I will devote all my efforts to completing the reversal of your spell. It's my absolute top priority." He looked away, off to the far end of the field, and rather awkwardly and uncomfortably said, "And, my dear . . . something you mentioned this morning . . . I was wondering . . . oh, it's really nothing . . . but still, I . . . ." He looked at her hopefully.

She raised an eyebrow in inquiry.

"Well, you mentioned something to Conhoon about my appearance . . . what you thought I'd look like in a few more decades. Do I really . . . ? I mean, I'm scarcely more than a hundred and sixty. For a wizard, I'm practically a tot. Surely I'm not starting to show signs . . . to look . . . Am I?"

She patted his hand, gave an enigmatic smile, and very slowly, she winked. "*Brereep,*" she said.

···❧ *Seven* ❧···

cogito, ergo sam

KEDRIGERN AT LAST dug Isbashoori's *Guide To Countering Complex Curses, Subtle Spells, And Multiple Maledictions* out of the chaos left behind by Rupert and Eleanor upon their banishment, and located nearly every book referred to in the section on postcounterspell complications. But instead of raising his hopes, further knowledge had confirmed his darkest fears. The basic spell on Princess was capable of so many twists and turns and elegant sly involutions that he might work at undoing it for the rest of his days with no assurance of success.

There was one bright spot: Princess was in no mortal danger. A failed attempt to restore her speech would not cause her to burst into flame, or dissolve, or turn to stone. It would not even cause minor embarrassments like the sprouting of horns or instantaneous obesity. But it would drag on and on, draining Kedrigern's magic without result, and eroding Princess's patience and her faith in him.

The more he brooded on the situation, the more annoyed Kedrigern became at his own haste and carelessness. At their very first meeting back in the Dismal Bog, he should have taken the time to learn every detail of Princess's enchantment.

Ideally, he should have brought her home, ensconced her in a comfortable puddle, and done his research in a methodical fashion before undertaking the counterspell. But he had rushed ahead like an eager apprentice, with only the most perfunctory inquiry into the facts. Worse still, when she had her speech completely restored he had not taken the opportunity to quiz her closely. Considering the rhetorical style induced by Conhoon's medallion, her answer might have lasted several days, but under all the oratory there might have been the clue he needed to direct him to the proper remedy. Now it was too late, and there was nothing for it but trial and error. He dreaded telling this to Princess.

Actually, Kedrigern could understand Princess fairly well by this time; quite well enough for all domestic purposes, at any rate. Princess could communicate far more effectively with her croaking than Spot with its one-word vocabulary. Of course, Spot was a troll and Princess was a princess, capable of vivid gestures and a wide range of facial expression. That did make a difference. But even the most delicately nuanced "*brereep*" was an inadequate medium for explaining the finer points of a transformational enchantment, particularly when they were the work of a malicious bog-fairy who had taken time and care to weave an ingenious spell bristling with pitfalls for the incautious disenchanter.

There were questions to which one could not accept "*brereep*" for an answer. But with Conhoon's medallion restored to its proper wearer, Princess was unlikely to give any other answer for a long time to come.

These thoughts troubled Kedrigern on an otherwise perfect day in summer, as he loitered in the garden after breakfast, reluctant to confine himself indoors on such a lovely morning. He knew that he had a long series of days in the workroom ahead of him, and it was all his own fault. Despite blue skies, warm sun, and melodious birdsong, he scowled.

"*Brereep?*" Princess inquired with instant solicitude.

"Nothing at all my dear. I'm just thinking of how hot and stuffy it's going to be inside on a day like this." He stood by the gate and looked out over the slope of the long meadow to the misty valley far below. "It's a shame I can't work outdoors. It would be nice to set up my things out here. Or maybe under the oak."

"*Brereep*," she suggested.

"It wouldn't do. Most of my materials can't take fresh air and sunlight. Half my books would crumble into dust."

She came to the gate and took his arm, laying her head against his shoulder in a silent gesture of sympathy. They stood for a time looking over the meadow, then Kedrigern raised a hand to shade his eyes.

"Is that someone approaching, my dear?" he asked.

"*Brereep?*"

"Over that way. See?" he said, reaching into his tunic for his medallion, muttering as he did so, "This place is becoming a madhouse. Buroc, then Conhoon, now somebody else . . . might as well have built an inn on the high road . . . crowds, and noise . . . never a minute's peace. . . ." As he peered through the Aperture of True Vision, his mood brightened. "I recognize that livery. It's a messenger from Vosconu."

"*Brereep?*"

"Vosconu the Openhanded, my dear. One of my favorite clients. His problems are usually straightforward and uncomplicated. It's always a pleasure to do a job for Vosconu." He waved an arm, and the distant figure returned his greeting. Leaving Princess at the gate, Kedrigern took up the silver bell from the table and rang for his house-troll. When Spot burst into view, he ordered light refreshments for his visitor, then returned to Princess's side to await the messenger's arrival. "I think you'll be impressed by the calibre of Vosconu's servants, my dear. He's extremely generous to them, and they in turn are fiercely loyal. I'll probably have to force this fellow to take a few minutes to refresh himself, he'll be that eager to get back and put his master's mind at rest," he said.

She turned to him thoughtfully and said, "*Brereep.*"

"Are you certain, my dear?" he replied with mild surprise. "The fellow might have some news that would interest you. Vosconu's court is a busy place. Always someone interesting passing through."

She shook her head resolutely. "*Brereep.*"

"I understand. You go on inside, and I'll talk to him out here. There's no reason for you to see anyone if you prefer not to. I'll tell you the whole story over lunch."

Kedrigern brushed the crumbs of bread and cheese from his fingertips, sipped his ale, and smiled contentedly. "It appears to be a very simple curse, the work of a rank amateur. It should give me no trouble at all. And Vosconu always pays promptly and generously. If we should have to resort to purchasing a counterspell, we'll need the money. The only hitch is that my presence is required, and that means a trip to Vosconu's lands. I do hate to travel, but I can't let an old client down." He was silent for a moment, then he said, "Why don't you come with me, my dear? It wouldn't be at all like our excursion with Buroc. The accommodations at Vosconu's palace are magnificent. We could turn it into a little vacation."

"*Brereep*," she said firmly.

"It's no trouble at all. Spot can watch things. I'll put a protective spell on the house and grounds to help out. I'm sure you—"

"*Brereep*," she repeated.

"But you wouldn't *have* to talk to anyone. You could remain mysteriously silent." She looked at him as if he were raving. He shrugged and said, "Or I could tell everyone you had laryngitis." When her expression did not change, he nodded in acquiescence. "Ah. Well. No need to come if you don't wish to, my dear. I'll get there, get it over with, and get back as quickly as I can. There shouldn't be any complications. In fact, there may not even be a curse. Vosconu tends to worry about things. A regular fussbudget." He laughed softly and held out for her inspection the long letter, in tight script on both sides of six sheets, that the messenger had delivered. "Just look at that, my dear. In Vosconu's own hand, no less. Have you ever seen anything so methodical, such attention to detail?"

"*Brereep*," she marveled.

"Nor have I." Kedrigern looked over the missive and sighed. "Now, if we had something like *this* to describe the exact circumstances of your spell, it would be a matter of . . ."

He stopped in midsentence. He and Princess stared at each other with a wild surmise, and then Kedrigern sprang up and raced inside, to emerge moments later with a pen, an inkhorn, and a sheet of clean parchment. Placing the materials before Princess, he stood back expectantly, beaming in anticipation.

Princess took up the pen, dipped it in the ink, and readied herself to write. She sat poised for a full minute, then rested her chin in her hand and looked thoughtfully into the distance, a faint frown creasing her brow. An artist fond of cliché might have done a quick sketch of her and entitled it "Poet Awaiting the Muse." At last she put down the pen and looked up at Kedrigern with tears glistening in her eyes.

"*Brereep*," she said in a barely audible voice.

"Nothing at all, my dear? Not a single detail?"

"*Brereep*."

"Oh dear me." Kedrigern rushed to her side and took her up in his arms, the better to comfort her. "Everything will be all right. We've lost a bit of time, nothing more. No need to be upset. I'll keep looking, and before you know it you'll be speaking as eloquently as you could wish."

"*Brereep*," she sobbed.

"There's nothing wrong with your memory, my dear. It will return. It's shock, that's all. You've been subjected to so much magic in so short a span that your system hasn't had time to adjust. You've blanked out the cause of it all. I've seen this sort of thing before."

"*Brereep?*"

"Oh, dozens of times. And they all got their memories back. No need to worry."

Princess seemed to take comfort from his words. With a squeeze of her hand, Kedrigern led her to a comfortable chair. He took the writing implements indoors and emerged with a small tankard.

"Drink this, my dear. It will cheer you up," he said. "I'm going to my workroom and start making a list of spells."

At dinner that evening, Kedrigern was silent, as if too preoccupied to speak. Later, strolling in the arbor, he broached a new idea to Princess.

"It occurred to me while I was working. I recalled the first time I helped Vosconu," he explained. "The poor man was certain he was being haunted, and he wanted me to drive the tormenting spirit off. I settled the whole thing to everyone's satisfaction, and now Amos owes me a favor, and I thought—"

"*Brereep?*" Princess interjected.

"Oh, Amos is the ghost. He didn't really intend to haunt Vosconu's palace, he was just looking for a place to stay, and he rather overdid his ghostly presence and upset everyone. If it hadn't been for me, Vosconu would have had him exorcised, and that's a very unpleasant experience for a ghost. Amos promised that if he could ever do me a favor, he'd drop everything and place himself at my service. Now's his chance."

Princess looked at him in puzzlement. He smiled, rubbed his hands together briskly, and explained, "If Amos can contact someone who was present when Bertha placed the spell on you, then we may be able to learn the exact phrasing and the subspells attached to the basic spell. Once I know all that, I'll have you speaking within the hour."

"*Brereep?*"

"Absolutely. I think it's our best chance. Mind you, I generally avoid summoning up departed spirits. If they've gone to a better life they resent being disturbed, and can't wait to get back. They give you curt answers, and get all fretful and impatient when you press them. And if they've gone anywhere else, they keep pleading to stay here, or they threaten, or try to bribe you. They're a difficult lot to work with, either way. But Amos shouldn't be a problem. Someone Out There lost his records, and so he has to wander about, homeless, not quite here and not quite there, until The Proper Authorities can get to his case. It's a lonely afterlife, and Amos appreciates any human contact that's offered."

"*Brereep,*" said Princess, softly and sympathetically.

"Not all that sad, actually. In fact, I think Amos rather enjoys it. There's one drawback, my dear. Amos can only contact a fellow ghost. Since you've been out of touch with the family for a while, you might be in for a nasty shock. . . . I mean, if he should mention someone, you'll know that . . . well, that they've gone Out There since your eighteenth birthday."

Her eyes widened in sudden alarm, and she raised a hand to her lips. Taking her other hand, Kedrigern said, "What I can do—if you'd rather not know—is ask Amos not to contact anyone in the immediate family. I can tell him to stick to courtiers and officials."

Princess nodded, and said "*brereep*" with obvious relief.

"All right, then, I'll get in touch with Amos. I'll go inside and start setting up the spell. Come to my workroom as soon as it's dark, and we'll do it," said Kedrigern.

Princess entered the wizard's workroom at the appointed time to find the table pushed back against one wall and a figure marked in colored chalk on the floor. Two fat blood-red candles stood on either side of the figure, and two slender tapers waited, unlit, in candlesticks on the table. Kedrigern closed the door behind her and led her to a chair, one of a pair facing the figure. Lighting both tapers, he gave one to her and seated himself in the other chair.

"One more thing, my dear. At the first sign of Amos's approach, I'd like you to act terrified," he said softly.

"*Brereep?*"

"No, he's as harmless as a kitten. It's just a thing with Amos. It makes him happy."

In the candlelight, a look of growing impatience spread over Princess's features. Hitching his chair closer to hers, Kedrigern said, "Amos used to be as nice and quiet a ghost as you'd care to meet. He skulked about in the shadows, not making a sound, scarcely ever showing himself. Whenever he did appear, he tried to smile and look friendly, so no one would be frightened. Then he picked up a book of ghost stories somewhere. Amos was always an impressionable sort, even when he was alive. In no time at all, he was rattling chains, and leaving ineradicable bloodstains, and carrying his head under his arm, and leaping out at—"

A low, hollow laugh reverberated through the chamber. The candles fluttered and began to burn with a blue flame.

"That'll be Amos," said Kedrigern. "Would you please act frightened?"

"*Brereep!*" Princess whispered angrily.

"Please, my dear. It means a lot to Amos. We can't offer him anything to eat or drink. We might as well make him feel good."

Frowning, Princess sighed, put her hands over her eyes, and shrank back into the chair, all the while making little terrified noises. She peeked out from between her fingers.

"Perfect, my dear," Kedrigern whispered. Then he gave a melodramatic start, looked about wildly, and cried, "What fearsome denizen of the worlds beyond comes to fill us with fear and trembling? Speak, dread ghost, and harrow our poor frail hearts no longer!"

Another peal of deep hollow laughter filled the chamber, echoing eerily and rattling all the loose objects on tables and shelves. "Are you frightened?" a ghostly voice demanded.

"We are limp with horror," Kedrigern replied.

"Oh, that's very nice. Really very nice," said the ghostly

voice, softening. "It's all right, you know. You're perfectly safe. This is Amos."

"Amos? Really?"

"None other. You did summon me, didn't you?"

"I did, Amos. But for a moment there, I thought I had somehow come in contact with a spirit of cataclysmic malevolence. Such a paroxysm of sheer cosmic terror came over me, I couldn't believe it was anyone I knew."

"Sorry if I gave you a start, old chap. I didn't realize there was a lady present, or I'd have gone easy. Has she fainted in horror?"

"Quite possibly," Kedrigern said.

"I do apologize. If I had known . . ."

"Not your fault, Amos. As a matter of fact, it's for my wife's sake that I've asked you here."

"Your wife? Congratulations, old man!" said the ghost heartily. "What's the lady's name?"

"Princess. She's a princess. We're having a bit of a problem with an enchantment that was placed on her, Amos, and I was hoping you could help us out." Kedrigern described the situation briefly, to the accompaniment of little grunts of amazement and sympathy from Amos.

"A terrible thing, dear lady," Amos said. "Tell me the names of your parents, and their kingdom, and I'll get right to it."

"*Brereep*," Princess said, extending her hands in a gesture of helplessness.

Kedrigern interpreted. "She can't remember. She doesn't remember *anything*, Amos."

"That may complicate matters."

"Couldn't you just ask around? If anyone knows anything at all about a beautiful princess turned into a toad on her eighteenth birthday, it could be a great help."

Amos sighed. "All right, Kedrigern," he said.

"You'll do it, then?"

After a brief silence, Amos said, "I've done it."

"So quickly?"

"You forget, time moves differently Out Here. I've found a chap who claims to be a court philosopher. His name's Sam. He's right here, if you wish to conjure him to speak."

Kedrigern looked to Princess. She shrugged, and gave no sign of recognition. "Maybe you'll remember the voice," he said, patting her shoulder for reassurance. Raising his hands, he said in a clear, ringing voice, "Speak to me, Sam! Spirit, I conjure thee, speak!"

Out of the profound silence that followed the wizard's words came a soft voice. In calm and reasonable tones it said, "This point is then agreed between us: I am to speak, *viva voce et omnes impositura*, and you are to listen, *cymbae citharaeque in horas peste futura*, and thus to perceive, immediately through the senses, the insensible sense of my signification, *ut trepidas in rebus*. Is that not so?"

Kedrigern hesitated, frowned, looked at Princess, shook his head in confusion, and asked, "What?"

"Though my words, once spoken, exist *tergo diluxisse quae non manet*," the voice went smoothly on, "Yet you do not perceive their meaning, for to exist and to be perceived are different states. Thus the perceived and the unperceived, *praetulerim delirius paplitibus*, like the negative and the affirmative sides of a question, contain between them all possibility, *non alium videre patres*, and by containing all, contain nothing. And thus we see that though I speak, I cannot answer, for while speech may exist without perception, it cannot be perceived without existence, *quid quisquae vitet*. Is this not likewise true?"

"Wait a minute, now. . . ." said the wizard uneasily.

"For it is impossible to deny real existence to a primary quality when one affirms the existence of the secondary qualities, *ille tamen inclusium*, without which the primary quality cannot be perceived, *minaequae murorum ingentes*, by the senses."

"I think—" Kedrigern attempted to interject, to no avail.

"Therefore, since to be perceived it is necessary first, *non elaborabunt in aeternam*, to exist, and to exist is, *mos olim*, to perceive, then it follows that that that . . . that which which that . . . which thus, *iam desiderium insomnia . . . quicquid delirium* . . . that that which perceives must be perceived first, to exist, and secondly, to be perceived to exist before, thirdly, being perceived to perceive that which exists, *odium melodiumquae sperabitur*, and that that which is, is, *per se* and *ad hoc* . . . that which . . . is perceived as . . . *et cetera inter alii* that which exists," the ghost of Sam concluded uneasily.

"*Brereep?*" murmured Princess, utterly befuddled.

"Balderdash!" cried Kedrigern. "Gibberish! Absolute drivel from beginning to end! What kind of philosopher have you got there, Amos? He sounds like someone who's read every other page of an epistemology text written by an alchemist!"

"He said he was a philosopher. He seemed all right to me," Amos said, sounding miffed. "You didn't give me much to go on, Kedrigern."

"I'm not blaming you, Amos. Sam! Don't try to slip away," the wizard snapped. "I want a simple straightforward answer from you. No more Latin. What do you know about Princess?"

After a pause, Sam said, "To know, what is it but to perceive? And as I have proven, to perceive—"

"You don't know a thing about Princess, do you? You've never heard of her before, have you?"

"To a philosopher, all knowledge is one; *ergo*, to know of a princess is to know the essence of princessness, and to one who grasps the essential—"

"Where do you get off calling yourself a philosopher?" Kedrigern demanded angrily.

"All men are philosophers. I am a man. *Ergo*, I am a philosopher. Is that not so?" Sam inquired, composed once more.

"It is not so. It is nonsense, like everything else you've been yammering. Your major premise is one of the silliest things I've ever heard. All men are not philosophers, and you know it. And even if it were true, it's irrelevant—you're not a man anymore, you're a ghost."

Sam was quiet for a moment, and then he said, "All right, then. Some ghosts are philosophers. I am a philosopher. Therefore . . . therefore, I must have been a man."

"That syllogism is the ultimate proof that you are no more a philosopher than my house-troll," said the wizard coldly.

"What are you trying to pull, anyway?" Amos demanded, his voice menacing. "Are you trying to make me look silly in front of a wizard and an enchanted lady? An enchanted *princess!* You said you knew something about the curse on her."

"What you perceived me to say is not necessarily what was said, nor was I necessarily the speaker nor you the auditor, *per ipse nullius dubitantur;* for that which is, and that which is perceived, and that which the perceiver perceives to be that which is and is, *quomodo,* perceived, is neither substantially nor accidentally—"

"Oh, be quiet!" Kedrigern said angrily. "Just tell me this, Sam: are you connected in any way at all with the court of Princess's parents?"

"Are not all things connected? In this universe of infinite gradations, all that exists exists in harmony with all, and that which—"

"I take it you're not connected with the court or with her parents any more closely than you're connected with my right foot," Kedrigern broke in.

"In the cosmic sense, all things are joined in an indissoluble bond. In the narrow sense in which I perceive you to speak . . . no," Sam confessed. "I am not."

"Then why did you volunteer? Why did you take up Amos's time, and Princess's, and mine, with all that jabber?" the wizard demanded.

Sam remained silent for a moment, then he howled in a bitter voice, "What do you know? What does anyone? No one knows, no one cares! Do you know what it's like to be a jester?"

"No," Kedrigern said. "Do you?"

"I was a jester all my life. Can you imagine what it's like to be a jester? He's a man way out there in the blue, riding on a smile and a coxcomb. He's always on, always expected to be funny—a riddle, a jape, a pun, a pratfall, a silly face, a bawdy song . . . and when they start not smiling back . . . Have you any idea what it's like to have to be funny on demand?"

"Difficult, I imagine," Kedrigern said.

"Difficult, he says!" Sam wailed, setting every small object in the room to shaking. "Difficult! What does a wizard know about difficult? Does a wizard get roused out of bed when he's half-crippled with rheumatism and have to cut capers for a bunch of drunken knights? Does a wizard have to hop around strumming a lute and singing 'tirra lirra lirra and a hey nonny no' when he has a headache that makes his skull feel like a cracked eggshell full of hot pebbles?"

"What are you whining about?" Kedrigern demanded indignantly. "Does a jester have to undo enchantments of fiendish intricacy that could turn him into a bedbug if he mispronounces a single syllable? Do jesters confront giants and demons and barbarian swordsmen? Are jesters always being accused of being in league with the devil?"

"All right, so wizards have it tough. So do jesters," Sam retorted. "And nobody gives them sympathy. Nobody understands. Nobody cares."

"Do you think people care about wizards?" Kedrigern shot back.

"I guess I was lucky. I was a shoemaker," Amos said.

Ignoring that, Kedrigern asked, "But why did you pretend to know about Princess, Sam? Why did you try to pass yourself off as a philosopher?"

"I wanted respect. Nobody respects a jester, or pays any attention to what he says. But when a philosopher opens his mouth, people listen. They don't understand a word he says, but they listen. They make me feel like somebody."

"Well, yes, they listen, but after they've listened to a sentence or two they realize that it's all gibberish," Kedrigern pointed out.

"You did, but you're a wizard. I can handle ordinary people. I just give them the stuff I remember hearing around the court, and they eat it up. Amos was impressed. Weren't you, Amos?"

"Yes . . . but what does a shoemaker know about philosophers?" Amos said grudgingly. "All I remember is that they were hard on shoes."

"All right, Sam. You had your moment. Attention was paid. Now go away and let Amos find us someone who can help Princess," Kedrigern said.

"Look, is there anything I can do?"

"No, Sam."

"Would you like to hear a funny song? A joke? How about a joke to cheer everyone up?"

"No need for that, Sam. Just let us get on with what we're doing."

"I could have made it if I hadn't run into a wizard. I could have been an authority. It was the Latin that gave me away, wasn't it? If I hadn't tried the Latin, I would have passed for a philosopher, wouldn't I?"

"You were a little shaky with the syllogisms, Sam."

Suddenly an unfamiliar and rather nasal voice called out sharply, "Amos! Amos, are you here?"

"Right here, Your Honor!" Amos cried.

"I've been looking everywhere for you. Your papers have

turned up, and we'd like to attend to your case right away, but if you're going to go wandering off . . . what are you doing, anyway?"

"Nothing, Your Honor, nothing at all. Just a chat with a few friends."

"Well, say good-bye and hurry over to the Routing desk. Who are *you?*" the nasal voice demanded.

"Who, indeed?" Sam answered. "Let us consider the question under its constituent headings: first, the existence of I-ness; secondly the existence of not-I-ness, or otherness; thirdly, the perception of I-ness by other, and otherness by the I. And let us, furthermore, consider each of these considerations in the light of both the interconnectedness and the distinctness of I and other," he went on, his voice slowly fading.

"You must be a philosopher," the other voice observed, faint with growing distance. Sam's response was lost, drowned out by Amos's close whisper.

"I have to go now, Kedrigern. You heard the Chief Clerk —they've found my papers!"

"But Amos . . ."

"Sorry, old chap. Must rush. Did my best. Good luck with your search, my lady," Amos said as his voice, too, faded into silence.

Kedrigern stood for a time, listening. The stillness in his workroom was profound. At last he called upon Amos, and receiving no reply, on Sam. No answer came. He stalked to the table, blew out his taper, and said, "Ghosts!" in a tone of deep loathing. "Can't depend on a single one of them. Can't believe a word they say." Turning to Princess, he said, "Well, you saw them. You heard the whole thing. They're utterly irresponsible. I was foolish to think I could trust Amos. I was silly to waste my time on Sam. I must have been an idiot to think I could accomplish anything with the likes of them!"

Princess rose and smoothed her gown. Smiling, she blew out her taper. *"Brereep,"* she said.

···⁙ *Eight* ⁙···

a welcome bit of assistance

THE ALE WAS warm and insipid. Kedrigern retained it in his mouth for a moment, uncertain whether to spit it out on the floor or swallow it. Gentilesse won out over inclination. He closed his eyes and gulped it down. It tasted like a distillation of the venial sins of petty-minded men.

He set his greasy, dented mug down on the undulate surface of the sticky tabletop, made a wry unhappy face, wiped his lips on his sleeve, and wished he were home. He loved his home. He hated travel.

Home meant comfort and tranquility and the company of Princess; travel meant a noisy, smelly press of strangers. Home was cold ale in a silver tankard, not scummed-over ditchwater in a filthy mug. Home was the prompt attentiveness of his faithful house-troll, not the shuffling dereliction of a surly, blotchy tapster. Kedrigern dwelt long on absent pleasures and resolved that once home, he would not soon leave again, not even for Vosconu the Openhanded.

Thinking further, he wavered. Vosconu had certainly lived up to his name. Forty casks of wine and a purse of gold was munificent payment for lifting one small, amateurish curse from Vosconu's vineyards.

Preoccupied with thoughts of reward, Kedrigern sipped his ale without thinking and nearly gagged. His resolution firmed and set. No, never again. Helping Vosconu meant traveling, and traveling meant stopping at verminous sties like Hossel's Inn. Better one's own plain ale at home than Vosconu's finest vintage at such a price.

A husky man with a tangle of black hair and beard merging to enclose a patch of weather-browned face settled on the bench across from Kedrigern. "What news, traveler?" he said amicably, setting his bow against the table and laying a quiver of arrows on the bench beside him.

"The world is going to hell on horseback," said the wizard morosely.

"That's no news at all."

"It's the best I can manage. Sorry."

"No need to apologize, traveler. There's little enough news these days, good or bad," said the other. Swiveling in his place, he bawled for ale, then turned to Kedrigern once again. "I've got some news, though," he said with a smug wink.

Kedrigern raised an eyebrow to suggest a mild interest he did not truly feel. He disliked having strangers intrude upon his privacy, particularly when he was brooding over injustices and pondering suitable retaliation. All the same, he tried to be civil. One never knew what one might learn from a chance remark.

"Oh, yes, I've got news you won't hear in every tavern," said the bowman, nodding and giving another wink.

"How very lucky you are," Kedrigern observed.

"Yes. Big news. Of course, I can't go telling everyone, you understand. Not until I've informed the proper authorities."

Kedrigern was in no mood to coax the news out of him. He fell silent and resumed his brooding, so it was not until the innkeeper, Hossel himself, brought the fellow's ale that the bowman, as if surrendering to universal pleading, said, "Oh, I suppose there's no harm in telling a few honest men."

"Telling what, Fletcher?" asked the innkeeper.

"My news, cousin. My good news."

"Oh. What is it now?" Hossel said. His tone suggested that he had heard his share of good news from this man and was not eager to hear more.

"I've slain a dragon," Fletcher announced in a voice that

carried through the entire ground floor of the inn. Two heads popped out of the kitchen, gaped for a moment, then disappeared as Hossel shook his fist at them. The low buzz of conversation at the other table was stilled for a moment, then went on. "Yes, it's true," Fletcher said, gratified by the reception. "I've slain a dragon."

"Where?" Hossel asked.

"At Belford, on the west road. He had just finished his filthy work there. The place was thick with smoke." The conversation at the other table died, and three dirty faces turned toward Fletcher. Hossel leaned against a post and folded his thick arms. Kedrigern felt his interest growing.

"I didn't notice him right away," Fletcher went on, after a theatrical pause. "My eyes were on the ground, not the sky. I was alert for barbarians. It looked like their handiwork, you understand. Then I saw it—just a speck, far off to the north, very high. It circled the churchyard once, then dropped to treetop level and came in fast over the town. It was heading right for me."

Fletcher glanced around the room. He had them now. The trio at the other table sat open-mouthed. Heads were poked out of the kitchen once again, and Hossel showed no sign of objecting. Even Kedrigern was listening attentively.

"I admit it, friends . . . I was frightened. A dragon is no ordinary beast. But I nocked an arrow and concealed myself behind the ruin of a wall. And as the dragon passed overhead" —here Fletcher sprang up and pantomimed his deed—"I loosed my arrow and took the monster in its heart!"

One of the men at the other table cheered. Fletcher nodded to him graciously, and the man and his companions raised their mugs in a salute.

"How big was it, Fletcher?" Hossel asked.

"The body was about the size of a haywain. Wingtip to wingtip was . . . oh, just a bit over the length of the inn."

"Must have made a terrible crash when it fell," said the man who had cheered.

"Ah, but it didn't fall. Wavered a little, but didn't fall. They never do, you know," said Fletcher knowingly.

"They don't?"

"Of course not. You've never heard of anyone coming across a dragon's carcass, have you?" Fletcher allowed his little audience an interval to reflect on that fact, then went on,

"Once they've taken a death-wound, they fly north. Up there, beyond the Last Forest and the Glass Mountains, there's a valley where all the dragons go to die. No man has ever laid eyes on it."

"How do you know about it, then, cousin?" Hossel asked.

Fletcher turned a cool gaze on him. "I heard it from Bess, the Wood-witch. She saw it in a vision."

The others exchanged significant glances and nodded solemnly to one another. They had heard Authority cited, and accepted the word without question. Kedrigern, who was acquainted with Bess, was unimpressed. Considering the stuff she brewed in her cauldron, it was no wonder she had visions. He had once drunk a small bowlful, on a professional visit to her hovel, and been unsteady on his feet for much of the following week. Vision, indeed.

Fletcher left him, to join the more appreciative trio at the next table, and Kedrigern returned to his ruminations. Nothing remained but to decide on Hossel's punishment, and he would then be on his way. He ran through the customary plagues—rats, mice, fleas, mildew, bad smells—and rejected them one by one. In Hossel's Inn, such things were part of the ambience. A poltergeist would serve nicely, but poltergeists were troublesome to deal with; Kedrigern's own workroom was still a mess from Rupert's visitation. Besides, all these measures would bother the guests as much as the innkeeper, and Hossel's guests were subjected to enough suffering merely by being here. Kedrigern was not one to punish the innocent with the guilty if it could be helped. A plague of boils seemed to be the only workable solution. Unimaginative, and rather crude, but under the circumstances as good as one could manage. Something had to be done, for the sake of future travelers.

He worked the spell, settled his bill, and went to the stable for his horse. A ragged, dirty boy helped him mount, and looked admiringly at the shaggy black steed.

"That's a fine horse, sir," the boy said.

"Yes, he is."

"Looks like a barbarian's horse to me, sir."

"You're very astute, my boy. As a matter of fact, I did get him from a barbarian." Kedrigern thought of Buroc, now no more than a scattering of gravel in a desolate valley. "He had no further use for horses."

The stable boy looked around cautiously, and with lowered

voice asked, "Are you a wizard, sir?"

"What makes you ask that?"

"Why, sir, you look like a wizard. You have the way of a wizard."

The boy was perceptive, Kedrigern thought. "What makes you so sure I'm not a scholar? Or an alchemist?"

"Oh, you look too bold for a scholar, sir. And too honest for an alchemist," the boy said promptly.

An amazing lad, Kedrigern marveled. Much too clever to be a stable boy. "What do you know of alchemists?" he asked.

"They stop here now and then, sir. A nasty lot they are, too."

A boy of excellent discernment. Reassuring, to find such a bright young lad in these dull and blundering times, when the alchemists seemed to have deceived everyone with their jabber and jargon. "Absolutely right, my boy. Never trust an alchemist," said Kedrigern.

"No, sir. Please, sir. . ." The lad looked up with wide imploring eyes.

"Yes, my boy?"

"Please, sir, would you let me come with you and be your apprentice?"

Kedrigern studied him closely. His clothes were tattered and absolutely filthy. He reeked of the stable. He was very young, and probably had no manners at all. On the other hand, he had a keen mind and was an excellent judge of character. His eyes were clear and bright, his features more refined than those of the locals, all of whom resembled turnips.

"Please, sir."

"I'm considering, boy."

An apprentice would be helpful. Not that the burden of work was so great, but wizardry could be a lonely business, and an apprentice would be someone with whom he could talk shop. Princess—quite understandably—was still chary of things magical, and Spot, while useful, was hopeless as a professional associate. It would be handy to have someone who could reach the upper shelves and speak in complete sentences. Too, a fresh, young outlook might liven up the house, and make things a bit more cheerful for Princess when he was taken up with business. And there was something about this eager, intelligent lad that reminded Kedrigern of himself a century and a half ago. He could not turn the boy away.

"All right. If your master agrees, you can come along."

"Hossel's not my master, sir. He lets me sleep in the straw and eat from the kitchen slops, that's all, sir."

"How very egalitarian Hossel is: he treats you exactly as he treats his guests. Very well, then. Get your things and follow me."

Kedrigern kept the slowest pace he could, but by midday the boy had fallen far behind. Kedrigern dismounted and sat on a log to wait for him.

"Sorry, master," the boy said, panting, when he caught up.

"It's all right. Sit down. We'll eat something, and rest awhile."

When it was time to continue, Kedrigern looked down on the ragged, pinched little figure and was moved to pity. He thought of himself comfortable on horseback while the lad hurried along the rough road, and felt a twinge of guilt.

"I think you ought to ride awhile," he said.

"Oh, no, master! I could never ride while my master walks!"

"You must learn to do as I say, boy. If I tell you to ride, you must ride," said Kedrigern sternly.

"If you say so, master," the boy said, springing eagerly into the saddle.

"And what's your name? I can't keep calling you 'boy.'"

"It's Jum, master."

"Jum. That's a muddy sort of name. Well, let's move on . . . Jum."

With Kedrigern leading, they headed west, to the junction of the great highway, and then turned north, toward the mountains. They proceeded in silence. Jum was lost in wonder at his new surroundings, craning and swiveling his neck to stare at each unfamiliar sight. He had no breath left for speech, and Kedrigern savored the spectacle of the boy's excitement.

Kedrigern felt more benevolent with each step. He had saved a bright lad from a lifetime of malodorous drudgery in Hossel's stables, and won a promising recruit for the wizard's calling. Jum badly needed a scrubbing and a few weeks of healthy food, but he was good raw material. He would require a new name, too; something a bit more dignified. Jum would do for a stable boy, or a jester, or an alchemist—perfect name for an alchemist, he thought—but never a wizard.

They went on, Jum gawking and Kedrigern ruminating and neither one saying a word, and the landscape around them became gradually more barren and bleak. Here stood the blackened ruin of a crofter's hovel, there the wild tangle of a long abandoned wheat field. The bleakness soon turned to menace. When he saw a blasted maple hung with a score of corpses in various stages of decomposition, Kedrigern worked a quick early warning spell. He could not be sure who had done all this, but he wanted to know if they were nearby.

"Is that the doing of barbarians, master?" Jum asked in a subdued voice.

"It probably is. But whether it's the work of invaders from the east or our local talent, I can't say. It might also be the outcome of a holy war, or a persecution. Or perhaps a family feud. Or the penalty for tax evasion. They all seem to come out the same in the end," Kedrigern said, sighing.

"Rotten barbarians . . . ought to skin them all alive!" Jum said with great vehemence.

Kedrigern was about to reprimand the boy, but he checked his tongue. Jum was young, and had plenty of time to learn restraint. His outburst might well be the fruit of some personal tragedy—he would not be the first young wizard's apprentice to suffer at the hands of marauders—and it would be cruel to silence him. Time would do the teaching.

A league farther on, they passed another small farm, burned to stubble, and two leagues beyond that, the smoking remains of an inn. Kedrigern felt a warning tingle in the back of his neck and looked all around. It was Jum who spotted the danger. Kedrigern heard his cry, followed his pointing finger, and saw a dot in the sky, approaching them at great speed.

He drew out his medallion and raised it, to peer through the Aperture of True Vision. He saw a dragon. It was not the size of a haywain, and its wingspan was not the length of Hossel's Inn, and it was getting on in centuries, but it was a dragon, all the same. It was, in fact, a very angry dragon. An arrow had transfixed its left foreclaw, causing considerable discomfort but no loss of mobility or power.

"So much for Fletcher the dragon-slayer," said Kedrigern, replacing the medallion and rubbing his eyes.

"Is it a dragon, master?" Jum cried.

"It is, Jum. Don't worry. We have protection."

"Kill it, master! Kill the dragon!"

"That's not my line of work, Jum."

"But it's a *dragon*, master! Dragons exist only to be slain!"

"That will be enough, Jum," said Kedrigern firmly.

The boy fell silent. Kedrigern worked a short, simple spell against flame and smoke, and then, stepping back and laying a calming hand on the horse's neck, he awaited the arrival of the dragon.

It came straight for them, dropping to just above head-height as it closed, and when it was within range, it spewed forth a burst of flame. Jum cried out in fear, but the flames rolled to either side without singeing a hair of their heads or a thread of their garments.

The dragon soared sharply, made a tight banking turn, and came at their flank. Again its flame was rendered harmless to the stationary figures, although it devastated what little of the inn was still standing. After the failure of its second aerial pass, the dragon landed gingerly a short distance away, wincing as its injured claw touched down. Inhaling deeply, it poured out a rolling ribbon of flame that completely encircled them. Jum howled; the horse whinneyed; Kedrigern stood firm; they were unscathed. The dragon took one look at them and drooped. Laying its head on the charred ground, it began to cry.

Kedrigern stepped forward and halted a few paces from the dragon's head. His command of dragon was limited, so he spoke in his own language, low and reassuring, as one would address a large strange dog. "It's all right, old fellow. I'm not an enemy."

The dragon raised its head slightly, blinked, and studied him. At that moment, Jum cried, "Kill it, master! Kill it!" Kedrigern snapped, "Shut up, Jum!" and the dragon burst out weeping afresh.

"I really mean it. I'm not your enemy," Kedrigern said.

The dragon rumbled mournfully:

"False-speaker to Fingard
In mendacious man-language!
Villainy of varlet
Has injured by arrow-point—
Now stranger comes stalking
To deal dastardly deathblow."

"I don't do that sort of thing, as a rule. I'm a wizard, not a dragon-slayer," Kedrigern said.

Fingard raised its brassy head. "Wizard?"

"Kedrigern of Silent Thunder Mountain. I'm sure you've heard the name. Then again, you're a long way from home, aren't you?"

> *"Fingard the far-faring*
> *Misses misty mountaintops,*
> *Glittering of glaciers,*
> *Blustering of blizzards."*

"Yes, I could tell you're a northern dragon. The alliteration is a dead giveaway."

Fingard raised its head still higher, until its slitted golden-green eyes were level with Kedrigern's. The wizard returned the chilling gaze steadfastly, one hand behind his back, ready to work a quick supporting spell if the need arose. The dragon again addressed him.

> *"Is wizard all word-skill,*
> *Proud without proof,*
> *Or can he help heal arrow-hurt,*
> *Fix Fingard's foreclaw?"*

Kedrigern folded his arms and adopted a stern expression. "I'll want some assurances first, Fingard. I'm not going to heal you so you can go about igniting homes and farms," he said.

The dragon raised its injured claw and placed it on its heart. Holding its head high, it intoned:

> *"Fingard the falsely accused*
> *Denies foul farm-burning,*
> *House-harm and people-hurt!*
> *Swears by Fafnir, far-famed fire-father,*
> *Dean of all dragons,*
> *That burning and butchery*
> *Were work of wicked warriors."*

Kedrigern was not entirely surprised to hear this. With so much fire and pillage going on in the world, it was all too easy to lay the blame on dragons. Still, appearances were against Fingard. Its recent intentions had certainly not been friendly.

Jum cried shrilly, "Liar, liar! The thing's lying, master! Blast it with a bolt of power! Shrivel it up into a pair of slippers! Destroy it!"

"Be quiet, Jum. I'm working," Kedrigern said. Turning to Fingard, he asked, "Why did you attack us?"

Fingard's head sagged until it hovered just off the ground. The golden-green eyes filmed over as the dragon pondered the question. Its reply came in a subdued, shame-filled bass.

> *"Fingard forgot himself,*
> *Had tiny temper-tantrum."*

His voice hard, his manner severe, Kedrigern demanded, "And did you have a tiny temper-tantrum at Belford, too?"

> *"In full faith, Fingard*
> *Swears solemnly by Fafnir:*
> *I burned no barns at Belford,*
> *Scorched no citizens,*
> *Charred no chattels!*
> *Simply went sightseeing,*
> *Flew over forests and farms,*
> *Until arrow came unexpected,*
> *Hit hard and hurt.*
> *Now wizard knows well*
> *The cause of this confusion—*
> *Will Fingard find friendship?*
> *Is healing help at hand?"*

"I suppose I can do something. But I want to settle on my payment first," said Kedrigern.

When the dragon responded, its deep rumbling voice had shrunk to the fawning whine of a street beggar. Its color faded, its head drooped, its eyes grew moist.

"The finances of Fingard are fragile,
Though gold-greedy gossips
Spread rumors of riches,
Musty mounds of precious metals,
Hoary heaps of high-piled treasure.
Fingard, in fact,
Guards gaudy geegaws,
Sits on scant silver,
A jumble of junk jewelry
And rust-rotted armor . . .
Dire days, these, for dragons."

Kedrigern raised his hand and shook his head. "No need to go on about your treasure hoard, Fingard. I know how you dragons are about treasure. What I want from you is some blood."

"Blood?" rumbled the dragon, its voice deeper and more resounding than ever.

"That's right, blood. You'll lose a little when I remove the arrow, and I probably won't require more than that. And I also want your solemn promise, no more temper-tantrums when you're around people."

"Blood?" Fingard roared, arching its neck high to glare down on the wizard.

"Stop showing off. If you want the arrow out, it will cost you two vials of blood. And you'll have to swear by Fafnir *and* Ladon *and* Nidhogg that you'll control your temper whenever you're within ten leagues of human beings. Take it or leave it, Fingard," said Kedrigern.

With a thin, steamy sigh, Fingard lowered its head and held out the arrow-pierced foreclaw, meanwhile intoning the solemn oath prescribed by the wizard. As Kedrigern examined the wound, the dragon winced, shut its eyes, and began to mumble gloomily.

"Still same sad story:
One man makes misery,
Another pockets profits
From injury to innocent."

"Stop feeling so sorry for yourself, Fingard," said the wizard, preoccupied with the wound. He cut off the arrowhead, gripped the shaft, and said, "This may hurt a bit. Don't get excited and start flaming and smoking, do you hear?"

"Fingard will show fortitude,
Suffer in silence, smokeless."

"See that you do. Ready?" Kedrigern gripped the arrow shaft in one hand, the scaly foreclaw in the other, and jerked the arrow free. Fingard emitted a little puff of steam, but no smoke or flame. "Thank you for not smoking," said Kedrigern, and proceeded to collect his fee and bind up the wound.

Fingard, subdued, muttered its thanks, unfurled its wings with the crackle of sails in a strong wind, and took its leave. As the dragon flapped off into the evening sky, Kedrigern turned to his apprentice. Jum sat waiting, watching, a dour expression on his face.

"Well, I hope you learned something today, Jum," the wizard said.

"Dragon lover!" the boy cried hatefully.

"Now, see here, Jum—"

"You're soft on dragons! You healed that monster, and you should have slain it!"

"Wizards are not dragon-slayers. We may, on occasion, have to do severe damage to another wizard, or a barbarian swordsman, or a fiend, in self-defense, but we do not wantonly kill injured dragons. If you can't get that through your angry little head, you'll never be a wizard."

"I don't want to be a dirty dragon-loving wizard! I hate wizards!"

Kedrigern closed his eyes and took a deep breath to calm himself. In a cold, level voice he said, "All right, then, Jum. Get off the horse. If you hurry, you can be back at Hossel's Inn by nightfall. Perhaps you'll be happier there."

"I will! I will!" the boy cried defiantly. "They're not a bunch of dragon-healers like you!" He dropped to the ground and stood glaring at Kedrigern for a moment. Then his expression softened; his eyes filled with tears, and he rushed to the wizard, weeping, and threw his arms around Kedrigern's waist. "Please, master, forgive me," he blubbered. "I hate dragons. I can't help it, master."

"I understand, my boy. You'll be happier apprenticed to a swordsman, I'm sure," Kedrigern said, patting Jum's head.

"Am I forgiven, master?" the boy asked, turning up his tear-streaked face.

"Of course you are, Jum."

"And you'll not send a punishing spell after me, ever? Do you promise that you won't do that to me, master?"

"Of course, Jum. No punishing spells, I promise."

"Then I'd best be on my way," said the boy, stepping back and wiping his eyes and nose on a filthy sleeve. "Good day, sir. Remember, no punishing spells."

"I'll remember, Jum. And don't worry about traveling. I'll see that you get to the inn safely."

"Thank you, sir," said the boy, turning to set off down the road.

Kedrigern mounted and headed north at a brisk pace. He wanted to put the burnt inn and all that had happened there out of his sight and memory. For some inexplicable reason, he felt uncomfortable, and that bothered him.

Clearly, the boy had not been cut out for wizardry, and the sooner he learned that, the better. Kedrigern had actually done him a great service. Why, then, did he feel guilty? Why had he extravagantly promised a protective spell *en route?* Such things cost good magic.

And why had the lad been so apprehensive? Was he such an ogre that small children feared punishing spells for a single angry outburst? It was a sobering thought. Kedrigern had come to think of himself as a kindly man, a loving husband, good with trolls, trusted by dragons; yet Jum had feared his vengeance. It was puzzling and unsettling. He decided that he would not mention Jum's reaction to Princess.

He consoled himself by thinking of the profits of this trip. Vosconu's wine would vastly improve the dinner hour for a long time to come, and he also had the two vials of dragon's blood, which, as an ingredient in advanced spelling, were worth ten times the value of Vosconu's entire vineyard. As an item of barter, they might well get him just what he needed to hasten Princess's complete despelling. He had in mind a deal with Bess the Wood-witch for a certain crystal in her possession, a matter he meant to see to immediately upon his return home. And aside from his expenses at Hossel's Inn, the trip had cost him nothing.

Absently, he reached down for his purse. It was not in his belt. He patted his belt all around, then his pockets, then the recesses of his garments. No purse. He reined in the horse, dismounted, searched himself and his saddlebags thoroughly, even removed his boots and turned them upside down. No purse.

Kedrigern remounted, and was about to retrace his way when the truth burst upon him. The tearful embrace. The carefully extracted promise of no punishing spell. The sudden willingness to be off and away. And he, like a fool, had even volunteered a safe passage for the mean little sneak. Well, we would see about that, he thought darkly.

He turned to face south, extended his hand—and remembered his promise. He had given his word as a wizard. There was no going back on it. He sat for a moment, fuming in silence, then flicked the reins and resumed his northern journey.

Good riddance to Jum. The whole idea of an apprentice—Jum's idea—was preposterous. Very few of the wizards he knew had ever taken on an apprentice, and the ones who had were continually complaining about them. One could always summon up temporary help when it was needed, and be sure it was first quality help. No such guarantee with an apprentice. Not these days. If Jum was serious about an apprenticeship, let him sign on with an alchemist. He was a fine prospect: he already knew how to lie and steal.

By the time he had gone a few leagues, Kedrigern had composed himself. His only remaining annoyance was over the promise of no punishing spell. One should not be able to steal from a wizard and escape scot-free. It set a bad precedent, and worse still, if colleagues learned of it they would never let him live it down.

His head came up and his eyes brightened when he realized that the promise referred only to Jum. Well, of course he would do nothing to the boy. A wizard's word was inviolable, and he had promised no punishing spell. But he had not said a word about the purse, or its contents. Not a word.

He rode on, smiling, humming a little tune to himself as he weighed the possibilities. It was amazing what one could fit into a purse with just a single small nonpunishing spell.

···⚜ *Nine* ⚜···

the crystal of caracodissa

KEDRIGERN SLIPPED FROM his study, pale and bloodshot of eye, and eased shut the door behind him with trembling hands. He made his cautious way to the breakfast nook, pausing on the threshold of the sun-drenched room to sigh and swallow loudly. Narrowing his eyes to slits and shielding them with his hand, he entered, slowly.

Princess was already seated. She looked particularly fresh and lovely in a soft green robe, with her black hair loose about her shoulders. Kedrigern scarcely noticed. On this particular morning, the sight of Venus herself rising from the jam jar would have made little impression on him. Princess glanced up as he entered, and her look was cool and disapproving.

"*Brereep?*" she asked politely.

"Awful, thank you," Kedrigern replied, gingerly lowering himself onto the seat opposite her.

"*Brereep,*" she said, with a tight, self-righteous smile.

"No, it does *not* serve me right, my dear. I had no choice in the matter," said Kedrigern in a fragile voice. He listened to his stomach gurgle threateningly, gulped, and went on, "I know what kind of stuff Bess brews, and I watered my drinks as much as I could. She just kept refilling my bowl."

"*Brereep.*"

"You don't know Bess, my dear. She's a good-hearted old thing, but she takes it terribly to heart if you refuse a drink in her hovel, and I didn't dare risk offending her." Kedrigern gave a shuddering, desolate sigh. "Would that I had. I don't know how she survives it. Her stomach must be lined with stone. That stuff of hers isn't fit for an alchemist."

"*Brereep?*"

"Worse. I think it could paralyze a full-grown troll."

As if on cue, Spot came skidding into the breakfast nook on huge flat feet. "Yah! Yah!" it shrieked in jubilant greeting. Kedrigern made a little whimpering sound and buried his face in his hands.

"No, Spot. Quiet. Please," he said faintly.

The little house-troll waited by his knee, panting and freely salivating, while the wizard recovered. Kedrigern rubbed his eyes, then blinked and glanced down on Princess's plate, on which lay a generous portion of grilled kidneys, a fried egg, and half a sausage. He quickly shut his eyes again.

"Plain porridge, Spot. A very small serving. A dab. And bring it silently," he said.

Spot careened out, ears and hands flapping. Kedrigern looked again at Princess. Her expression of superior disapproval was unchanged.

"I wasn't too bad last night, was I?" he asked.

"*Brereep.*"

"I did? Funny . . . I don't remember that at all. Are you positive?"

"*Brereep!*" she said indignantly.

Kedrigern raised his hands before him defensively. "Certainly, my dear. If you say so. I'm terribly sorry."

She glared at him, but said nothing.

"I didn't . . . I didn't try to work any magic, did I?" he asked apprehensively.

She solemnly shook her head in the negative.

Kedrigern let out a sigh of relief. "I'm glad to hear that. Working spells when one is . . . when one has had . . . well, it's irresponsible. I've heard of conventions where everyone wound up invisible just because some silly wizard . . . anyway, we don't have *that* to worry about."

From her expression, Princess was not comforted by this observation. She did not speak. Spot caromed into the breakfast nook, eased a bowl of porridge and a pitcher of milk silently onto the tabletop, and departed. Kedrigern ate, in small, cautious helpings, and still Princess was silent. At last he laid down his spoon and looked directly into her eyes.

"In any event, my dear, I got what I was after. It meant a long trip, and hard bargaining, and an excruciating hangover, and the price was absolutely outrageous, but it was all worthwhile," he said.

"*Brereep?*"

"More than that. Much more. I had to give Bess a full vial of dragon's blood. But I don't begrudge a drop of it. I'd gladly spend all the dragon's blood I've got, to make you happy."

"*Brereep?*" she asked. Her voice had softened.

"All for you, and you alone, my dear." Kedrigern reached out and laid his fingertips gently on her hand. "It's a slightly belated wedding present: the crystal of Caracodissa. At this very moment it stands on my worktable. And as soon as my head is clear—"

She squeezed his hand in both of hers. With a *brereep* of sheer joy, she ran to his side, threw her arms around his neck, and kissed him repeatedly. He took her in his arms and drew her close.

"*Brereep?*" she whispered.

"Oh, no doubt at all. It's the genuine article. I know the markings too well to be fooled. The inscription runs completely around it, in letters that burn like fire:

"Magic of the helping kind,
Seek it here, and ye shall find,
Wake the spirit that indwells,
Find the spell to loose all spells."

I'll work on it first thing tomorrow morning, and by dinnertime tomorrow you'll be speaking as clearly as ever."

She drew away, and looked in dismay at Kedrigern. "*Brereep?*" she asked.

"No, tomorrow. Please, my dear. My head is throbbing. I'm in no condition to attempt—"

"*Brereep!*" she cried.

"Of course I love you!" Kedrigern said, wincing at the loudness of her voice. "That's why I'm being cautious. We're dealing with very delicate magic here, my dear. I can't approach it lightly. I must have a clear head and a steady hand, and at the moment . . ."

"Brereep?"

"No. I can't. There's nothing to cure a hangover. Not even magic. We'll just have to wait until tomorrow."

Princess slumped dejectedly. She sat huddled by his chair, looking up at him with wide, sad blue eyes. A tear welled up in each eye, brimmed, and coursed down her pale cheeks.

"My dear, I can't. A great deal of preliminary study is required. It would be very risky to barge ahead."

She gave a little sob. More tears came. She buried her face in her hands and wept, silently.

Kedrigern's resolve lasted less than a minute. Rising, he laid his hand on her shoulder and said, "Perhaps I can do something today, after all. At least we can look it over and get an idea. . . . If Spot can bring me a cold compress."

Princess sprang to her feet and clapped her hands once, sharply. Kedrigern twitched at the sound, which brought Spot reeling into the breakfast nook.

"A bowl of very cold water, and a clean cloth, Spot. Bring them to my workroom at once. And don't make a sound," said the wizard in a low, strained voice.

The cold compress helped ever so slightly. Kedrigern wiped his brow, dried his fingertips on his shirt, and turned his attention to the crystal cube that stood in a cleared space on his long worktable. Princess, too, gazed upon it with fascination.

It was a perfect cube, about a hand's length to a side, and it glowed from within, where a misty radiance swirled like a slow sinuous current. Around all six sides in letters of reddish gold that flickered like living flame ran the inscription. In the darkened room, Kedrigern read the familiar words aloud in a subdued voice, while Princess looked on in attentive silence.

"Wake the spirit that indwells,
Seek it here, and ye shall find,
Find the spell to loose all spells,
Magic of the helping kind."

Something nudged at his memory. He had not been at his most alert when he read the inscription earlier, but it seemed to him that the verses had been in different order. He picked up the cube, turned it over in his hands—it was oddly light in weight—and setting it down, read the inscription once more.

> *"Seek it here, and ye shall find,*
> *Wake the spirit that indwells,*
> *Magic of the helping kind,*
> *Find the spell to loose all spells."*

He drew out his medallion and studied the inscription through the Aperture of True Vision. It was unchanged. He let out a weary groan and reached for the compress. This was going to be more difficult than he had anticipated. Princess, seeing his look of concern, lent her aid, plunging the cloth into the bowl, wringing out the excess water, and applying the soothing compress gently to Kedrigern's forehead. He accepted her ministrations silently, his eyes fixed on the glowing crystal surface.

"Our task will not be simple, my dear. Not simple at all. What we have here is a permutational spell . . . very tricky thing to deal with," Kedrigern said abstractedly. He turned, and began, "It really would be best to wait until I . . . ," but the abandoned look in Princess's eyes silenced him at once.

He returned his attention to the cube. The radiance at its center was slowly swirling, like dyes dropped carefully into still water. He whispered a melodious phrase, and then another. The glow deepened, and clotted. He gestured for Princess to go to the opposite side of the table, facing him, and as she moved he took up a longer incantation in an utterly strange language of soft liquid syllables which flowed into one another without pause.

When Princess stood opposite him, he reached out, took her hands, and placed her palms flat against the sides of the cube. He placed his own hands over hers. The light within the crystal drew in upon itself, congealed, and solidified into a golden cube within a cube.

Kedrigern's head was throbbing. Sweat ran down his forehead and into his eyes. He blinked it away, staring hard at the letters slowly coming into view on the face of the inner cube. The print was tiny, the light was painfully bright, his vision was blurry and his head felt as if it were about to burst; but there was no stopping now. Squinting and cocking his head, he read off the words of the unbinding spell as one by one they came into sight. When he spoke the final word, the golden cube burst into a million tiny fragments of light that glowed, and faded, and left the crystal and the room in semidarkness.

Princess was slumping forward, dazed. Kedrigern rushed around the table just in time to catch her as she fell. He carried her to the bedroom, placed her on the bed, and summoned Spot.

"Get the cold water and the compress from my study, Spot. Bring them here at once," he ordered.

Princess was pale, but her breath and heartbeat were regular. Kedrigern began to swab her brow and cheeks as soon as Spot arrived, and in a very short time, her eyelids fluttered. He set to wiping his own brow as she opened her eyes, looked up at him, and smiled.

"Can you speak, my dear?" he asked eagerly.

She took a deep breath, and softly said, ".Yes"

"Wonderful! How do you feel?"

".well Very .Well," she said.

Kedrigern let out a great sigh of relief. "I'm so glad to hear. For just a moment there . . . I had some difficulty making out the words of the spell, you see. But apparently I got it right."

She frowned, shook her head, and said, ".wrong it got you think I .No"

"What?"

"!backward thing silly the recited You"

"Backward?"

".backward, right That's"

"Oh, dear."

"?!say can you all *that* Is ?dear, Oh"

"Well . . . at least I didn't recite it sideways, my dear," Kedrigern said, grasping at the first straw that occurred to him. "There's no telling what you'd sound like if I'd done that. This way, if you're careful—"

"?life my of rest the for backward talking be I Will ?careful, mean you do What !Careful"

"Oh, dear," Kedrigern repeated.

".say to you for Easy ?dear, Oh," Princess said bitterly.

"Look at it this way: it's a start. You're speaking, and that's the important thing."

".Backward," she muttered.

"It beats croaking, doesn't it? If you just keep to simple sentences, everything will be fine. Meanwhile, I'll read everything I've got on the crystal of Caracodissa and permutational spells, and we can try it again in a few days. Everything's going to be all right. You'll see," Kedrigern said cheerfully.

Princess looked him in the eye, still dubious but trying not to show her doubts. At last she smiled and held out her hands to him. ".up me Help," she said.

Kedrigern was much relieved when she rose, stretched, and then walked out of the bedroom in completely normal fashion. When, at dinner, she did not begin with dessert and end with soup, he was reassured. And when Princess showed no sign of waking up before going to sleep that night, his mind was put completely at ease. The spell had affected only her speech. Kedrigern was confident that, given time to bone up, and a clear head, he could set everything to rights.

He spent the next day in his study, reading closely. When he came out, in midafternoon, to take a short breather, he received a shock to see Princess preparing an upside down cake for dessert that evening; but this was sheer coincidence. He sighed with relief and sat on the kitchen bench.

"?hard working you Are," she asked.

"Yes. The crystal of Caracodissa is an amazingly complicated device. It seems that whenever one summons up the spell, it appears in slightly different form in each face of the crystal. Only one form is the right one, but there's no way to tell which it is."

"Princess frowned in puzzlement ".one only saw I ?six were there sure you Are"

Whichever face you look into appears to be the only one with a spell showing. It was centuries before a young witch named Moggropple discovered the secret."

"?mirrors use you Could"

"Moggropple tried just that. She surrounded the crystal with mirrors and recited all six spells, one after the other. She's been trapped in the mirrors ever since. Six of her. No one knows the spell to get her out. They can't even be sure which one is the real Moggropple, and what might happen if they let out one of the reflections. I don't think it pays to get too clever with the crystal."

"?do you will What"

"If we have one chance in six of finding the right spell, I

suppose we just have to keep trying."

". . . .now, minute a Wait," Princess said, holding up her hand.

"It didn't hurt, did it?"

"No," she admitted.

"And you did get your voice back."

"Yes," she said reluctantly.

"Well, there you are. We'll try again tomorrow morning. There's nothing to worry about," Kedrigern said confidently.

"?out inside Or ?sideways talking start I if What"

"You're worrying yourself unnecessarily, my dear," said Kedrigern, rising. "Now, if you'll excuse me, I have a few references to check out. I'll be working late tonight, I'm afraid. I want to have everything ready for tomorrow morning."

The next morning, both Princess and Kedrigern were too edgy to eat a proper breakfast. Spot had scarcely cleared away their half-emptied plates when they went hand in hand to Kedrigern's workroom. Kedrigern at once set to work, bustling about, covering his nervousness with activity and a stream of chatter.

"Now, if you'll take your place opposite me, just as you did the other day . . . that's right, my dear, right there . . . hands by your sides, relaxed . . . nothing to worry about," he said in a gentle, reassuring voice. "I'll just clear away these empty bowls . . . there we are. Now, I'll turn the crystal so . . . and see what happens when I read the spell in the next face. It won't be any time at all, you'll see. I'll read the spell, and you'll be speaking beautifully. Only one or two little things to attend to before we . . . there . . . and then . . ."

"!it with on get, Oh," Princess cried sharply.

"Certainly, my dear, certainly," Kedrigern said with a soothing gesture. "I'm practically finished. There. Now. Are you ready, my dear?"

"Yes," she said, through clenched teeth.

He nodded, took a deep breath, and commenced the summoning of the spirit in the cube. At his first words, the inner radiance came to life, and stirred, and began to glow. It spun and twisted, and Kedrigern began the incantation that would raise it to readiness.

Motes and streamers of light danced in the crystal cube,

ever closer and denser, moving in upon one another until a single glow hung shimmering in the center. Kedrigern reached for Princess's cool hands, placed them on the sides of the crystal, and covered them with his own, just as he had done before. The light formed a brilliant inner cube. Once again, letters began to take shape before Kedrigern's eyes, and he read off the spell slowly revealed to him.

As the last word left his lips, the light burst into fragments. Kedrigern looked up quickly. Princess stared at the crystal, vacant-eyed, for a moment, then looked at him fully alert and aware.

"No, it isn't," she said.

"Is everything all right?" Kedrigern asked anxiously.

"Well, I'm not. Something's gone wrong again."

"You sound fine, my dear."

"Listen to me! I'm one sentence ahead of you, that's what happened!" Princess cried.

"What could have happened?"

"—Ridiculous!"

"But that's—"

Kedrigern waved his hands frantically for silence and restraint. Princess folded her arms like a gate shutting and looked at him with Armageddon in her eyes. With a flurry of soothing gestures, Kedrigern prepared for an immediate new attempt. He gave the crystal a quarter-turn. He wiped his damp forehead on his sleeve, rubbed his eyes, took three deep calming breaths, and for the third time, spoke the spell of summoning.

The light this time was sluggish, moving slowly as winter honey in the center of the crystal cube. Kedrigern could sense the reluctance of the spirit within; but having once begun, he could not turn back. That was a fundamental rule of the wizard's trade.

When the summoning phrases were spoken, Kedrigern paused for breath. The cube was faintly glowing now, with a sallow, grudging light. Princess had relaxed; her hands were by her sides; and her eyes were fixed on the crystal.

Kedrigern began the incantation. The inner light swirled fitfully, like a fish on a line, but its color brightened and deepened. As it gathered, Princess placed her palms against the sides, and Kedrigern enclosed her hands in his. The light rose, and flared, and died, and they stood in the fading afterglow exhausted, their bowed heads almost touching over the crystal cube.

"Are you all right, my dear?" Kedrigern asked when he had his breath under control.

Princess nodded. She took a long, deep breath, then another, and raised her eyes to meet Kedrigern's.

"Say something. Just a short phrase. Anything," Kedrigern said.

She cleared her throat. *"Peererb,"* she said.

Kedrigern recoiled in shock, but quickly recovered his poise. "We'll try again, my dear! A few minutes' rest, that's all we need, and then we'll try it again," he said quickly.

"Peererb! Peererb!!" Princess cried, enraged.

"Now, my dear, you must be patient. These things happen sometimes when you work with magic. It's a momentary setback, nothing more. You mustn't let it—Princess, what are you doing?!"

Kedrigern sprang forward an instant too late. Princess swept up the crystal of Caracodissa in both hands and raised it over her head. With a furious *"peererb"* that drowned Kedrigern's cry of horror, she hurled it with all her might to the stone floor.

From the wreckage rose glimmering motes of golden light. They merged, and danced together in a flashing spiral, and then, with a tinkle of crystalline laughter, the spirit of the crystal of Caracodissa floated out a crack in the shutters and vanished into the light of day, forever free.

"Princess, speak to me!" Kedrigern cried, rushing to her side.

"Brereep," she said, flying to his open arms.

He clasped her tight to still her trembling and hide his own. "It's all right, my dear. The spirit of the crystal was obviously determined not to be helpful. We're well rid of it. I promise you, I'll get your speech back as soon as I possibly can. But we've had quite enough magic for one day. Let's have Spot make up a picnic basket. We've earned a holiday. What do you say to that, my dear?"

"Brereep," she said.

··⌇ *Ten* ⌇··

quicker than the eye

PRINCESS, IT TURNED out, had had quite enough magic for that day and for many days to come. For some time following her unfortunate experience with the crystal of Caracodissa, she showed open detestation for magic in all forms. Since she shared the house with a practicing wizard, this was not an easy course of action, but Princess was a determined woman. At the first hint of a spell, at the slightest gesture that might be the prelude to an enchantment, her features froze and she uttered a single admonitory *"Brereep."* It was warning enough for Kedrigern, who on such occasions withdrew to his study. Sometimes he continued his magic there; more often, he sulked.

It was obvious to him that Princess was losing confidence in his powers, and this seemed unfair. By his magic he had delivered her from toadhood, filled this house with elegant furnishings, and rescued her from the clutches of a barbarian. On two occasions he had actually had her speaking again. One would think that a woman who had witnessed and experienced such things would live in a constant state of unshakcable faith.

But not Princess. She chose to look always on the darker side of things. She remembered not Rupert's meticulous trans-

porting of precious goods, but his derangement of Kedrigern's
workroom and library; not the conjuring of a spirit to aid her,
but the duplicity of the spirit summoned; not that the crystal of
Caracodissa had restored her speech, but that it had restored it
in a somewhat unusual manner. Worst of all, she overlooked
the fact that she had been liberated from a powerful enchantment, and dwelt angrily on the fact that her speaking arrangements continued to be of the batrachian kind. Such an attitude,
thought Kedrigern, was counterproductive. If Princess could
not trust him fully, she might as well abandon all hope of
regaining her human voice. The wizard-client relationship was
deteriorating.

Far worse in his mind, and the cause of most of his sulk-
ing, was the atmosphere of skepticism daily encountered in his
own home. It was dispiriting. He could not imagine Charle-
magne's wife going around the palace muttering that the Holy
Roman Empire was all nonsense, or William the Conqueror's
wife saying that invading England had been a foolish waste of
time. Politicians' wives were supportive. Even barbarians'
wives were willing to pitch in, or at least shout words of
encouragement, when things were tough. But Princess was
showing in every way she could that she trusted magic no
more than Kedrigern himself trusted alchemy. It was enough
to undermine a man's faith in himself.

The letter from Vosconu came very close to being the last
straw. It arrived on a short, dark day in winter, delivered by a
solemn messenger who stood silent and impassive by the fire,
awaiting the wizard's reply. It was very long, written in a tiny
even hand, and contained a circumstantial account of the unpleasant aftermath of Kedrigern's visit. In the opinion of
Vosconu's council—and of Vosconu himself—Kedrigern had
not removed the curse, he had only shifted it. The vineyards
were now healthy, but Vosconu's cattle were beginning to suffer from loss of appetite and exhibiting signs of lameness.
Clearly, it was the wizard's fault, wrote Vosconu, and something had better be done about it quickly or the world would
learn that a certain wizard dwelling on a certain mountain was
going about collecting inflated fees for counterspells and dis-
enchantments that ceased to operate once he was off the prem-
ises.

Kedrigern contained his anger only with great effort. The
curse on the vineyards had been a clumsy patchwork job un-

worthy of a wizard's attention. Left to itself, it would have dissipated within a few days. But to placate the worrisome Vosconu, he had worked a first-class counterspell that would keep the vineyards safe from bad magic for generations to come. And this was his reward: doubts and accusations. First Princess, now Vosconu. It was difficult not to be bitter. It was, in fact, impossible.

As winter closed in, Kedrigern kept more and more to his study, seeking the counterspell that would restore Princess's speech and her confidence in him. He examined, one by one, the books that stood in tottery stacks about the room, or were jammed without system or order onto the shelves. It was a Herculean task, and his progress was agonizingly slow. Day after day he sought the necessary passage, and though he found a great many interesting things, he did not find what he wanted.

The first snow fell, and soon melted away. The next snow remained, and another soon covered it, and before long the little cottage lay snug in a hollow carved by the wind, surrounded on three sides by a rising, sweeping curl of snow. Only in the front of the house was the ground swept clear by the wind that blew unimpeded up the valley and over the meadow. On sunny windless days Kedrigern and Princess, warmly cloaked, took lunch in the dooryard, enjoying the sunshine and crisp air all the more for their long confinement withindoors.

But there was no talk of magic during these *al fresco* luncheons. Deprived of his chief topic of interest, Kedrigern, who had no fund of small talk, was reduced to observations on the weather, a subject soon exhausted. One afternoon, having remarked that it was warm for the time of year, but not as warm as it might be, and that in any event, snow seemed unlikely for the next few days, he leaned back in his chair, turned his face up to the sun, and clasping his hands over his well-filled stomach, drifted off into a light doze, from which he was awakened by a startled *"Brereep!"*

He snapped awake and saw Princess standing by the gate, shading her eyes from the glare of the sun and snow as she peered out over the meadow. She turned to him, pointed into the distance, and repeated, *"Brereep!"*

"Are you sure, my dear?" he said, climbing to his feet. "It's not the season for traveling."

"Brereep," she said, pointing to a tiny dot far in the distance.

"Yes, it does," he agreed, digging under cloak and tunic for his medallion, drawing it forth and raising it to his eyes. "It is. It's Axpad!"

"Brereep?"

"From the guild I belong to. Used to belong to, anyway. The one Conhoon was in. That's where we got our medallions," he explained. "Only good thing I ever got out of the foolish organization was that medallion. Now, what on earth could bring Axpad . . . ?" He fell silent, looking out at the speck trudging across the white expanse, and then, in sudden rage, he roared, "The medallion! He's come to ask for it back, so they can hand it over to some sneaking alchemist! That's what he's here for!"

Princess took a step backward, alarmed by the outburst. Kedrigern, glowering, bunched up his fists.

"We'll see who wears this medallion. Not Axpad, not the whole lot of them with all the magic they can muster and the help of their weasely, skulking alchemist friends . . . ," he blustered, subsiding into red-faced silence, inarticulate with righteous wrath.

"Brereep," Princess said.

"Why else would he come here? This certainly isn't the season for casual visiting. He's not just passing by. Well, he won't get it. That's the last straw!" Kedrigern howled, waving his arms wildly as he stalked about the dooryard. "First *you* treat me like a clumsy apprentice, then *Vosconu* claims that I'm a fraud, and now *this!* It's the absolute last straw! They'll never get this medallion off my neck! Never!"

Taking his arm, Princess led him to his chair. When he was seated, calm once again but still scowling, she patted his hand reassuringly and said, *"Brereep."*

"That's true. Yes, that's true, my dear," he said, brightening. "But if Axpad's not here for the medallion, then why *is* he here?"

"Brereep," Princess suggested.

"Do you really think so? It would be . . . no, it's not possible, my dear. He'd never come all this way in winter just to apologize. More likely the guild wants something. That's bound to be the reason for this visit." Kedrigern's eyes narrowed and his voice grew steely. "Let him crawl. Let him grovel, let him beg and whine and cajole, let him apologize on his knees with tears steaming down his face and dripping from his beard and freezing into icicles. I will never lift a finger to help the Wizards' Guild. Never! After the way they hounded me out . . ."

Again patting his hand, Princess kissed him and whispered, "*Brereep*."

Rising and taking her in his arms, kissing her warmly, he said, "No call for you to be sorry, my dear. I did botch it with the crystal. Only natural for you to be a bit chary when I suggest a spell, after what you went through."

"*Brereep*."

"It won't happen again, I assure you. I'll work no magic to get your voice back unless I'm absolutely certain of the results. Trust me, my dear. And let us prepare to receive our visitor."

Axpad staggered into the cottage about a half-hour after they first caught sight of him. Kedrigern led him to a soft chair by the fire, Spot brought him a tankard of mulled wine, and Princess tucked a blanket around his skinny legs. He barely managed to gasp a feeble hello before falling into a deep exhausted sleep.

That evening, over a late dinner, Axpad was talkative, but not overly informative. He retailed the latest news of the guild, snickering at Hithernils's measures for collecting late dues, frowning at Tristaver's little intrigues, shaking his head in wonderment over Conhoon's sudden aggravated enmity toward barbarian swordsmen. Kedrigern did nothing to interrupt the smooth flow of anecdote and gossip. At appropriate moments he would interject a monosyllabic expression suitable to the context, or show by a raised eyebrow or polite smile his feelings of concern, amusement, or surprise, but he made no attempt to open a dialogue. He knew that Axpad had not walked for days through cold winds and hip-deep snow merely to share a chuckle over the idiosyncrasies of mutual acquaintances. With patience, the whole thing would come out; Kedrigern knew he need only wait.

Since Princess chose to remain completely silent, Axpad was not long in running out of chat. When they had settled in soft chairs before the fire, and Spot had brought a fresh bottle of Vosconu's choicest vintage, Axpad sighed, gazed thoughtfully into the flames, and turned a melancholy gaze on his host.

"It's Quintrindus," he confessed.

"Ah," Kedrigern responded, nodding.

"You were right."

Kedrigern raised an eyebrow and remained silent.

"He's a fraud. It's bound to come out. The guild will be a laughingstock. 'Professor-Doctor-Master Quintrindus' indeed! The man never got past his apprenticeship. And he's not just a fraud, he's a swindler, as well!" Axpad cried, his voice rising.

"Oh?"

"Transmutation of base metals. Lead into gold. That's how he got us, Kedrigern: greed. Greed, pure and simple. It was our own greed that did for us."

Shaking his head sadly to conceal the warm inner glow of self-righteous pleasure that flooded through him at Axpad's words, Kedrigern refilled his guest's goblet. "To the guild," he said, smiling.

"What's left of it," Axpad muttered, raising his goblet half-heartedly.

"Why don't you tell me the details, Axpad?"

His visitor drank, closing his eyes and sighing softly to express his sheer rapture. "Marvelous wine, Kedrigern. Your vines?"

"A client's. The details?"

All rapture vanished from Axpad's voice, manner, and countenance. He grumbled wordlessly, scowled at the fire, and said in a low unhappy voice, "It's not an easy thing to tell anyone. Especially the one who warned us. We were complete dupes."

"You've already told me that. Presumably you haven't come here to brag about the fact, and you certainly haven't come looking for sympathy. I assume, then, that you've come for my help or my advice, or both. And I can give you neither until I know what Quintrindus has done," Kedrigern said patiently, savoring every word he uttered.

Axpad drew a deep breath and began his long account. It was a textbook case of swindling. Quintrindus had filled everyone's ears with his talk of transmutation of base metals. "Lead into gold" became a catchphrase among the members of the guild. The traditions of wizardry were forgotten amid endless prattle of the Philosopher's Stone and the White Elixir, both of which remained tantalizingly just out of reach. Then one day Quintrindus burst into a meeting, hollow-eyed and pale from long effort, to display a pinch of gold dust in a vessel and proclaim success at last. The secret was within his grasp. All that he needed now was financial backing. The assembled wizards—wise old Belsheer, suave Tristaver, and all the rest—practically fell over one another to offer their worldly goods. Hithernils moved that they place the guild treasury at the alchemist's disposal, and the motion passed unanimously, amid loud cheering.

Quintrindus thanked them humbly and tearfully, as they pressed their wealth upon him. He begged leave to retire to his chambers to rest and prepare himself for the final great effort, and took his departure to a chorus of good wishes.

For the next two weeks, all the wizards could talk about was their shrewdness in admitting Quintrindus to membership, and their prospect of immense riches and eternal fame. For a day or two into the third week there was excited speculation on the alchemist's progress. Then came a day of uneasy curiosity about his long absence; and after that, revelation. Tristaver returned pale and breathless from a visit to Quintrindus's laboratory to announce that alchemist and treasury were gone without a trace.

There were mutterings of vile enchantment by rival wizards or jealous fellow alchemists. But a close search of the laboratory turned up a mocking note in Quintrindus's own hand that revealed his deception. Long planned and perfectly executed, his plot to swindle and humiliate the guild had been a complete success, thanks to the enthusiastic cooperation of the wizards themselves.

"And that's all we know," Axpad concluded. "Quintrindus has vanished from human ken. We've tried every kind of spell at our command, and it's as if he'd never existed."

"He, or the treasury," Kedrigern pointed out cheerily.

"That, too," Axpad admitted.

"What exactly do you want me to do?"

"Find the treasury and get it back to the guild before that rotten swindler reveals to the whole world how he's duped us. If you can find Quintrindus, or turn him into something more loathsome than he already is, that's fine with us. Get his dog, too, while you're at it."

"His dog?"

"Quintrindus got himself a dog after you left. A nasty little mutt named Jaderal. Used to snap at all the wizards."

"I know Jaderal well. He used to snap at wizards even before he was a dog. But why bring me into this, Axpad? I have no love for Quintrindus, but if all the efforts of the guild can't turn up anything, what do you expect of me?"

"Well, we thought there might be a spell involved, and you're the expert on counterspells."

"Quintrindus couldn't cast a spell with a catapult. There's more to it than a spell, Axpad. It's impossible for a man to stay hidden if the most accomplished wizards in the world are looking for him."

Axpad waved off Kedrigern's concern. "Quintrindus isn't that important. All that really matters is getting the treasury back, so we don't look ridiculous. This could do us a lot of harm."

"Yes, it certainly could. It could ruin you," Kedrigern said with a broad smile.

"It could ruin *us*," Axpad said, with careful emphasis.

"Us?"

"Well, you were a charter member of the guild. You're well known in the profession. What's bad for wizards is going to be bad for you, Kedrigern. Once people start gossiping, they don't pause to make fine distinctions. You'll be tarred with the same brush as the rest of us."

Kedrigern was stunned into silence by this appalling prospect. He pictured Vosconu filling page after feverish page with disparaging remarks in his tiny script, spreading word of the guild's folly throughout the literate world and giving him, Kedrigern, a totally undeserved leading role in the fiasco. No one would believe that he alone had seen through Quintrindus, had warned his friends and colleagues and been ignored. And what Vosconu invented, others would rush to embellish. Ruination would be upon them. Trust in wizards would vanish, and in its place would come laughter and alchemy. The alchemists would sweep all before them. Wizards would be reduced to healing boils and telling fortunes.

"That's outrageous. It's completely unfair," he said angrily.

"Oh, it is, I agree. But you know it's true. That's the way of the world, Kedrigern," said Axpad, looking at him with studied innocence.

Kedrigern made a sour growling noise. He did indeed

know that it was true, and that he had no choice but to help the guild. His long-awaited gloating time had come, and had vanished in the wink of an eye. He gulped his remaining wine and slammed the empty goblet down noisily on the table.

"You'll help us, then?" said Axpad.

"Yes," Kedrigern snarled.

"We do appreciate it. If I can help in any way, I'm at your service."

"Thank you," said Kedrigern bitterly.

"We're in this together, after all. Must stand shoulder to shoulder at this time of trial. Do our bit. Put aside personal differences. Think of the greater good."

Only by a heroic effort did Kedrigern refrain from throwing himself on Axpad, seizing him in a throttling grip, and howling "Shut up, you idiot! Shut up!" He bit his lip, nodded, and was silent.

"Any assistance I can give, Kedrigern. You need only ask," Axpad went on.

"My books," Kedrigern said.

"Certainly. What about them?"

"They're a mess. You can help me get them in order, so I can research this thing properly."

"Happy to be of service. I don't mean to pry, but this does puzzle me. Is something wrong with Eleanor of the Brazen Head? As I recall, she used to do your cataloguing, and she was quite efficient."

"I had to let Eleanor go. She got involved with a poltergeist." Kedrigern was silent for a moment, then said, "Too bad. She might have been able to catch a glimpse of Quintrindus."

"Is there any possibility of summoning her back?"

"None whatsoever."

Kedrigern refilled Axpad's goblet and his own. When he turned to Princess, she shook her head, rose, delicately covered a yawn, and with a kiss for her husband and a wave of the hand for her guest, silently took her leave of the men.

"A lovely woman, your wife. Quiet, too," said Axpad.

"Yes. Princess isn't one for small talk."

They sipped the excellent wine, gazed pensively into the fire, and passed the time in companionable silence. Kedrigern began to mellow. Axpad was a decent sort, all things considered. The rest of the guild were good fellows, just a bit too easily impressed by flashy mountebanks. And when all is said and done, a man must stick up for his friends and his profession. Especially against alchemists.

"Did Quintrindus leave any clothing behind?" he asked abruptly. "If Spot could get a scent, he might be able to track him."

"No. All he left was the note."

"That would do."

Axpad shook his head. "We tore it to shreds and burned the pieces."

Again they drank in silence. This time it was Axpad who made a suggestion. "I've heard of a miraculous crystal ball that allows one to see distant people and places. Perhaps we could obtain it. . . ."

"I don't work with miraculous crystal objects of any kind," said Kedrigern flatly.

They took up their goblets, which by now were nearly empty. Kedrigern refilled them, and they imbibed of Vosconu's best once again. The next thing Kedrigern was aware of was coming suddenly awake to the sound of snoring. Axpad was sunk deep in his chair, mouth gaping wide, making sounds like a man drowning in thick syrup.

There was no point in trying to rouse him. Being a wizard, inured to the rigors of the road, Axpad could sleep as comfortably in the chair as anywhere. Kedrigern rose stiffly, stretched, yawned profoundly, and shuffled to Axpad's side. He raised his guest's feet and rested them on a cushioned stool, then covered him with a blanket. And then to bed.

After an early breakfast, the two wizards withdrew to Kedrigern's workroom to begin putting his library in proper order. It was a slow business, for neither of them could take up a book without leafing through it, or leaf through a book without pausing to read an interesting passage that caught his eye, or read an interesting passage without sitting down in the nearest cleared space and reading on until forcibly interrupted. And since each was engrossed in the contents of the book at hand, the interruptions were few. By the end of the first day they had organized eleven books into three neat stacks, and confronted the necessity for more speed and less browsing.

On the second day they made heroic progress, and by the third morning they were halfway through their task. Kedrigern's workroom began to approach something like order, and he and Axpad paused to admire their work.

"You have a lot of books that I haven't seen in other wizards' libraries," Axpad said.

"You never know what's going to come in handy," Kedrigern replied.

"But histories? Memoirs? *Jest books??* Come, now."

"Well, the jest books are strictly to help me relax, but the others . . . this one, for instance," said Kedrigern, taking up a fat volume that chanced to be near at hand and opening it at random. "They're full of odd bits of information. Take this anecdote about Zluc the Decisive, for example," he said, propping the book up before him and reading aloud. "'But the oxen of the kingdom, which for greatness of body and sweetness of flesh were without equal in the world, did then fall prey to a strange rot. Whether from drinking of hurtful waters or grazing in unwholesome fields or from the machinations of wicked men I know not, they began to lose their appetite and to walk with halting gait, as if lame, and soon to die and give forth a great stink. Which when Zluc learned, he gave order that all infected cattle were to be put to death forthwith, and buried in quicklime in a far . . .'" Kedrigern looked up with a sudden wild grin and began to laugh and clap his hands. "Do you hear that? Wonderful! It's wonderful!"

Axpad gaped at him in utter bewilderment. "Is that a jest, Kedrigern? If it is, you'll have to explain it. I don't get the point."

Kedrigern bounced up and said, "It's a jest on a picky client of mine, Axpad. It's an example of chance working at her lovable, unpredictable best. It's exactly what I was talking about—you simply never know when one of these books will come in handy."

"No," said Axpad, befuddled.

"Let's have lunch. It's a propitious time for lunch. A marvelous time for lunch!" Kedrigern said exuberantly, leading his guest from the workroom with a sprightly step.

Princess joined them for lunch. She remained silent, communicating by means of dazzling smiles and graceful gestures and completely captivating Axpad. He replied in monosyllables to Kedrigern's cheery flow of anecdotes, but his eyes remained on Princess. As they put down their napkins at the end of the meal, a knock sounded at the door.

"Yah!" Spot cried from the kitchen.

"Never mind, Spot. I'll get it," said Kedrigern, rising. Smiling, he told Princess and Axpad, "I have an odd feeling that I know who it is."

Axpad looked blankly at Princess, who shrugged and shook her head. Kedrigern's voice boomed from the hall in merry greeting, and he entered with his arm draped over the shoulder of a snow-covered, red-cheeked, sniffling youth, whom he led to a bench by the fire.

"You sit right there and have a good warm, my boy, while I read your master's message," he said. Returning to the table, he seated himself, and with elaborate care, opened the seal and perused the contents. Here he chuckled, there he frowned; he clucked disapprovingly at some passages, nodded at others, and several times muttered, "Oh dear. Temper, temper." At last he refolded it, tucked it in his tunic, and said, "It's from Vosconu, my dear. His cattle are still doing poorly. Well, I must correct that forthwith, as Zluc the Decisive would say. Will you excuse me while I write a reply?"

He left the room, returning in a short time with a packet which he gave to the messenger. "Just tell your master to follow my instructions to the letter, and the murrain will be lifted from his herds. He must do exactly as I've set down. I'll attend to all the necessary enchantment at this end. You're welcome to sit by the fire until you're ready to leave, my boy."

"Oh, no, master, I'll delay no longer. My good lord awaits your response eagerly," the messenger said, rewinding his scarf and pulling on his mittens. "I must leave at once."

"Good lad. That's loyalty for you. Vosconu deserves no less," said Kedrigern warmly, slipping a coin into the messenger's pocket and pressing a slab of cheese and some buttered bread into his mittened hand. "Must keep up your strength. You've a long hard road ahead," he said, ushering the youth from the room.

When he returned, beaming happily on Princess and Axpad, he said, "What a wonderful day! It's a whole new day dawning—I can feel it!"

Axpad stared out the window for a time, then turned to Kedrigern and said, "It's early in the afternoon, and the weather is terrible."

"Only out there." Kedrigern thumped himself on the chest.

"In here, it's the first day of spring. A lovely day. Everything's coming to life again. Winter is over, the clouds have passed, the gloom is gone. Come, Axpad, to work! The guild must have its treasury."

Princess nodded reassuringly to her uneasy guest. Axpad rose and accompanied Kedrigern to his workroom, where they labored into the night to finish their cataloguing. Kedrigern was as brisk and chirpy as a sparrow through it all, and showed no sign of hunger or fatigue when Axpad slipped the last book into place and collapsed in the wizard's chair with a great sigh.

"Well, that's done," said Kedrigern, rubbing his palms together eagerly. "Now I can get to work."

"Now, Kedrigern?" Axpad asked in dismay.

"No time to waste. First I'll need the book with the spells for summoning up things. If Quintrindus is getatable, that book will give me a spell to get at him."

"It's after midnight!"

"Best time to work. No distractions. Princess understands —she won't be annoyed."

"Kedrigern, I can barely move!" Axpad wailed. "My eyes feel like hot pebbles. My bones have turned to slush. I'm ready to collapse."

"Good. That's fine," Kedrigern muttered, oblivious now to everything but the task at hand. He plucked the black book from its new niche, opened it to the instructions for summoning up an essence of known identity but uncertain location, and set about his preparations. When Axpad began to snore loudly and distractingly, he interrupted his work just long enough to carry the sleeping wizard to the guest room and dump him on the bed, then returned with swift purposeful steps to his workroom, where he remained. And remained. And remained.

Days passed. Spot carried Spartan meals to the workroom and left them outside the door without knocking. Each morning it removed the empty tray, but there was no trace of Kedrigern.

Axpad, who knew too well that no one, not even a wife or colleague, disturbs a wizard in the midst of spelling, tried to control his impatience and stay out of the way. Ordinarily not a sociable man, he sought to engage Princess in polite conversation whenever their paths crossed, which was frequently, but could initiate nothing more than a series of monologues, he doing the talking, she responding with smiles and nods, or frowns and shakings of the head, according to the drift of his talk. He wondered if Kedrigern had married a mute, or if Princess had, for some reason, vowed a life of silence; but he vaguely remembered Conhoon's remarking on the sweet voice and astonishing eloquence of Kedrigern's wife. Was this, perhaps, a new wife? If so, what had become of the eloquent one? Or was Conhoon exaggerating; or, perhaps, Axpad's own memory slipping? It was a great perplexity. Too many things about Kedrigern were a perplexity. His wife was a mystery, his behavior was eccentric, his house-troll was grotesque, his dwelling remote. On the other hand, his wine was excellent, his table abundant, and his guest bed comfortable. Axpad bided his time, assuring himself that Kedrigern's protracted sequestration would end in the resolution of all his puzzlement.

On the morning of his ninth day of seclusion, Kedrigern appeared at the breakfast table looking like a man delivered from long hard servitude on a poor diet. He was pale and noticeably thinner, and his eyes had the grainy red-rimmed look of long waking and close watching. But he was in the best of spirits, and had the appetite of a family of active giants. With a quick kiss for Princess and a word to Axpad, he began at once to devour a breakfast consisting of heroic amounts of porridge, eggs and rashers, bread and jam, more eggs and rashers, sausages, most of a plate of muffins, a few grilled kidneys, and two more slices of bread and jam, washed down by a large pitcher of milk. When the last morsel was gone, he leaned back in his chair, sighed with repletion, covered a single elegant belch with his fingertips, smiled lazily on his wife and guest, and said, "Marvelous breakfast. Best I've had in forty-three years. The muffins were superb, my dear. And your strawberry jam . . . ! Ambrosial, positively ambrosial. And Spot has never fried an egg so expertly." He shut his eyes and sighed again in utter contentment. "A marvelous breakfast."

"I'm sure you've earned it," Axpad ventured.

"You bet I have," said Kedrigern without opening his eyes. "You *have?*"

"Yes." Kedrigern yawned a long, wrenching yawn and settled deeper in the chair. He neither moved nor spoke, but a satisfied smile spread over his face.

"The treasury . . . is it found? And Quintrindus?" Axpad asked in a low, anxious voice.

Kedrigern drew himself slowly up out of the chair, yawned once again, and smiled benevolently on his fellow wizard. "The guild will get its treasury back, and Quintrindus will never bother anyone again." Raising his hands to dam the flood of Axpad's questions, he said, "I'll tell you the details when I wake up." Turning to Princess, he asked, "Were there any messages while I was working, my dear?" She shook her head, and he said, "If any should arrive, please don't wake me. They'll just have to wait." With a farewell kiss for Princess, he plodded off to bed and slept through the day and night.

When Kedrigern and Princess appeared for breakfast the next morning, the wizard's appetite was on a more human scale: he had only a large helping of everything, no seconds. Axpad nibbled impatiently at his muffin and egg, darting eager curious glances at his host and hostess every few seconds. Kedrigern ate methodically and silently. When he popped the last morsel in his mouth and pushed back his chair, Axpad could contain himself no longer. "What happened?" he cried.

"To whom?" Kedrigern replied coolly.

"To the guild's treasury! To Quintrindus!"

"Oh. Oh, yes, I promised to tell you, didn't I?" Kedrigern said, shaking his head as if bemused by his lapse of memory. "Well, it wasn't all that difficult, really, once I found out— may I have a muffin, please?—once I learned about Quintrindus. That was the puzzling part. And Jaderal. Jaderal was the key to the whole thing. He's the one to watch out for now. Thoroughly rotten, that Jaderal."

"The dog?" Axpad asked, pressing the muffin dish upon Kedrigern.

"That's right. Would you pass the jam, please? It seems that Quintrindus agreed to despell Jaderal in return for his help in distracting the guild members from too close attention to the lead-into-gold process. I assume he did a lot of barking, and nipping at hands and ankles—that sort of thing."

"Yes, he did. He was a terrible nuisance. But you say he was under a spell?"

"Jaderal was once an apprentice of mine. He didn't work

out at all. I finally had to turn him into a dog. Thought it might improve his character—teach him loyalty, that sort of thing—but apparently it didn't. When Quintrindus despelled him, Jaderal played a very nasty trick on Quintrindus. He sent him off to another plane on a one-way spell. That's why no one could find any trace of him. You should have been looking for Jaderal."

Kedrigern took up the bread, which he had been spreading thickly with Princess's strawberry jam, and bit off a sizeable chunk. Axpad was silent for a moment before asking, "How did you ever find this out?"

Mouth filled, Kedrigern winked and said, "Uh hum muh wudd."

"You what?"

Swallowing, Kedrigern said, "I have my ways. The hard part was getting a fix on them after all this time, and with Quintrindus gone elsewhere."

"The treasury! Did you locate the treasury?"

"Certainly." Turning to Princess, Kedrigern said, "May I have the pitcher, please, my dear?"

"Where is it?" Axpad cried.

"Right over there, by the bread," Kedrigern said, pointing.

"No, the treasury! The treasury!"

"Oh. The treasury is hidden in a stable. I had to put a quick spell on it to deceive Jaderal, but I'll give you the counterspell. It's a very simple one." As Kedrigern began to pour the milk, a loud knock came at the front door.

"Yah! Yah!" Spot responded from a distant room.

"Answer the door, Spot. Take your time about it," the wizard called, beaming at Princess and Axpad and raising his milk-filled mug, as if in a toast.

Another knock came, then the sound of Spot's huge feet slapping in the flagstones of the hall, the creaking of the door, the customary startled cry of the visitor at the sight of Spot, and then a babble of deep voices. Half turning in his chair, Kedrigern shouted, "Show our visitors in, Spot!"

Four large men, heavily armed, wearing the colors of Vosconu the Openhanded, entered the room, respectfully removing their helmets at the sight of Princess. Their leader saluted Kedrigern and stepped forward, looking uneasy.

"Have you a message for me, Captain?" the wizard asked.

"I do, Master Kedrigern," said the guard captain, ducking

his head and blinking nervously. "My lord Vosconu the Open-handed sends his profound thanks for your loyal and faithful assistance in his hour of need, and his assurance that all who converse with him shall hear of the wisdom and great power of the matchless wizard Kedrigern of Silent Thunder Mountain," he recited in a loud monotone, red-faced with the strain of remembering.

"Well said, Captain. Anything else?"

"Yes, Master Kedrigern. You are to disregard my lord Vosconu's previous message, which was written in great heat and under the baneful influence of jealous and suspicious men."

"You may inform Lord Vosconu that I have forgotten it completely," said Kedrigern with a smile and a casual wave of the hand.

"And I'm to give you this, Master Kedrigern," the captain said, drawing from his tunic a pouch about the length and thickness of a man's forearm and placing it in Kedrigern's hands with a solid clinking of coin against coin. "And I'm to advise you that as soon as the snows are melted and the roads are passable, my lord Vosconu is sending you forty casks of his choicest wine as a token of his gratitude and esteem."

"My lord Vosconu outdoes himself in generosity. Please assure him that I am ever ready to assist him. And now, Captain, perhaps you and your men would like a flagon of ale and a light repast to fortify yourselves against your return trip. If you'll just follow my house-troll, it'll see that you and your men have your fill, and it will pack a nice lunch for the road," said Kedrigern, rising and gesturing toward the doorway, where Spot awaited.

"Yes, Master Kedrigern. Thank you," the captain said, backing out, and his men joined their expressions of gratitude to his.

Turning to Axpad, who sat in awed silence, Kedrigern said, "It's always so nice to receive good news at breakfast, isn't it? Lovely way to start the day."

Axpad nodded slowly. He could think of nothing to say.

With his mission fulfilled, Axpad was eager to leave, and the prospect of an armed escort made it desirable to go this very day, when he could set out with Vosconu's men. He needed only the counterspell to restore the guild's gold, and

Kedrigern copied it out as Axpad rolled up his few belongings. Vosconu's men were gratefully packing bread, cheese, and dried meat and filling their water bottles for the journey. Their hearty voices could be heard at the front door, where the two wizards stood.

"I'm grateful, Kedrigern. We're all grateful. It was most kind of you, after the way we . . . after what . . . ," Axpad said awkwardly, trailing off into an uncomfortable silence from which he emerged with, "You had every reason to bear a grudge."

Clapping him on the back, Kedrigern said, "As you reminded me, old friend, we're in this together. We must stand shoulder to shoulder. Do our bit."

"About the spell you put on the treasury," Axpad said. "What exactly did you do?"

"Oh, that. I disguised it. Camouflage, you know. Didn't want Jaderal to recognize it."

"Very farsighted of you. How did you disguise it?"

"I had to act quickly, you understand. It was in a stable, and I thought . . . well, to put it simply, I turned it into horse manure. It just . . . blended right in."

"Brilliant! And all we need do is recite the counterspell, and it will be gold again!"

"That's all there is to it. *Practically* all," Kedrigern said, looking away. "As I said, it . . . it blended right in . . . with the real thing."

"Blended?" Axpad repeated dubiously.

"Well, you know how stables are. All that moving around, and . . . mixing together," said Kedrigern, with a vivid churning gesture, adding cheerfully, "Once it's cleaned up, no one will ever suspect where it's been. You'll just have a few unpleasant moments separating . . . the wheat from the chaff, as it were."

Axpad gazed at him blankly. "The wheat . . . from the chaff," he repeated in a dull voice.

"In a manner of speaking. Ah, here come Vosconu's men! And Princess, to see you all off. What a fine brisk morning to be traveling! Spring is just around the corner, no doubt about it," said Kedrigern, breathing deeply of the keen air as he steered Axpad to the gate.

"Good day to you, Master Kedrigern, and our thanks for

your hospitality," said the guard captain. His men raised their hands in a salute to the wizard.

"Our pleasure, Captain. Please convey to Lord Vosconu our warm friendship and our deepest gratitude," said Kedrigern, pressing a few coins into the man's hand, adding, "A little something for you and your men."

"We'll drink to your health, Master. And to yours, my lady," said the captain, bowing to Princess. He turned to Axpad. "We'll be leaving now, sir, if you're ready."

"Look after him, Captain. He's an old friend."

"I will, Master Kedrigern."

They walked off into the bright clear morning, turning at the crest of the hill to exchange one last wave of farewell with their host and hostess. When they dropped from sight, Kedrigern took Princess's hand and raised it to his lips. "You're a gracious hostess, my dear. And patient, as well."

"Brereep," she said, smiling.

"You're too modest. Axpad can be trying, especially if one is left alone with him for days. Sorry about that, but I couldn't interrupt the spell once it was working."

"Brereep," she reassured him.

"Thank you, my dear. It's been a busy fortnight for us both, but a most rewarding one." He looked out benevolently over the shrunken snowfields, where here and there a patch of ground showed through. "Oh, my, yes, a very rewarding one for all concerned."

"Brereep?"

"Well, my colleagues in the guild have learned the consequences of trusting an alchemist. Vosconu's herds have been saved, and he's learned not to write accusing letters in the heat of the moment. And I have my library in order at last—which means that I can finally find the proper counterspell for you. I'm going to concentrate on herbal remedies. Spring is almost here, and I'll soon be able to gather good fresh materials. Believe me, my dear, you'll be speaking in a very short time," he said, squeezing her hand.

She smiled at him noncommittally. He waited, but she was silent.

"Surely you have no more doubts. You do trust me now, don't you, my dear?" he asked.

"Brereep," she said.

···⊰ *Eleven* ⊱···

a rarebit of magic

THE SUN WAS warm, but not too warm for comfort; bright, but not dazzling to Kedrigern's overworked and slightly near-sighted eyes. Birds sang, but not too loudly, and every note rang clear. The mild breeze was freighted with rich fragrance. It was a perfect spring day.

Kedrigern made his unhurried way along the forest path, humming a little wordless tune which he made up as he walked to where his horse awaited. He was in excellent spirits and at peace with the world. In plain fact, this spring day had filled him with the ebullient, unfocused glee of a small boy on holiday, and he was in a mood to do handsprings and cut capers right here on this green-roofed pathway. Only the pouch at his side, filled with freshly gathered herbs of great virtue, prevented him. The herbs were much too delicate to withstand gymnastics.

On an impulse, he set the pouch down gently at the foot of a tree. He sprang into the air, tapping his heels together. Selecting an open patch of green beside the path, he did a head-stand. At last, laughing for pure joy, he tumbled onto his back and lay looking up at the sunny sky through the tapestry of new leaves.

And then he heard a distant moan.

He sprang up quickly and brushed himself off. His expression became somber. It would not do for ordinary citizens to see a respected wizard bounding about the woods like a silly lamb. Taking up his pouch of herbs and simples, he proceeded in the direction of the mournful sound, guided by frequent repetitions which became louder and more distinct as he pressed on. His gait was stately, but rapid, and before long he came upon a huddled figure by the wayside.

It was a young man, dressed in once gaudy finery which now was much stained and worn from travel. He sat with his back to a flat rock, his bare feet stuck straight out before him. His hands were limp and forlorn in his lap, his head slumped forward in a posture of desolation. Looking about, Kedrigern saw a single boot lying a good way down the road, as if it had been vehemently flung away. Something unusual was going on here, he thought, and resolved to find out what it might be.

He cleared his throat, and in his most disarming voice said, "Good morrow, traveler. Is all well with you?"

At the first syllable, the young man jerked up his head. He brushed back his tangled jet-black hair and gazed up at Kedrigern with large, sad brown eyes. "Look you, sir, how I am crippled entirely with the curse of ingrown toenails, and it not ten days since Black Ivor Gruffydd placed it on me," said he in a deep voice, speaking in a lilting manner halfway between oratory and incantation.

"Ingrown toenails can be very painful. Particularly if one is required to do much walking," Kedrigern said sympathetically.

"That is the plain truth. And a *cerddor* must do much walking, and that is to say nothing of the taking care of his harp, and the keeping his head filled with sweet sound, or he will be forced to sleep in the woods and feed on nuts and berries," the young man lamented.

"Ah . . . you're a minstrel, then."

"I am a minstrel now. But despite my youth, I was near to being *bardd teulu*, household bard to a great lord, look you, and would now hold such a fine position except for the dirty underhanded scheming of the Gruffydds to snatch away what was justly mine and hand it over to whining whey-faced Red Gruffydd."

Kedrigern shook his head, puzzled. "I thought it was Black

Ivor who did this to you. How does Red Gruffydd come into it?"

"There is sharp you are, mister," said the young minstrel appreciatively. "Red Gruffydd does not curse well enough to curdle milk on a hot day. It was his brother, Black Ivor Gruffydd, put the curse on me, indeed, and him known as Black Ivor not for the color of hair or eyes or skin but for the black of his nature. I had not seen him, nor he me, since I left my home these two years gone. But I saw him at the fair ten days ago, where he was peddling his bawdry and lechery, and I said for all to hear what kind of a nastiness is in him. And it is then he put the curse of ingrown toenails on me."

"What do you plan to do?"

The young man's eyes flashed. "I will soak my feet in a pail of the Gruffydds' blood, that is what I will do, as soon as I can walk without the pains of hell to cripple me."

"That's a bit drastic, isn't it? Surely it won't do anything for your toenails."

"There is peace of mind it will give me, mister," the minstrel said grimly.

Kedrigern nodded to acknowledge the desirability of peace of mind. He seated himself at the minstrel's side. For a time, neither of them said a word, then Kedrigern, looking off into the trees, said casually, "The local overseer of law and order is a man named Panglunder the Unyielding. He got his name from his practice of tracking down and punishing everyone suspected of crime in this part of the kingdom. As a rule, he hangs murderers, but now and then he impales one. Just for a change."

"I would be away from here like the smoke, look you. No man would find me."

"When you can hardly walk? Give it up, my boy. Revenge is very entertaining on the stage, but totally unworkable in everyday life," Kedrigern said with a wise, avuncular smile.

"There is foolish I am, and have been always," said the minstrel with a deep despairing sigh. "When we were lads, studying at the feet of the great *penceirdd* Twm ap Tudur, the Gruffydds learned all the spells for rapid advancement and discomfort to enemies, and far it is that their wicked knowledge has brought them."

"From your manner of speaking, and the terminology you employ, I gather that you are no ordinary minstrel, but one of the Cymric bards," said Kedrigern.

"That is what I am, mister," said the young man proudly.

"And while the Gruffydds were mastering their nasty spells, what were *you* learning?"

"Every charm for eloquence and sweetness of speech in the *Green Book of Maelgwyn* I have by heart. I can make the stones of the ground to sing, look you, and the croaking toad to converse with the voice of an angel. And I would trade it all for a spell to cure my ingrown toenails."

Kedrigern turned a broad, beaming smile on the woebegone minstrel and clapped a hand solidly on his shoulder. "It's a deal, my boy," he said.

"There is cruel you are to mock me, mister," said the youth.

"I'm not mocking you. I can get you back on your feet in no time. In exchange, I want you to use your spells for eloquence—specifically, the one that makes the croaking toad converse with the voice of an angel. I'm a wizard. Semiretired at the moment, but I do a lot of private work, especially in counterspelling. The name's Kedrigern," said the wizard, extending a hand.

"And I am Rhys ap Gwallter," said the minstrel, accepting the proffered welcome. "Though it is small need you have of my spells, to hear the speaking of you."

"It's not for me. You'll see when we get to my house. We should arrive just in time for lunch," Kedrigern said, rising and brushing himself off.

"I will be slow in the walking, look you. More like it will be breakfast time two days hence," Rhys warned.

"No need to walk at all. I'll summon my horse."

Rhys looked up, wide-eyed. "A great excitement it will be to me to see how a true wizard summons his horse."

Kedrigern looked at him, puzzled. "Why? All I'm going to do is whistle."

"Oh," said the minstrel, crestfallen.

Kedrigern thrust two fingers in his mouth and gave a sharp, long whistle. In a very short time, the sound of measured hoofbeats echoed up the forest path, and soon a shaggy black horse came into sight.

"That is a horse I would expect to see a great barbarian warrior riding, and not a kindly wizard," said Rhys, hauling himself painfully to his feet.

"It belonged to a barbarian warrior once," Kedrigern said. "He doesn't ride anymore. Got all stiffened up."

With a bit of assistance from Kedrigern, Rhys ap Gwallter mounted the black horse. Kedrigern handed up the minstrel's harp and skimpy pack, and his own pouch of herbs, and they started off for the wizard's home, where Princess awaited.

As they emerged from the forest, and Silent Thunder Mountain loomed before them, far across the rolling grasslands, Rhys uncovered his small harp and began to play a sweet, sad melody. It was a very fine performance, but not at all suited to Kedrigern's mood, which was improving with every homeward step. He requested something merry, and the minstrel obliged.

Kedrigern was certain that he had at last found the solution to Princess's difficulties. The power of the charms over speech and eloquence known to the Cymric bards was the envy of wizards everywhere. Kedrigern had more than once given serious thought to making the long and perilous journey westward in hopes of obtaining bardic help for his wife, but every time he had been discouraged by remembered accounts of the bards' notorious reluctance to share their magic with an outsider, even a wizard offering an exorbitant price. And now the magic of the Cymri was his for the asking, in exchange for a small, simple healing spell. It seemed to him to be a sign that the universe was in good hands after all. He smiled placidly and began to hum along with the harp.

They arrived at the cottage just at midday. Kedrigern was helping Rhys down from the horse, and suddenly he felt the minstrel stiffen.

"What is that, now?" Rhys cried in alarm.

A grotesque little creature was bouncing up and down on the flagstones of the dooryard, salivating liberally. It cried "Yah! Yah!" in joyous welcome.

"Tell Princess I'm back, Spot," Kedrigern called, waving a greeting. As the little apparition bounded into the house, he said to the minstrel, "That's our house-troll. A good hard worker, and absolutely devoted to me."

"That is a thing I have never seen," said Rhys guardedly.

"No, I suppose not. You have to get them young, or it's no use at all, and it's very difficult to find a nice clean tractable young troll. Spot is a real treasure."

"Look you, sir, my charms were not meant for trolls, young or old."

"Don't worry, Rhys. That's not what I have in mind," said Kedrigern. Spot reappeared, and the wizard sent it off at once to fetch a basin of warm salt water. "You can sit here in the sun and give your feet a good relaxing soak until lunch is ready. After lunch we'll get down to business," he explained to Rhys.

At that moment, Princess appeared in the doorway. She wore a pale green robe, trimmed with white. Her ebony hair hung loose to her waist. A slim golden circlet bound her brow. Rhys ap Gwallter looked on, bedazzled by her beauty, as Kedrigern kissed her warmly, then took her hand and conducted her to their guest. She curtseyed deeply to his bow, then she smiled a smile that made the spring morning seem dull and cheerless by comparison. Without having spoken a word, she withdrew.

"There is a fine-looking woman your wife is, Master Kedrigern," said Rhys reverently. "I have seen queens and princesses and fine ladies, but next to her, look you, they are all as ugly as toads."

"Funny you should put it that way," Kedrigern said. "Would you believe, Rhys, that only a few—"

The arrival of Spot, bearing a great wooden tub of steaming water, interrupted Kedrigern's response. The troll set it down in front of a chair, and Rhys, at Kedrigern's bidding, immersed his pained feet in the tub with a long, low sigh of relief.

"Nothing like a nice restful soak when your feet hurt," Kedrigern said. "Make yourself comfortable. Lunch will be ready shortly. As I started to say," he went on, pulling up a chair for himself, "you'd hardly believe that only a few months ago—just under a year—that beautiful woman was hopping about in a bog."

"In a bog, you say? There is strange in that, now."

"Nothing strange about it. She was a toad."

"A toad, you say?"

"Yes. A lovely little toad she was, too. I knew there was something special about that toad the minute I laid eyes on it."

"A grand toad she was, I am sure of that. But why would such a woman want to be a toad altogether?" Rhys asked.

"It wasn't her idea. Her parents had neglected to invite a local bog-fairy to Princess's christening, and so the bog-fairy put a curse on the child. On her eighteenth birthday, Princess turned into a toad. Didn't even get to open her presents. Bog-fairies can be very mean-minded when they think they've been slighted."

"And it was you changed her back into the lovely lady, then, with the magic of you?"

"Yes. As I mentioned earlier, I specialize in remedial magic. Counterspells and such. Undoing other people's nastiness. Been remarkably successful with it, too, as you can see. There's only one—"

Princess emerged from the doorway bearing a silver tray on which rested a chunk of deep golden cheese, a round of dark bread, and a square of pale yellow butter. Behind her bounded Spot, with a frost-coated pitcher in one hand and three stone mugs clutched in the other.

Kedrigern, rising and bidding Rhys remain seated, pulled up a chair for Princess, kissed her cheek, and took the tray.

"Brereep," she said, smiling gloriously as she seated herself facing the minstrel.

Rhys gave a little start. Water sloshed from the tub.

"As I was about to say, there's only one small problem left to deal with. Nobody wins all the time, even a wizard. But I have absolute faith in *you*, my boy," said Kedrigern.

"There are always the complications," Rhys said sympathetically. "Things there be that we cannot control. Well I remember a love-chant I wrought, of great potency it was, look you, but I could not get it to work for the complication of the lady's name." He sighed and shook his head slowly. "A great beauty she was, but she had a name to her that not one man in all the kingdom could pronounce properly, and so there was no wooing her. How is a man to woo a maid, I ask you, if he is unable to speak her name? There is frustrating it was."

"Whatever became of the poor lady?"

"She changed her name to Ann Jones, and was married in a fortnight."

Kedrigern nodded approvingly. "The simple solutions are best in some cases." He turned to Princess. "I was just telling Rhys about our first meeting, my dear, and how I used my arts to restore your proper—and most attractive—form. Rhys is having a bit of a problem himself right now. Someone has placed a curse on him."

"*Brereep?*" she asked.

"I am, my dear. And in return, Rhys will place at our disposal his knowledge of the Cymric spells for eloquence and sweetness of speech which he has learned from the *Green Book of Maelgwyn*. I believe we have solved your problem at last, my dear," Kedrigern said, squeezing her hand reassuringly.

"*Brereep? Brereep!*" she cried happily.

Rhys looked from one of them to the other, his apprehension evident. "Look you, now, this is a bit more complicated than I thought it would be."

"Surely the charms of the *Green Book of Maelgwyn* can deal with a little croak," Kedrigern said, pouring foaming ale into the first mug.

"A great difference there is, Master Kedrigern, between taking a tongue-tied *cerddor* and instilling in him sweetness of discourse, and taking a lady who croaks like a toad—a very fine and melodious croak it is, lady, I do assure you—" he quickly added, "and putting eloquent words to her tongue. Oh, a very great difference, indeed."

"I have every confidence in you, Rhys, and in the *Green Book of Maelgwyn*," Kedrigern said, pouring into the second mug. "And if my confidence is misplaced, you may find your toenails growing out the top of your head."

"*Brereep,*" Princess said softly. She shook her head and placed her hand on Kedrigern's forearm.

Kedrigern's face fell. He nodded and said, "Yes, of course, my dear. You're absolutely right. No bullying. It's bad form." Handing Rhys ap Gwallter the foam-capped mug, he said, "There will be no reprisals, my boy. You must do your best for Princess, and in return, I will free you of Black Ivor's curse. Agreed?"

"Agreed," the minstrel said, raising his mug in salute and looking much relieved.

They partook of a leisurely and satisfying lunch. When they were finished, and Spot had cleared away, and Rhys had dried his feet and donned a pair of soft slippers provided by his host, it was time for business. Rhys took up his harp, struck a few notes, tightened two of the strings, played the notes once more, and then cleared his throat.

"For my first charm, I would like to attempt Ceiriog's spell of unlocking," he announced. "It has always been a great favorite of mine. It is much favored for stirring speech in those who appear reluctant or incapable."

"Do you want me to leave? I'd love to stay and watch, but if I'm going to make you nervous . . . ," Kedrigern said, half rising.

"I am accustomed to an audience, Master Kedrigern. Stay," said the minstrel.

The wizard smiled gratefully and resumed his seat. Rhys struck a chord, then began to play a simple melody, like a child's song, to which he sang lyrics of great subtlety and very sophisticated poetic technique. When he was done, he and Kedrigern both turned to Princess.

"How is it with you, lady?" Rhys asked, setting down his harp.

Princess took a deep breath, swallowed, let out the breath, blinked twice, drew a more normal breath, and slowly said, "I can talk."

"That's marvelous, my dear! Well done, Rhys!" Kedrigern cried.

"Oh! Oh! I can talk!" Princess repeated, rising from her chair.

"On the first try! Oh, this is wonderful, my dear!"

"Do you hear me talk?"

"Yes. It's lovely!"

"Look! Look!" she shouted, and the two men twisted their necks in sudden alarm. But they saw only the little troll, who had reappeared and was now running about, picking up scraps and tidying the front yard.

"See Spot run!" Princess cried. "Run, Spot, run!"

"Yes, my dear," said Kedrigern, glancing uneasily at Rhys. She turned to Kedrigern, and the look in her eyes was enough to break his heart. "I can talk. Do you hear me talk? I talk stupid!"

"Considering that it's only a starting point . . . ," Kedrigern began, looking to Rhys for encouragement.

"Look you, Ceiriog's spell is a great thing for the children, but I am thinking that maybe it is not so good for a grownup," Rhys said.

"I talk like a baby. I am a lady. I want to talk like a lady. I do not want to sound like a baby all my life," said Princess. Kedrigern noticed that she was getting a bit flushed.

"Maybe you'd better try something else," he suggested.

"There is dangerous it is to work too many spells too quickly on one person. If the lovely lady is patient, everything will be fine."

"How patient?"

"Oh, a few years, no more than that, and she will be talking like a grownup," Rhys assured him.

Princess glowered at them. "I am getting angry. Do you see me getting angry? Soon I will be *very* angry, and that will not be nice. Do you want me to get very angry?"

"I will try something else," Rhys said.

"Oh! Oh! I hope it works. If it doesn't—"

"Now, my dear," Kedrigern said, reaching out to take her hand. "We mustn't upset this young man. He's doing his best."

Princess seated herself demurely, folding her hands in her lap. "I will be good," she said. Kedrigern noticed that her knuckles were white.

Rhys took up his harp once again. This time, the melody he played was so intricate, and so lively, that it filled Kedrigern and Princess with wonder to see it played by a single player, with only two hands and ten fingers. The chant that accompanied this whirlwind of music was dark and harsh and impossible to follow. Kedrigern recognized the signs of a powerful charm, and kept a close eye on Princess. She seemed fascinated by the web of words and sound, but quite alert.

At last Rhys laid his harp aside and wiped his brow, damp from the strain of concentration. In the silence, Princess spoke. Her words came slowly, as if she were groping for each syllable and placing it as carefully as an artisan might place the stones of a mosaic.

> "Mute, tame, Oh! long my tongue lay,
> Maelgwyn's words made go away
> Toad's gruff croak. 'Twas good coming
> Brought Rhys, best bard, to sing."

Rhys ap Gwallter looked at Princess with awe, and joy, and an expression that rapidly came to resemble that of a man who has scuffed his foot in the pebbles of a pathway and come upon a potful of precious gems. He turned expectantly to Kedrigern, who was gazing vacantly at his wife.

"Look you, now, there is poetry for you!" Rhys cried proudly. "That is the true *cywydd,* embellished with the beauties of *cynghanedd.* Oh, that is grand, indeed."

"Is she always going to talk that way?" Kedrigern asked without taking his eyes off Princess.

"She will improve with practice. There was a bit of weakness in the second line, where the rhyme should properly have come on an unstressed syllable, and I did not count more than three consonants recurring in any line. But it is very good for a first effort. In a few years the lady will be a great bard," Rhys said, looking very pleased with himself.

"A great bard," Kedrigern repeated, dazed.

> *"Great bard? I grant better days*
> *May follow—but must always*
> *I be rhyming? Right cramping*
> *'Twould be; word-bound. Better sing*
> *Small songs, some lesser in grace,*
> *Quite modest, neat, commonplace;*
> *Speak as plain lass, prosily—*
> *So my dear deciphers me."*

Kedrigern scratched his head, working on her utterance. The last line was promising, but he was not sure about what had gone before. Poetry was not his forte.

"That was an excellent first line," Rhys said. "Six consonants I counted, repeated in order. You do not often find that in a beginner, lady. Are you certain you do not wish to speak forever in *cywydd,* adorning your verses with *cynghanedd?*"

Princess smiled to acknowledge the compliment, but she shook her head decisively. After a pause, she said:

> *"Plain discourse will please me best;*
> *Simple speech is the sweetest."*

Kedrigern breathed a sigh of relief. Rhys ap Gwallter shook his head slowly, sadly, as if at a great waste of good, but took up his harp once more.

"For my third charm, I will recite something that has long been a popular favorite. It is a simple rhyming spell that is attributed to Hywel Morgan," said the minstrel.

"Don't you know anything that doesn't involve rhyming?" Kedrigern asked.

"I have tried the best nonrhyming spell I know, and it was a disaster, with this lovely lady speaking like a four-year-old, and not a very clever one, look you."

"Just asking. Go right ahead with Hywel Morgan's charm."

Rhys began again, and this time his music was merry and bright, a tune to dance to. His small audience could not refrain from tapping their feet in time with the harp. The words were quick and clever, and several times Princess and Kedrigern glanced at one another and shared a smile. Rhys ended on an abrupt note and looked at Princess with an expectant grin.

"Speak to us now, lady!" he said.

"Your music has worked like a charm! It's done me all good and no harm."

"I have done it this time," Rhys said proudly.

"But she still speaks in rhyme," Kedrigern pointed out.

"Stop complaining, and give me your arm!" said Princess.

Kedrigern did as she bade him. Princess pulled him to his feet, and with arms linked, they danced around the beaming young minstrel. At last, flushed with exertion and out of breath, they fell into their chairs, laughing for sheer joy. Princess leaned forward and laid her hand on Rhys's. Giggling a bit, brushing back a loose strand of hair, she said, "Young man, you're an absolute winner! I insist that you join us for dinner. I'll give orders to Spot—something lovely and hot."

"You speak well, my dear, for a beginner," Kedrigern observed.

"Look you now," Rhys asked, "could you fix up my feet? There is pain."

"Do it promptly, my sweet," Princess said. "I'm sure you know how."

Kedrigern rose, saying, "I will see to it now."

"There is plenty of time till we eat," Princess assured him.

She left them, and Kedrigern set about his part of the bargain. Black Ivor Gruffydd's spell turned out to be a simple one, and he removed it easily. As he pronounced the last word of the counterspell, Rhys's face lit up with relief and he heaved a great sigh.

"There is good you are with your magic, Master Kedrigern," he said, "I did not feel a thing."

Kedrigern gave a self-deprecating smile and waved off the compliment. "No reason you should. It was a small spell."

"It did not feel small when it was in my feet."

"They never do. Rhys . . . I'm curious about something."

"I will answer you gladly," said the minstrel, rising.

"Well, it seems to me that when we were talking with Princess just now, everything was falling into rhyme. Is that right?"

Rhys took a few gingerly steps. He grinned at Kedrigern, walked firmly around his chair, then did a vigorous little dance. "Better than ever I am, look you, Master Kedrigern. I could walk from here to the sea without stopping, thanks to you. Yes, we were all rhyming. The charm is fresh and new, you see, and it spreads out around the lady, touching others. That will pass. Indeed, if she does not remain in constant practice, she will be speaking prose in a week's time," he said.

Kedrigern smiled. "All things considered, that would be for the better."

That night, the three of them dined lavishly and drank deeply of Kedrigern's most treasured stock, the very best from Vosconu's vineyards. It was well past midnight when the last song was sung, the last health drunk, and the last limerick limned. With muffled yawns and weary goodnights, Kedrigern and Princess led Rhys to the guest room and made their way to their bedchamber.

Kedrigern awoke to a bright morning, refreshed by a night's unbroken rest. He yawned and stretched, and turned to Princess. She was already awake, and was staring up with a preoccupied air.

"My dear, did you have a good sleep?" he asked.

She replied thoughtfully, "For a time, it was restful and deep. But I woke with a cry—"

"Did you really? But why?"

"I dreamed I'd relapsed to '*Brereep.*' "

He took her hand and pressed it for reassurance. She snuggled closer, and they lay comfortably warm and quiet for a little while. Then Princess said, "Did you notice, my dear, that we rhyme?"

"It will go away in a short time," Kedrigern replied without thinking. Then, recalling his words of moments ago, he realized that he was once again falling into the rhythms of his wife's speech. It was harmless, he knew; but something in him made him resist the spells of others. "Let us rise," he said.

"Yes," Princess cheerfully agreed. "It's best we remember our guest."

Kedrigern nodded, but said not a word in reply. This was really getting out of hand. He threw on his robe and went to see about breakfast, and found Rhys up and about, walking in the dooryard, taking evident pleasure in every step. Kedrigern signaled to the minstrel wordlessly. Rhys, seeing his gesture, grew confused and cried, "Look you now, what is this pantomime?"

In exasperation, Kedrigern said, "Oh dear me, is there no way around it?"

"What? The rhyming?" Rhys asked.

"Yes!"

"No," said the minstrel with a shrug.

"Well, confound it, it's going too far! After all, Rhys—" Kedrigern replied, only to be interrupted by Spot's morning "Yah! Yah!" of greeting. He clapped his hands over his mouth and rushed from the room, nearly colliding with a footstool Spot had set down in the process of removing it from the kitchen. Princess entered just in time to see Kedrigern's departure. Noticing the stool, she said, "Spot, put this thing back where you found it."

Kedrigern gave up the struggle. All that day and the next, any conversation that took place in the house or on the grounds was in limerick form, and there were no exceptions to the rule. Even Spot's outbursts fell into the pattern. But when, on the morning of the third day after his arrival, Rhys ap Gwallter left them, the rhyming charm seemed to depart with him. Princess spoke in a voice as sweet and musical as an angel's, but she spoke in prose.

As they sat over lunch, Kedrigern said, "It took a long time, my dear, but you have your voice back at last."

"Thanks to you, Keddie. I know you'd do it."

"Well, I needed Rhys's help to bring it off."

"But if it weren't for your own powers, Rhys would never have helped you. I've heard you say dozens of times that the bards of Cymri are very close with their magic. More ale?"

"Just a drop, thank you." Kedrigern reflected for a time, and said, "Yes, I suppose you're right. It's all professional courtesy, but nothing would have been done if I weren't a wizard of some standing."

"Exactly. So the credit is yours."

"It was a privilege, my dear. And now that you have your voice, what shall we do to celebrate? Shall we have a little party?"

"Whom would we invite? I still can't recall anything about my family, and all my friends are toads," Princess pointed out. "Not much point inviting *them*. And your friends are scattered all over the place."

"True," Kedrigern said, nodding. "It would be nice if you could meet people, though. Even strangers. Even if it meant..." He paused, swallowed hard, and in a lowered voice said, "... traveling."

"Traveling?"

"There's a convention coming up. I hadn't planned on attending, but if you'd like to... Give it some thought. No need to decide now."

"It's hard to think. Actually, all I want to do for a time is talk. To anyone at all, about anything and everything. I want to talk about the meaning of life, and gossip about people I barely know. I want to discuss great art and literature and music, and tell silly jokes, and sing songs, and recite poetry, and complain about the way you leave indescribable things lying around the house when you're in the middle of an enchantment—"

"—I'll try to be more careful—"

"—And congratulate you when you work a difficult magic just right. And I want to be able to talk with another woman about all the things that don't interest you at all."

"We could invite the wood-witch over for a weekend."

"That's a start, I suppose. I want to say everything, Keddie—except for one thing."

"What's that, my dear?"

"Must you ask?" she said.

...⸙ *Twelve* ⸙...

the student, princess

WITH PRINCESS SPEAKING in her own voice, employing the cadences of normal prose discourse and sentences that came out front end first and followed in orderly sequence, the atmosphere of the cottage on Silent Thunder Mountain became noticeably more cheerful as the summer proceeded. There were bright salutations upon waking, pleasant conversations over breakfast, heartening exhortations from time to time throughout the day, witty banter at the dinner table, and a sweet "Good night" upon retiring.

Princess was delighted by her restored power of speech, and made all possible use of it, often speaking for the sheer pleasure of speech itself. When she was not conversing with Kedrigern she talked to Spot, or to the growing things in the garden, or the birds, or the trees, or the little bright-eyed creatures that dwelt in the dark corners of Kedrigern's study, or the winds, or to herself. She recited long poems of chivalry and blighted loves; mnemonic rhymes for Latin prepositions taking the accusative, the signs of the zodiac, and the months of the year with their proper number of days; multiplication tables as far as fifteen times fifteen; and, in relaxed moments, nursery rhymes. Sometimes, when dinner was over and they were strolling over the meadow in the twilight, she sang a ballad; and she sang so sweetly that Kedrigern, who had never cared very much for ballads or for singing, urged her to sing again.

In about six weeks, though, the novelty wore off, and Princess was silent for longer and longer periods. She sang infrequently, and recited hardly at all. She spoke only to Kedrigern and Spot, and her words to the house-troll were few and of a purely utilitarian nature. Kedrigern noticed the growing silences, but made no mention of them, assuming that this was a normal reaction and would work itself out eventually. And it did.

"Keddie, I want to start a program of studies," said Princess one fine spring morning as they sat down to breakfast.

"An excellent idea. Keep the mind alert. Very sensible, my dear. What do you plan to study?"

"For one thing, I want to improve my vocabulary."

Kedrigern nodded in approval. He reached for a biscuit.

"And I want to study magic."

Kedrigern paused in the act of breaking the biscuit, and his eyebrows rose. But his only comment was, "May I have the jam, please?"

"That's not a very enthusiastic response," said Princess, pushing the jam pot in his direction.

"I'm sorry, my dear. Actually, it's a very good idea. I'm surprised that it didn't occur to either of us before this, that's all. You've been exposed to quite a bit of magic, and you appear to have coped very well. You seem to have a natural affinity for magic."

"Do you think so?" she asked with evident pleasure.

"It's very likely. Did you have a particular type of magic in mind?"

"Not really. I like what you do, but I'm not ready to specialize."

"Very sensible," he said, nodding and taking a bite of biscuit. He chewed slowly and thoughtfully, and at last added, "Plenty of time to make those decisions later on, when you know your strengths and weaknesses. The first thing to do is master the basics."

"When do we begin?" she asked brightly.

"This morning, if you like. Now that my library is in order I can easily find my old textbooks. I'd say *A Handy Book Of*

Basic Spells and *Enchantment For Beginners* would be best to start with, and then you can go right on to *Spells For Every Occasion.*"

"How long will it be before I'm casting spells?"

"Hard to say. If you really have the gift, you might be able to work a small spell before the leaves turn."

Her face fell. *"That* long?"

"My dear, that's no time at all. I don't want to name names, but I know several people of considerable standing in the profession who were ten years learning to spell properly. What I do may look easy, but I didn't learn it overnight."

Princess sighed and gazed out the window; then she rose resolutely and, placing her hands on her hips, said, "If that's the case, Keddie, the sooner we start, the better. Let's get to it."

Though it showed signs of frequent use, Kedrigern's library was still in unaccustomed good order. Here and there a book lay opened, face down, on stool or table, and a small stack was rising on either side of the wizard's reading chair. But the shelves were tidy, and the categories remained clearly delineated. No longer were collections of spells commingled haphazard with collections of counterspells, or books of formulae, or architectural drawings; dictionaries were not flanked by gazetteers and jest books, nor were atlases the neighbors of analecta or enchiridions. Primers of wizardry had their own individual niche, as did glossaries, lexicons, and thesauri. There was a place for everything, and practically everything was in its place, or so close by as to make no real difference. Kedrigern felt almost embarrassingly well organized, and covered his awkward feelings with a great show of efficiency, snatching down a book here, leafing rapidly through it and replacing it with a censorious frown, taking down another from there, examining its index critically and then tucking it under his arm while he scanned the shelves for others.

Princess seated herself in his big comfortable chair and put her feet up, looking on with interest as he made his selection. He turned to her at last with two books under his arm and a third book in his hand. One by one he placed them in her lap, identifying each as he did so.

"This blue one is *Enchantment For Beginners*. It's the best introduction to the field. Very clear and easy to understand," he said as he presented the first book.

"What spells does it contain?"

"No spells in here. It's purely introductory. It gives you all the basic dos and don'ts, all the laws and rules and necessary precautions."

"It looks awfully thin. Aren't there a lot of rules to learn?"

"There are quite a few precautions, but they're all common sense. There are only three laws of magic."

Princess looked incredulous. "Only three?"

"Let me see . . ." Kedrigern closed his eyes, pressed his fingertips to his brow, and began to recite. "First Law: Subjects of spells remain spelled unless despelled by some external power. Second Law: Enchantment and spelling are proportional to, and of a kind determined by, the spell or enchantment invoked. Third Law: To every spell, there is an equal and opposite counterspell, and the same goes for enchantments." He looked up, blinked, and said proudly, "I had to memorize them a hundred and forty years ago, and I've still got them word perfect. No, it was nearer a hundred and fifty years ago. Think of that."

"Have they been any help?"

"Oh, my, yes. The third law, for instance, keeps one from becoming overconfident. Overconfidence is one of the great hazards of the profession. You really must have all the laws and rules and safety precautions by heart before you start learning other things."

"All right, I'll learn them," she said with a resigned sigh. "But when do I start learning to spell?"

He flourished a slender book and said, "This is *A Handy Book Of Basic Spells*. You must get it by heart, and practice every day for at least eight hours until everything in here is second nature."

"Eight hours?" she repeated in dismay. "Every day?"

"That's the minimum, my dear. It's a difficult business, magic. If it were easy, you'd have wizards everywhere you turn. They'd be as thick as alchemists." He laid the book in her lap and held up the third for display. "When you have *A Handy Book of Basic Spells* down pat, you go on to *Spells For Every Occasion*. It's an advanced speller."

"Do I have to memorize *that*, too?" she asked. The book was bound in black, like the introductory speller, but at least five times thicker.

"It would be best if you did," Kedrigern said as he put the book down, "but that will all come in time. *A Handy Book Of Basic Spells* will give you the necessary fundamentals. You'll learn the essentials of transformations, transmutations, transportations, appearances, disappearances, invisibility—"

"Keddie, wait! You're confusing me."

He pointed to the blue book. "That will explain things."

"But they all sound the same! What's the difference between transformation and transmutation?"

"Well, a transformation—turning a man into a pig, say, or a woman into a crow—is really just a matter of reshaping what's already there. Feet into hooves, or arms into wings, and so forth. Rather simple, actually. But turning someone into an anvil, or a swamp—transmuting them—takes a bit more effort. There's not much in common between the before and the after, you see."

"Yes," she said thoughtfully.

"And then you have the alchemists throwing the word about, talking of 'transmutation' when they really mean their foolishness of turning lead into gold, which—if they could actually do it—is transformation."

"I see," said Princess, nodding. "So when you turned Buroc into stone, you worked a transmutation, and not a transformation."

"You could say that. Actually, the precise technical term for what I did to Buroc is 'translation.' Any petrifaction spell is a translation."

"Oh."

"Very simple, actually, because it's just a taking away of qualities. It can be done quickly, too. Good in an emergency, but not very impressive stuff."

"It impressed Buroc."

"Any decent spell impresses the spellee. I meant the informed onlooker. The connoisseur. Compared with what the Drissmall sisters did to Metalura, my spell on Buroc was nursery games. On the instant, they worked a self-renewing petrifaction in beautifully textured gray stone, exquisitely detailed. Sheer artistry," said Kedrigern.

"Who are the Drissmall sisters? And who is Metalura?"

"No time to talk about them now. You must learn your basic spells, and no distractions. Let me see, now . . . transportation is, as you might expect, getting yourself, or someone, or something, from one place to another without the bother of traveling through all the space in between. It eats up magic, but it's a real timesaver."

"I can see how it would be. And I understand what an appearance spell must be. But aren't disappearance and invisibility the same thing?"

"Oh, my, no. Not at all. When you make something invisible it's still there. You just can't see it. But when you make a thing disappear, it's *gone*."

"Where?"

Kedrigern shrugged. "Anywhere you like. It's your spell."

Princess stared at him in silence, wide-eyed, then looked with new respect on the books in her lap. After a time, she said in a subdued voice, "That's a lot of power to have at one's command."

"It certainly is," Kedrigern agreed cheerfully.

"I don't know whether I really want to be quite that powerful, Keddie."

"My dear, my dear," he said, taking her hands in his, "You're an intelligent woman. You've had experience with magic, and you have a sense of responsibility. After all, you're a princess. You're not going to turn people into newts just to see the expression on their faces, are you?"

"No."

"Well, there you are. Besides, it isn't all that easy. Magic doesn't grow on trees, you know. Sensible people don't squander it. If you're profligate with your magic, and use it for amusement, or convenience, you can find yourself all out when you need it most. That's what happened to Conhoon, as you recall. And even more so to poor Yoligon. Or so I've heard. Yoligon was a friend of my old teacher, Fraigus. I never met him, myself. Not when I could speak with him, anyway."

"You've never mentioned Yoligon before."

"His is not a happy story. I don't like to think about it. But I believe you should be aware of all the pitfalls. Yoligon was a pretty fair wizard. He had one idiosyncrasy: he couldn't bear to have anyone around his house for more than a brief visit—anyone at all—so he kept no servants. On the other hand, he liked good food and a tidy house, so he used a considerable amount of magic for cleaning and cooking and general housekeeping." Kedrigern cleared a corner of his worktable and perched on the edge. He folded his arms, looked earnestly down at Princess, and went on, "The house was quite a showplace, from what I've heard. Everything spotless and gleaming, not a weed in the garden, not a speck of dust or a cobweb to be seen."

"It sounds lovely," said Princess. "Spot does its best, I know, but it misses the cobwebs."

"There are worse things than missed cobwebs, as the fate of Yoligon attests. For a long time, he had been feuding with a pair of elderly sorceresses over a strip of property running between their house and his. He decided to invite them to dinner and settle their differences amicably, so he did a thorough cleaning and sprucing up of house and grounds, and prepared a marvelous seven-course dinner. All by magic. Well, the sorceresses enjoyed the dinner—even asked for seconds on the dessert, I've been told—and after dinner, while they were all strolling in the garden, they leveled a spell at Yoligon. Ordinarily, he would have been able to defend himself, but he had used up all his reserves getting ready for his guests. So the spell took. They turned him into a lilac bush."

"A lilac bush," Princess repeated in a low soft voice.

"Yes. A very pretty one, too. I had a cutting from it by the old tower where I used to live. It was lovely in the spring."

Princess took up the three volumes of magic very cautiously and set them atop the stack of open books at her right side. "Maybe magic isn't really the thing for a princess. I might be wiser to stick to embroidery and the lute," she said. "For the time being, anyway. That's what people expect, after all. . . ."

"Ah, but my dear, you've got the gift, I know you have. It would be a shame to waste yourself."

"But Keddie, it's so complicated. . . . I thought it would be nice if I knew a little more about your work. It would give us something to share. I thought I might even be able to lend a hand with a spell now and then, when you were pressed for time. But I don't want to be turned into a lilac bush!"

Kedrigern came to her side, dropped to one knee, and took her hands in his. "The more magic you know, my dear, the less chance there is that anyone will *try* to turn you into a lilac bush. Or anything else. A toad, for instance."

"I suppose that's true," she conceded.

"Absolutely. If you had learned magic as a child, you could have been spared . . . on the other hand, we might never have met. Well, anyway. I think you should start to work this very day."

"I will," she said resolutely, taking up the three volumes she had set aside. "I'll go out into the garden and start on *Enchantment for Beginners*. Right now."

"Wonderful, my dear. And to break up the long hours of magical study, you can use this," said Kedrigern, rising and extracting a small green book from inside his tunic. *"A Storehouse of Serviceable Synonyms To Enlarge The Vocabulary, Enrich The Mind, Enliven Discourse, And Enhance The Expression Of Ideas*. The best little vocabulary builder I've ever encountered. Just ten minutes with this book, two or three times a day, and you'll soon be sounding like an academician."

She leafed quickly through the book, page after page of tiny print in triple columns. "There's a lot in here," she observed.

"Just think of how your vocabulary will grow!"

"Between this and my magic studies, I won't have a spare minute in the day."

"How fortunate you are, to have the time to devote to it, and all the lovely peace and quiet to study in."

"I certainly have peace and quiet," she said without enthusiasm.

"Nobody barging in on us at all hours, traipsing through our house making noise and slamming doors and disturbing our concentration. No intrusions at all. Just you and me and Spot," the wizard went on cheerily.

"Yes, just you and me and Spot. Day after day," she said, looking at him with narrowed eyes.

"We can come and go as we please, eat whenever and whatever we like, go to bed when we're tired and get up when it suits us. We can wear old clothes, and comfortable slippers, and just be ourselves. Our time is our own. No need to make small talk when we'd rather be working a spell," Kedrigern rhapsodized.

"Some people don't *mind* making small talk once in a while. Some people actually *enjoy* it," Princess said in a chilly voice.

"Oh? But surely now, with all this work . . . all the study you have to do . . ."

Princess advanced on him, books tucked under one slender arm. The other arm was extended before her, an accusing finger aimed at the wizard. "I recall some mention, Keddie, when I regained my proper speaking voice, of a change in our mode of life. A party. Friends for dinner. Neighbors for a chat. Travel. In short, a social life befitting a princess, not the seclusion customarily enforced upon a nun!"

"My dear, I was only trying to give you time to grow accustomed to speaking again. I didn't want to rush things," said Kedrigern, sounding aggrieved.

"You didn't?" she asked warily.

"Certainly not. I knew you'd need some time to adjust to your voice. It's only natural. And I was certain you'd want to do something like this—enlarge your vocabulary and acquire new skills before encountering total strangers. Once you're ready, we'll plunge into society."

"Is that a promise?"

"It is. I'll invite . . . oh, I'll ask Bess the Wood-witch to fly over for dinner. She's a great one for gossip and small talk."

"Is that your idea of plunging into society? Dinner with the wood-witch?"

"I need time to adjust, too."

"You didn't spend part of your life as a toad, and another part of your life croaking like one."

"Well, no. But I've lived alone for more than a century, and suddenly to be faced with the prospect of a stream of guests, visitors . . . a social life. . . ." He closed his eyes and shuddered.

"A normal life, Keddie. That's all I want."

"Normal life is awful. Why do you think I became a wizard? My family led a normal life, and they were miserable."

"My family led a normal life, and we were all very happy," Princess countered.

"Yes, but you were living the normal life of a royal family. There's a big difference. I was raised by peasants, and it was no fun, I can tell you."

Princess dropped the books and recoiled. "By peasants? Are you a *peasant?"*

"No, I was *raised* by peasants. They found me in a basket in the middle of a fairy ring on Midsummer Day. I was too big to be a fairy, so they assumed I was an abandoned child."

"Who could abandon a baby like that? What a cruel thing to do!"

With a shrug, Kedrigern said, "Whoever my parents were, they weren't altogether heartless. They left a purse of fifty gold pieces in the basket with me. That was more money than Hob and Mag dreamed existed on earth."

"Hob and Mag?"

"The peasants who found me. They treated me pretty well, actually. They always said that I was the best thing that ever happened to them. Considering the other things that happened to them, I suppose I was."

Princess sat down and looked at him sorrowfully. "What was it like, Keddie? It must have been awful!"

"Not at all. Hob and Mag were certain that I was the son of some great king who'd come to claim me one day, so they let me do whatever I liked. When I was about six, I discovered that a retired wizard lived in a cave not far away, and I used to visit him a lot. Nice old codger . . . Tarrendine, that was his name."

"Was it Tarrendine who introduced you to magic?"

"Not exactly. He never mentioned it. We used to fish a lot, and he told me some wonderful stories, but I never suspected that he was a wizard until . . . well, until later on. At the time, I had no interest at all in magic. I wanted to be a robber," Kedrigern said with a sad, nostalgic smile.

"What happened?"

"I came home from Tarrendine's one evening and found the hovel burned down. Hob and Mag were hanging from a tree, shot full of arrows. Once I saw that, I didn't want to be a robber anymore." He was silent for a time, then he sighed and went on, "I ran all the way back to Tarrendine. He let me stay and be his servant. I wasn't much of a servant, because I didn't know how to do anything except play, but he was patient, and I learned. Tarrendine taught me how to read, and one day I came across his old books of spells, and I guess that was how it all began." After a thoughtful pause he rounded on Princess and said, "It took me years and years of struggle and hard work to become a wizard, so if you expect to learn anything, you'd better get to it. No time to sit around listening to stories."

Princess rose reluctantly, clutching the books to her like a schoolchild. She made no move to leave the workroom. "Don't you want to tell me anything more about your early life?" she asked.

He looked at her blankly. "There's nothing worth telling. I worked and I studied."

"But didn't you ever seek your true parents? Didn't you wonder?"

Kedrigern hesitated for a moment, as if weighing the advisability of revealing a secret, and then said, "I've always believed that I'm related in some way to Merlin. If I'm not, I don't care to know."

"Surely there must have been some clue—a token of some sort, or a heraldic device on your blanket. Or a birthmark! Do you have a birthmark?"

"I did. Mag had a witch spell it away. She paid her with the gold locket that was clutched in my fist when they found me."

Princess gave a groan of frustration through tightly clenched teeth. "The blanket—was there a crest on it?" she asked.

Rubbing his brow, frowning with the effort to recall, the wizard said, "There was some kind of emblem woven on the blanket, I think. A coat of arms or something like that. Mag tried to tell me about it—I had chewed the blanket to bits while I was teething—but Mag didn't communicate well. She had a vocabulary of about forty words, all of them concerned with work or suffering, and it's hard to describe fancy needlework under such circumstances."

"Keddie, aren't you curious? Don't you ever wonder who you are?"

"I *know* who I am. And I'm curious about what's going to happen, not what's already happened. I'm not an historian, my dear, and I'm not a genealogist. I'm a wizard."

She shook her head slowly, dazedly, in disbelief. "I don't understand. I can't see how anyone can go on so calmly not knowing who or what his parents were. It bothers me *terribly*, not being able to remember."

"My dear, I tried," he confessed. "Naturally, I tried. But when you've worked a difficult spell with exacting care and had an ominous voice from the heavens tell you that the spell is temporarily out of service, you begin to wonder. And when you try a half-dozen other spells, and none of them get through, you accept the fact that there are things someone doesn't want you to find out."

"Is that what happened?" Princess asked, alarmed. "Oh, Keddie, that's awful! You poor, piteous, tragic man!" Her eyes grew moist. "You dear, sad, thwarted creature!" She wiped away a tear. "You wretched, unhappy—"

"It's not all that bad," he broke in. "I may not have names and addresses, but it's obvious that I'm descended from royalty on one side and wizardry on the other. And I learned a valuable lesson: even a great wizard doesn't always get what he goes after. So if you want to be even a moderately successful wizard, my dear . . ."

"I'd better get cracking," she said, and turned to go.

Learning magic is a slow and tedious business; improving one's vocabulary, on the other hand, is not, and Princess had such success in the latter endeavor that she bore the frustrations of the former with quiet patience. Days wore into weeks, and summer was fully upon them, and still she plugged away, morning to night, at her studies.

One evening Kedrigern came into their dining room and found Princess standing by the window, looking out to the west, where a beautiful late summer sunset was blazing in splendor down the skies. Her little green vocabulary book lay where it had been tossed aside. Her hands were planted firmly on her hips, the fingers drumming a silent tattoo. A slight spot of color glowed on her perfectly sculpted cheeks. The simple golden circlet on her brows was set at a determined angle. To Kedrigern, who had learned to read her moods, these were signs that the present one was not her best.

He cleared his throat very softly. She did not speak, or even turn, but the color in her cheek glowed a bit more brightly.

"Is anything wrong, my dear?" he asked.

She turned and pinned him with wrathful eyes. "Yes, Kedrigern, something is very wrong, amiss, and awry, and you know exactly what it is, and how many months it has been that way, and how to set it right."

"If—"

"I've had my voice back for nearly four months now, and

in all that time I haven't spoken to a soul but you and Spot. On the day I ceased to croak like a toad, and finally spoke good sensible prose like every other woman in the world, you promised me that our life would change. We would entertain. We would travel," she said, advancing on him. "There was a convention to attend."

"That's not for a while."

"And we were to have visitors. The house was to ring with persiflage, raillery, quips and cranks and badinage, wit of all sorts, and merry banter. But not so, Kedrigern. There has been no one. No one at all."

He stepped back. Raising his hands defensively, he said, "But your studies... the distraction..."

"A plague on my studies. I *want* distraction. I want to see people!"

"I asked Bess to come over just last week. She wasn't free."

"Always *your* friends. Why don't we invite any of *my* friends?"

"But my dear, as you yourself pointed out, all your friends are toads. Surely you wouldn't want—"

"Oh, that's right. That's the way to respond to my needs. Be as cruel, harsh, and unfeeling as you can be," she said, her voice rich with scorn.

"Cruel?" Kedrigern repeated, utterly bewildered.

"Go ahead, dig up the past, fling it in my face. Do everything you can to humiliate, degrade, demean, abase, and mortify me. Tell me once again how if you hadn't come along, I'd still be sitting on a lily pad in a dank misty bog waiting for the next fat fly to come along."

"My dear, I've never said such a thing."

"No, but you're always thinking it. You're ashamed of me. That's why you're always running off to your study to work a spell, charm, cantrip, or enchantment. I don't think you love me anymore."

"How can you say such a thing, my sweet?" Kedrigern cried. "Why, I love you more than ever!"

"You never say so. We never visit, or have guests. I think you want to keep me hidden, concealed, and sequestered here, like a guilty secret. The magic has gone out of our marriage," said Princess with a sigh.

"Now, *that* is patently false. If the magic ever went out of our marriage, my love, you would at once become a toad, while I—"

Princess gave a cry of anguish and buried her face in her hands. "You're shouting at me!" she said in a muffled voice. "You don't love me!"

Actually, Kedrigern loved Princess just this side of uxoriousness, but a very long lifetime spent in the solitary and often perilous study of magic had prepared him poorly for the everyday stresses of domestic life. He could face dragons, demons, and the vilest sorcery with aplomb, but minor arguments at home dismayed him, and the sight of Princess in tears turned him to jelly.

"There, now, my sweet," he said in his most soothing manner, enfolding her in his arms, rigid and unyielding though she was. "You know I love you, and I'd do anything to make you happy. If you really want to get away for a while, or see someone, we'll take a little trip. We'll go anywhere you like."

She raised her head. "Really?"

"Absolutely."

"When?"

Kedrigern hated travel. He loathed little trips as much as big ones. His idea of a good vacation was a sunny afternoon's nap on a bench in his own dooryard, and an extra glass or two of good wine with dinner. But he gritted his teeth, swallowed, and said, "Whenever you—"

And then a loud knock sounded at the door, followed at portentous intervals by a second and then a third.

"Are we expecting anyone?" Kedrigern asked.

"We're *never* expecting anyone," said Princess.

"No. . . . Odd time for a client. I think I'd better answer it myself. Spot does give people a start," Kedrigern said, turning toward the front door. A small grotesque form went bounding past him and he said, "No, Spot, I'll see who it is. You get back to the kitchen."

"Yah!" the little house-troll said obediently, pivoting on one huge foot and returning whence it came.

Kedrigern worked a quick protective spell—it was best to be cautious these days—and opened the door. Before him stood a tall, slender, black-bearded man dressed from head to foot in black, with a black patch over one eye. Removing a black-plumed black hat, the fellow favored him with a sweeping bow.

"Master Kedrigern, I presume?" he said in a high, rasping voice.

"I am he."

"I am the servant of Prince Grodz. My master has sent me to seek the aid of your wisdom. He wishes you to come to Castle Grodzik."

"Well, I'm not sure what I can do for Prince Grodz, or when . . . but come in. You must be thirsty."

Kedrigern led the messenger inside. At the sight of Princess, the man in black bowed once again, with great flourishes of his plumed hat.

"This is my wife, Princess," said the wizard.

The messenger bowed a third time, and said, "I am overwhelmed by the presence of such beauty and such wisdom in one room. Surely I am unworthy to remain within these walls. I beg you to permit me to deliver my master's request and then withdraw while you consider it."

"Whatever you like. Are you sure you're not thirsty?"

"It is not for the servant of Prince Grodz to be thirsty without Prince Grodz's permission," the visitor rasped.

"All right, then, don't be thirsty. What exactly is the problem?"

"A plague of rats is upon my master."

Kedrigern frowned. "I'm not a rat catcher, I'm a wizard. Grodz wants a rat catcher."

"Three rat catchers have come to the castle. All three have been devoured by the rats."

"I see. Well, I can refer you to a colleague of mine who specializes in this sort of thing. Conhoon of the Three Gifts is his name. He's rid whole kingdoms of rats and mice and moles. My field is really a bit different. I deal in remedial magic, mostly. Counterspells and such."

"That is why my master seeks your aid. This is not an ordinary plague of rats. They are enchanted rats."

"Are you sure?"

"They sing and dance on moonlit nights. They whisper unnerving phrases in the ears of sleepers. They scrawl disrespectful messages on the walls of the castle," the messenger said.

Kedrigern nodded. "That certainly doesn't sound like your

ordinary rat," he admitted.

"My master has no doubt."

"All right, then, you tell Grodz that I'll be—" Kedrigern began, stopping short when Princess tugged hard at his sleeve and looked at him irately. Recalling his promise to her, he winked and went on, "—over to see him sometime in the fall. Before the first snow. He can count on me."

"By then, all of Castle Grodzik will be eaten. You must come now, or we are lost, my master says."

"I have another commitment and I can't break it," Kedrigern said, taking Princess's hand. "Sorry, but I can't make it before the fall."

"My master will be disappointed," said the messenger, and there was a discernible quaver in his voice.

"It can't be helped."

"Prince Grodz has planned a great festival in your honor."

"Oh?" said Princess.

The messenger's words came out in a rush. "Feasting and dancing and the finest wines. Beautiful clever maids and handsome brave men, all of the very best and oldest families, all eager to praise you and drink your health. Sweet music and tasty delicacies at all hours—you need only request. Your lovely wife is, of course, to accompany you. My master would insist upon it, out of his great respect for the institution of marriage and the joy he takes at the sight of a happy union. The entire west wing of Castle Grodzik at your disposal, hosts of servants to obey your every command, stay as long as you wish. A generous fee. Plus a silver piece for each dead rat."

"I do not accept payment by the rat," Kedrigern said indignantly.

"My master will pay any way you wish. Only come and help us, I beg you," the messenger said.

Princess squeezed Kedrigern's hand. He turned, and at the sight of her expectant smile, he nodded. "We will pack tomorrow and leave for Castle Grodzik the following morning. You may tell Prince Grodz to expect us," she informed the messenger.

"Oh, thank you, gracious lady, most lovely lady, thank you, thank you!" the messenger said, falling into a fit of bowing, and the air of the room was soon filled with dust from the sweeping flourishes of his hat and cloak. Still bowing and babbling his gratitude, he backed out the door, ran to his waiting black horse, and rode off to bring the news to his master.

Kedrigern was silent and thoughtful at dinner, and all through the evening. Princess was so excited by the prospect of society that she kept a lively conversation going with no need of assistance. It was not until the following evening, when dinner was over and the packing almost complete, that she became aware of Kedrigern's reflective mood.

"Cheer up, Keddie," she said, sitting beside him and taking his hand in hers. "I know how you feel about travel, journeying, and peregrination. But you need to meet some new people. You'll enjoy yourself this time."

"It's not the travel. It's Grodz."

"The poor man *needs* you. Think of all those awful rats nibbling away at his castle."

"The rat that worries me is Grodz. I've heard some very unpleasant things about Prince Grodz of Grodzik."

"What have you heard?"

"They're only rumors, mind you, but one can't be too careful. He's said to be extremely cruel, and he has a reputation as a colossal lecher. Always trying to seduce other men's wives, they say. I really don't like the idea of bringing you to a place—"

"Keddie, you gave your word, pledge, avouchment, and assurance."

"I know, I know. But still . . ."

"Do you really think I could be seduced by a prince? A mere prince, when I'm the wife of a wizard with royal blood?"

"Well . . . there could be danger."

"Nothing you couldn't handle."

He pondered for a moment, and at last, judiciously, he said, "No. No, there shouldn't be any problem. I'm worrying needlessly, I suppose. Grodz will turn out to be a charming host, and we'll have a wonderful time."

"Feasting and dancing and scintillating company . . . lovely surroundings . . . brilliant conversation . . . I'm sure we won't have a moment to ourselves, but I think I'll bring a few books just the same."

"Always a good idea," Kedrigern said crisply. "You've made impressive progress with your vocabulary builder. How have you done with *Enchantment For Beginners?*"

"Oh, I finished that long ago."

"Good. And *A Handy Book Of Basic Spells?*"

"Practically committed to memory. I'm having some difficulty remembering the basic invisibility spell, but I have the others almost by heart."

"Very good, my dear," Kedrigern said, taking his wife's hand in his. "The thing to do is master the basics. Get those spells down pat, and you can't go wrong."

"They're *hard*, Keddie."

"I know they are. Many a wizardly reputation is based on mastery of one or two of them, and oblivious ignorance of the rest. But you mustn't settle for that. Have you looked into *Spells For Every Occasion?*"

"Yes, I've . . . looked through it," she said uncomfortably. After an awkward silence, she blurted, "Most of the words are unpronounceable! It hurts just to try to form my mouth for them."

"Keep practicing. It's very good for the jaw muscles. And even though it may seem difficult, you do have a natural talent."

"Thank you, Keddie," she said, patting his hand and then rising. "We'd better finish packing. We want to make an early start, outset, and departure in the morning."

Kedrigern sighed and hauled himself wearily to his feet. He wished there existed some wondrous spell that would pack one's clothes, books, and minor necessaries in an instant, and leave no essential item behind. There was not. He set to work.

···❦ *Thirteen* ❦···

the hoppy prince

THE WEATHER WAS mild and the journey uneventful. To Princess, who was delighted simply to be somewhere other than the cottage on Silent Thunder Mountain, it was nevertheless very exciting. To Kedrigern, the lack of incident was a blessed relief. In the wizard's mind, travel invariably meant unpleasant surprises and unnecessary confusion; one met new people and had new experiences, all of them nasty.

One was always swindled while traveling. The currency changed from place to place, and everyone insisted that the local coinage was worth more than anyone else's, and charged accordingly. Distances were never certain, and asking directions was folly, since no two districts followed the same system of noting measurements. Drinks were of different sizes, and had funny names, besides; one could never be sure whether one was getting a bucketful of wine or a thimbleful of ale. The only safe rule seemed to be "the better the beverage, the smaller the portion." Food was awful. Beds were hard, lumpy, and filled with tiny living things that had appetites like wolves. The towels were always gray and scratchy, if towels were provided at all, which they usually were not because there was nowhere to wash and if there was the water was cold and greasy. All things considered, Kedrigern hated travel.

This trip, though, was only moderately horrendous, and

Princess's obvious pleasure helped make it almost endurable. They arrived at the gates of Castle Grodzik one dusty afternoon little the worse for their journey, and were admitted by a gatekeeper with a wooden leg. They proceeded to the castle entrance, where their baggage was taken by scurrying men, all of whom lacked an ear, an eye, or a few fingers. A limping stable boy led their horses off just as an elderly, distinguished-looking man in black emerged from the castle to greet them. He was missing one hand.

"Greetings to the illustrious wizard Kedrigern and to the beautiful Princess," he said. "I am Banderskeede, High Steward of Prince Grodz. I welcome you in his name. Did you have a pleasant journey?"

"Pleasant enough," Kedrigern said. He was already starting to feel homesick.

Princess, pinching his arm, smiled brightly and said, "It was a succession of memorable moments, Banderskeede. Marvelous weather, and the scenery was gorgeous, imposing, and picturesque."

"The prince will be pleased to hear that. I will convey your satisfaction to him."

"Will we meet Prince Grodz?"

"The prince is occupied with affairs of state at the moment, my lady, but he requests the honor of your company at a private supper this evening."

"We'll be delighted," Princess said.

Banderskeede led them down broad corridors and up elaborate staircases to their quarters in the west wing. Their bedroom was the size of a very large inn. The ornate canopied bed that stood against one paneled wall could have accommodated twelve restless sleepers in comfort. Rich tapestries decked the walls. The furnishings, though few, were exquisite.

"Is this satisfactory?" Banderskeede asked, ducking his head respectfully and rubbing his stump.

"It will do nicely," said Kedrigern.

Princess pinched him again, harder. "It's lovely! You must tell Prince Grodz that we're overwhelmed by his graciousness, exquisite taste, and generosity," she said.

"I shall do so, my lady," said Banderskeede, bowing and backing from the room.

When the servants had brought their luggage, unpacked,

and arranged everything to Princess's satisfaction, she dismissed them. Once they had limped and shuffled their way out, she made a slow circuit of the room, examining everything, looking into corners and behind tapestries, emitting little pleased sounds at the quality and cleanliness of all she saw. At last she joined Kedrigern on the broad balcony overlooking fields, river, and the distant hills. He was sitting in thoughtful silence, gazing up at the fat fair-weather clouds gently drifting southward.

"Isn't it lovely, Keddie? Everything is so beautiful I can hardly believe it," she said, skipping out onto the balcony in an exuberant mood.

"The people aren't so beautiful."

"They're not bad, for peasants."

"I didn't mean that. I've never been anyplace where so many people were missing so many bits and pieces. Haven't you noticed?"

She thought for a moment. "Maybe they're just clumsy."

"Maybe. Or maybe Grodz really is as cruel as rumor makes him out to be."

"No, Keddie, that's impossible. I mean, look at this room. A man with such impeccable taste could never be cruel."

"Good taste and cruelty are not mutually exclusive, my dear. One of the most exquisite pieces of workmanship I ever saw was a headsman's axe. The executioner had it made to order. It cost him a year's wages, but he said it was worth it to work with the best materials."

"I don't care about executioners, Keddie. I can see that Prince Grodz is tasteful, seemly, decorous, genteel, and discriminating. There's no reason to believe that he's cruel."

Kedrigern did not press the point. They watched the sunset, which was spectacular, and then re-entered their quarters to rest. A fire had been kindled against the chill of the late summer evening, and Princess stretched out on the thick bearskin in front of the fireplace to read for a time before changing for supper. Kedrigern, a bit restless, took the opportunity to explore the west wing. He saw nothing, and heard nothing, to verify his suspicions, and returned to the bedroom with a petulant air. Something was wrong, he knew, but he could not pin it down. The uncertainty nagged at him like an unidentifiable sound in the night.

Banderskeede arrived to escort them to the prince's private

apartments. They walked down unfamiliar corridors in procession, with torchbearers before and behind, and Kedrigern was silent until they were ascending the broad staircase that led to Grodz's rooms—then he realized what had been bothering him.

He drew closer to Princess and whispered excitedly, "I don't smell a rat!"

She turned and stared at him, bewildered by the announcement. "What on earth do you mean, Keddie?"

"They wanted me to come here because the place was alive with rats, don't you remember? Well, have you seen, or heard, or smelt any sign of rats?"

"Maybe they left."

"Then why weren't the people celebrating? I haven't seen anyone who looks happy."

"Would *you* look happy if you'd been through a plague of magic rats?" she whispered.

That was a point worth considering. He grunted, frowned, and said no more for a time. But the absence of rats still troubled him. Another thought occurred to him, and he whispered to Princess once again.

"What about the big festival? I don't see any sign of other guests. I tell you, my dear, something's wrong here."

"How can they have a festival until you get rid of the rats?"

"But there aren't any rats!"

"Of course there are, Keddie. Don't be so suspicious."

"Then why haven't we seen any trace of them?"

"Do you expect them to welcome you? You're here to exterminate them."

"They can't know that. Rats aren't *that* smart."

"These are magic rats, aren't they?" Princess whispered impatiently. "You can't expect them to behave like ordinary rats."

Another good point. Instead of reassuring Kedrigern, it troubled him all the more. He could feel something wrong in the very air of Castle Grodzik. For all its taste, refinement, elegance, polish, grace—and whatever else Princess might say of it—Castle Grodzik was an evil place. Something very nasty was going on here. But he could not say what it was, or where it was going on, or who was behind it.

He fingered the medallion that hung around his neck. On an impulse, he raised it to his eye, and peering through the Aperture of True Vision at its center, he took a quick look around. Everything seemed to be just as it should be. Nothing appeared wrong, and this infuriated him. Something *was* wrong, and he wanted to know what.

By this time, they were at the doors of Prince Grodz's private apartment in the north tower, and it was too late to work a spell without being obvious. Kedrigern thought of doing a quick protective magic for himself and Princess anyway, but he did not. After all, he could not be sure what he wanted to protect against. Assassins? Trapdoors? Poison? No. Perhaps he was being silly. Just because he was away from home, he was not necessarily surrounded by wickedness and danger. He promised himself that he would look into things that night, but in the meantime he would enjoy a good meal and the hospitality of Castle Grodzik. If Grodz was as fastidious about the cuisine as he was about the decor, supper should be a memorable experience.

Prince Grodz welcomed them himself, with a sweeping bow more graceful than any Kedrigern had yet encountered in this frequently bowing household. He was a large man, a bit soft around the jowls and ample about the waist; fleshy but not flabby. Handsome in a way that struck Kedrigern as oily and a bit too studied, Grodz was dressed in a short black robe trimmed with ermine, over a simple white shirt and loose black trousers tucked into high black boots that gleamed like polished salvers. His black hair, long and curling, shone almost as brightly as the highlights cast by the black candles that burned everywhere in the room.

"Welcome, a thousand times welcome to the beauty and the wisdom of the age," said Grodz in a voice like flowing treacle. He took Princess's hand and raised it to his lips, where he held it much too long for Kedrigern's liking. Flashing a smile crowded with small yellowish teeth, he gestured to a table set splendidly for three, where gold and silver and crystal glittered in the candlelight. "Do forgive me the simplicity of this humble setting. I indulge myself in an evening alone with my most honored guests before the rout arrive and my duties as a host deprive me of the pleasure of your company," he crooned.

"It's exquisite!" Princess cried. "Everything we've seen in Castle Grodzik so far has been sumptuous, elegant, luxurious, splendid—in a word, princely."

Kedrigern thought of other terms: pretentious, flashy,

tawdry, garish—in a word, tacky. He said nothing, merely nodded noncommittally to Grodz.

"The generous approval of one so beautiful gratifies me beyond utterance, fair lady. But Master Kedrigern is silent. Tell me, Master," said the prince, turning to the wizard with a look of appeal, "does anything displease or offend you? I will have it removed at once."

The thought of Grodz's having himself pitched out the nearest window was a pleasing one, but Kedrigern did not indulge it for long. Smiling politely, he said, "Oh, no. Everything's just fine."

"Ah, you reassure me, Master Kedrigern. I am unacquainted with the ways of wizards, and for a moment I feared I had committed some gaucherie."

"Of course you haven't, Prince Grodz," Princess assured him. "Everything is splendid."

"Again I thank you, gracious lady," said Grodz, offering his arm. "It is said by some that the view of the river by moonlight from this balcony has a certain uncommon beauty. Would you care to see it? And you, too, of course, Master Kedrigern."

"I'm not much for scenery," said the wizard.

"Ah, so. But you are fond of morels, I have learned. And if you lift the cover of that golden dish, you will find sautéed morels of uncommon excellence. I am sure your lovely lady would not object if you sampled them while she and I view the river."

"Thank you, Prince Grodz. I love morels, but I don't often have a chance to enjoy them."

"Then indulge yourself, dear Master. They abound on my lands. I will see that you have a generous supply to take home."

Grodz ushered Princess to the balcony. As soon as they were out of sight, Kedrigern lifted the golden lid of the chafing dish and savored the warm aroma that curled up to greet him. He closed his eyes and sighed. Sautéed morels were a weakness of his, enjoyed all the more because enjoyed so rarely. He began to think better of Grodz. Underneath that oily exterior, he must be a splendid fellow. It was outrageous the way gossip could defame a decent man. And even if he were a consummate swine, sautéed morels atoned for a staggering quantity of sin.

Kedrigern took up a crisp round of bread and spooned a generous helping of morels on top. He bit into it, chewed it slowly, savoring the delicate taste, and moaned softly in sheer delight. Finishing, he took another round of bread, topped it in similar fashion, and consumed it in two bites. A third and fourth helping followed. Then, as he raised the fifth morel-heaped slice of bread to his lips, a chill ran through him. He felt his limbs grow instantly numb. He tried to cry out, but his voice failed him; his paralyzed fingers could not work even a simple spell. Helpless, he crumpled to the floor.

His mind was alert, but his body was devoid of all sensation. Drugged, he thought; and a chilling memory returned, of vague and shadowy rumors about Castle Grodzik that he had so casually dismissed. Husbands and wives entered, the stories said; and if the wife attracted the eye of the prince, no more was heard of them. Kedrigern knew that he had been an absolute fool. Overconfident in his magic, he had never considered the possibility that he might somehow be prevented from using it; but a wizard who cannot speak or gesture is as helpless as a baby.

He lay in impotent rage for a time, and then he heard Princess cry his name and rush to his side. Grodz raised her, leaned over Kedrigern, and said, "Some poisonous mushroom was mixed with the morels. The cook will pay for this."

"But what about Kedrigern? What can we do for him?!"

"I will have him taken at once to my bedchamber. My personal physician will attend him."

"Oh, my poor Keddie! Can he save my Keddie?"

"Your husband will be up and about by morning, fair lady. If not, the physician will be flayed along with the cook."

"Flayed? Prince Grodz, you mustn't . . . ," Princess said, shocked.

"One must keep up standards. Otherwise, workmanship becomes shoddy. If you will permit me, Princess, I will summon men to bring your husband to my bedchamber."

Princess knelt beside Kedrigern, took his face in her hands, and gazed down on him with tear-filled eyes. He could not even blink to catch her attention. She kissed his forehead, and pressed her cheek to his. He heard her sobs, and he could do nothing.

Grodz returned with two sturdy, sullen-looking men. "This is Master Kedrigern, a great wizard and an honored guest in

Castle Grodzik," he told them. "He has suffered a mishap with the sautéed morels. He is to be conveyed at once to my chambers and placed in the bed of Prince Vulbash, do you understand?"

They understood. They lifted Kedrigern by shoulders and ankles and carried him from the room. The last sounds he heard were Princess's muffled sobs and the comforting voice of Prince Grodz.

As they made their way from the apartment, Kedrigern began to reconsider. Certainly, Grodz was doing his best to make amends. Cooks did make mistakes; especially with mushrooms. Rumors could not be trusted. And aside from the paralysis, he did not feel all that bad. Perhaps he had judged Grodz too hastily.

Then he became aware that they were going down, and had been going down for some time, flight after flight of stone steps. Down, not upward to the prince's bedchamber. Kedrigern began to feel very bad indeed.

Somewhere deep below the castle the stairs ended, and they entered a dark cell where the wizard was placed none too gently on a table, like a slab of meat. A torch flared to life somewhere out of his line of sight. He heard his two bearers settle into creaking seats, sigh with relief, and catch their breath.

"Heavy for a slim one, isn't he?" a voice observed.

"It's the drug. Makes them go all limp."

After a brief silence, the first voice said, "Time to get the bed of Prince Vulbash ready for the next guest."

The other gave a snuffly, sniggering laugh. "This one's been a long time coming. They'll give him a good welcome."

"It's either feast or famine down there."

The two were again silent. Then the first speaker rose, to the relieved creaking of whatever he had been seated on, and said, "Let's be about it, Jegg. Sooner we start, sooner we're done."

More creaking, and a great weary sigh, and the other man said, "Right enough, Thubb. Is anyone around to help us?"

"The other boys are all busy."

"I hopes we can manage. That lid gets heavier each time."

"We can handle it, Jegg. Come on."

Kedrigern, flat on his back staring at the shadowed ceiling, could see nothing of the goings-on around him. He listened carefully, for the brief conversation had stirred a fragile hope.

His immediate problem was to stop Thubb and Jegg from doing whatever it was they intended to do. He had no clear idea what or where the bed of Prince Vulbash was, but he was certain that it was not a place he wanted to be; he had a feeling that it involved rest of a permanent nature. He had to avoid it, and in his present state only an act of concentrated mental power could help him.

Unfortunately, mental enchantment was his weak point. As an apprentice, he had enjoyed working with his hands, and concentrated on gesticulatory magic. His advanced study had introduced him to incantations and verbal spells. Mental enchantment was a field he had left almost unexplored—and now it was all he had.

He heard much grunting and muted swearing, and the squeal of a rope in a pulley. Stone grated on stone. Grunting again, louder. Kedrigern gathered all the force he could and directed it to the object being raised by the two men, tripling its weight for a split second.

That was sufficient. He heard a great ringing crash. The room shook, and there was a howl of pain.

"Me back! Me back's broke, Thubb! I told you we needed help!" cried the voice of Jegg.

"Easy, now, it's just a strain," said his companion.

"I can't straighten up, you fool! I'm ruined for life! If Prince Grodz sees me like this, he'll toss me into Vulbash's bed with his own hands!" Jegg whined, his voice a mixture of pain and terror.

"The prince wouldn't do that, Jegg."

"Of course he would! And he'd probably throw you down with me!"

Thubb was silent for a moment, then he said, "Let's get you out where I can take a look at you. Maybe I can do something."

"Zinch, over in the west dungeon, is good with back problems. Can you help me over there, Thubb?"

"What about this one? We didn't get the lid open enough to drop him down."

"He's not going anywhere, is he? They'll come up and get him before long. They're hungry enough. Come on, Thubb."

Kedrigern heard footsteps, and then the slamming of a huge door, and then there was silence. He did his best to move, but his body was inert. He was able to shift his eyes slightly, and blink, but voice and body were still lost to his control.

He heard scuffling, and squeaking, and low small voices. There was a scratching sound nearby, and then he felt a weight on his stomach, and on his chest, and suddenly he was looking in the beady eye of a large gray rat.

"Why don't we ever get a nice fat one?" said a little voice near his head.

"He'll do. He's on the slim side, but he'll do," said another.

"What do you think, Fred? Is he all right?"

"Looks fine to me."

"You want to watch out for poison. That time they threw us the poisoned one, we lost some good chaps."

"You're always worrying, Jerry."

"Well, you can't be too careful. Why didn't they chuck this one down to us, like the others?"

"One of the jailers hurt his back. You heard him yell."

"All the same, it looks funny to me."

"Oh, shut up and eat your dinner, Jerry!"

The rat on Kedrigern's chest had been silent all this time. He sat on his haunches cocking his head this way and that, studying the wizard closely as he rubbed his forepaws together in a way that reminded Kedrigern unpleasantly of a man washing his hands before tucking in to a hearty meal.

"Here, now. Just a minute," said the gray rat. "I think I know this bloke."

"Introduce us, Alf, and then let's fall to," said a tiny voice, and general laughter followed.

The gray rat silenced the merriment with a glare. "If this is the man I think it is, he can help us."

Kedrigern's heart gave a leap.

"Who is he, then, Alf?" a rat cried.

"Yes, Alf, tell us who the fellow is!" demanded another.

"He's Kedrigern of Silent Thunder Mountain, that's who he is! He's a wizard!" Alf announced triumphantly. "He saved my brother Mat and all his friends from the barbarians!"

"Here, now, Alf—how can you be sure he's the one?" a rat asked.

"Mat described him to me a dozen times. And look here,

around his neck. It's a medallion of the Wizards' Guild! This is Kedrigern, right enough."

Angry crowd noises rose all around, and Kedrigern's spirits faltered. Despite Alf's enthusiasm, wizards did not seem to be popular with his fellow rats.

"Kedrigern knows more about counterspells than any other wizard alive, you silly nits!" Alf cried, rearing up and waving his forepaws dramatically. "He can change us back into men!"

"Can we trust him, Alf? It was a wizard turned us into rats, you know," someone said.

"You can trust Master Kedrigern," Alf said firmly, and Kedrigern silently blessed him for his excellent judgment.

"Look here, Alf, before we gets our hopes up—is he alive?" another rat asked.

"Of course he's alive. Look at his eyes. And do you smell the sautéed morels? That's how Grodz slips them the drug. He'll start coming round in a few hours. Meanwhile, we'd better get him to a safe place before the jailers come back. The end cell is empty—we'll take him up there. Jerry, you get the rest of the gang. Bob, you bring up a few rags and bones to scatter around, so's the jailers won't get suspicious," Alf said briskly, in the manner of one who is accustomed to command.

In a very short time, Kedrigern was gliding smoothly down the dimly lit passage, supported on the backs of two score husky rats. It was a much more comfortable way to travel than the method of his descent, and the rats were far more solicitous of his bodily well-being than Jegg and Thubb had been, but his mind was still in a turmoil. He had no idea how long he had been helpless; it was surely more than an hour. According to Alf, he could expect to be paralyzed for several hours more. And what was to become of Princess in that time?

She was innocent and trusting. She would be defenseless against the smooth and practiced guile of Prince Grodz. Magic might have protected her, but by her own admission, Princess had not yet mastered serious spelling. She would lack that instinctive sureness of touch, the instantaneous choice of just the right spell for the situation that came only with experience. Maybe she could run. There was no point in fighting—she was agile, but not strong; Grodz could easily overpower her and force his wicked will upon her. Even now . . . no, surely not until after supper, Kedrigern told himself . . . not even

Grodz was that depraved. If anything, he would delay, savoring her helplessness, watching and waiting, leering and sneering, as the gentle dove fluttered ever nearer the cruel snare.

If Grodz savored his victory long enough, Princess might be rescued before the worst had befallen her. And if not, then Grodz would answer for it; and his answer would be long and complicated, Kedrigern promised himself that.

Under Alf and Jerry's supervision, Kedrigern was deposited on a stone shelf in a dark, empty cell. Foul-smelling straw was heaped over him to conceal him from view, and then there was nothing for it but to wait. Alf perched near his ear. In a subdued voice, he explained the situation at Castle Grodzik.

"I know you won't care to wait around and listen to me once you're up and about, Master Kedrigern," said Alf, very sensibly, "so I thought I'd tell you what's going on here while we're waiting."

"Tell him about that rotten wizard, Alf," said a thin little rat angrily.

"All in its proper time, Jack. You see, Master Kedrigern, we were brought here under false pretenses, as I daresay you and most of the others were. We were just finishing up a wall-and-moat job for Martin the Inexorable, way up to the north, when Grodz's messenger came and made us a staggering great offer if we'd come and do some very confidential work for the prince. Secret staircases, hidden passages—that sort of thing."

"We're very good at that, sir," said a large, placid rat at Alf's side. "Done a lot of it, we have."

"Right you are, Dan. Anyway, down we came to Castle Grodzik, and we worked on this place for three years. It was just after Prince Vulbash the Kindly had dropped out of sight and Grodz taken over. We installed some of the neatest secret corridors and hidden entrances you'll ever see, Master Kedrigern, and we were right proud of our work. Then when we asked Prince Grodz for our pay—"

"Rotten stinking wizard turned us all into rats!" Jack blurted.

"That's the truth, Master Kedrigern," Alf said soberly. "For a time we tried to harass Grodz into changing us back and giving us our money, but he was too much for us. He's a cruel, hard man, Grodz is. He drove us down here, down into the pit where he had flung poor old Vulbash, and put that big stone slab over it. For a while, we thought we'd starve down here. It was bad times."

"Then he threw that wizard down," Dan said.

"Just in time, too," one of the crowd added, and his words were received with approving murmurs.

"It kind of went against the grain, Master Kedrigern, but food is food, and we were hungry. And after all, we're rats."

Kedrigern understood and sympathized, and wished he could say so. But all he could manage was a faint grunt. Small as it was, it sent Alf into a state of high exhilaration.

"Hear that, lads? He's coming round!" the rat cried in a joyous little voice. "We'll be men again before you know it!"

Kedrigern knew, and intensely felt, every passing instant; but in truth it was not long before he could move stiffly and speak intelligibly. As he swept away the straw covering him and pulled himself erect, the rats gathered in a semicircle, balanced on their haunches, looking up at him expectantly.

"You've saved my life, gentlemen, and—I sincerely hope —the honor of my wife. That remains to be seen. But first, is everyone here?" he said.

Alf made a quick headcount and assured him, "All here, Master Kedrigern!"

"Very well." Kedrigern extended his arms and looked down on his rescuers. "I want you to close your eyes tightly. Now, take five deep breaths, very slowly, and hold the fifth." He began to speak in a deep monotone, working intricate figures with his hands. The words came faster and faster, and then he brought his hands together with a loud clap, and suddenly the little cell was very crowded, as forty-seven husky working men, stonemasons and sappers and woodcarvers, stood where forty-seven rats had been an instant before.

Kedrigern raised his hands to silence their happy uproar. Alf sprang to his side to assist him, whispering, "Quiet, lads! We don't want them to know anything just yet."

"Where do we start, Alf?" said one large man in a deep slow voice.

"The armory, Dan. There's a passage that will let us in by a secret door. Once we're armed, we can spread out."

"Is there a way I can get to the west wing unseen?" Kedrigern asked.

"There's a private staircase, and a secret corridor that opens into the chimney corner. I'll show you the way."

"Thank you, Alf, and good luck. I'd like to be going with you, but when I think of Princess in that villain's clutches . . ."

"Say no more, Master Kedrigern. Just between us, I don't think we'll have much trouble. There's few in this castle willing to fight for Grodz."

Alf led the way from the dungeons to a staircase landing, where he paused before a blank wall of smooth stone. He studied the surface for a moment, then reached up and pressed three of the smaller stones in sequence. The wall swung open without a sound. Alf glanced at the wizard, a workman's pride in his eyes.

"Go to the left, up the staircase, and take the second door on the right," he said. "All you have to do is press. The doors all open from this side."

Kedrigern clasped Alf's hand firmly, and waved a farewell to all the others. "Best of luck, men," he said, and turned to the left.

His torch revealed a surprisingly neat passageway: no dust, no bats, and scarcely a cobweb to be seen. It appeared that the secret corridors of Castle Grodzik were busy thoroughfares.

At the second door he paused for a moment to choose his magic. Grodz was not going to get off easy, and if he had anyone with him, they were in for the same treatment. When he was set, Kedrigern worked an all-purpose protective spell, doing his best not to confront the fact that this is what he should have done hours ago, when he first suspected that something was amiss. He placed his fingertips against the narrow door and pushed very gently.

It swung open silently. Kedrigern slipped out into the chimney corner and stood for a moment, listening. He heard no sound save the crackle and the low mutter of the fire. He sidled around the flames and peered into the chamber. There was no evidence of disarray, no sign of pursuit and struggle. He wondered, for an instant, if Grodz had carried Princess off to his own bedchamber—and then he saw Grodz's gleaming black boots standing by the bedside.

He sprang into the chamber, arms flung wide, and cried, "Turn and face your doom, Grodz! It is I, Kedrigern of Silent Thunder Mountain, come to avenge—"

"Keddie! Is it really you?" said a startled voice behind him. "Princess!"

She jumped from the chair by the opposite side of the fire.

Books tumbled to the floor unheeded as she ran to Kedrigern's arms.

"You're well, fit, and sound! He didn't hurt you!" she said, her words muffled by the kisses she rained upon him.

"And you, my dear—he didn't—"

"He tried, Keddie. But he didn't succeed."

Kedrigern gave a long sigh of relief and held her close for a time, too happy to speak. She was safe, he was alive, Grodz was thwarted. All was well.

"What happened to you, Keddie? Did he poison you?"

"He put a paralyzing drug in the sautéed morels. He assumed that if I couldn't speak or gesture, I'd be helpless. And he was almost right."

"But you outwitted him!" she said, hugging him.

"I had some help. What about you, my dear? How did you escape him?"

"Grodz insisted on escorting me to our chambers. To protect me from the rats, he claimed. I remembered what you had said, about not smelling a rat, and I was especially observant, circumspect, and wary all the way here. There wasn't a hint of rat, so I began to suspect his motives."

"Good girl. Clever girl. Excellent thinking."

"He acted the perfect gentleman. He even insisted that I bolt the door from inside—"

"The insidious swine!" Kedrigern snarled.

"—But my suspicions were aroused. I changed into my robe, and settled by the fire with my books. I wanted to be ready. After a time, I heard a noise, and there was Grodz, standing by the bed, very quietly removing his boots. He must have slipped in by a secret door."

"He did."

"Well, it didn't take long to figure out what he was planning to do, so—"

"The villain!"

"—I let him have it. I read it straight from the book."

Kedrigern looked down into her jubilant face, puzzled. "You let him have a stream of synonyms? What good did that do?"

"Oh, no. I was reading the *other* book, Keddie," she said. She dashed to the scattering of books that lay beside the chair and brought one to him, displaying the words embossed in red on the black cover: *Spells For Every Occasion*.

"Wonderful, my dear! I'm proud of you, truly I am. Tell me, which one did you use? How did it work?"

Princess, looking very pleased with herself, pointed to the boots. "Why don't you ask Grodz?"

Kedrigern walked over, peered into one boot, and finding nothing, looked into the other. There was Prince Grodz, small and helpless and very very angry. Kedrigern let out a great roar of laughter. He took Princess by the hands, and they danced in a ring around the boot.

Princess collapsed on the bed, laughing. Kedrigern looked down at Grodz, a broad smile on his face. "Well, Prince Grodz, how do you like it?" he asked cheerfully.

The prince, enraged, attempted to hop out of the boot but fell back. He glared up at Kedrigern with his jeweled eyes and puffed himself out in his most threatening manner.

"Brereep!" he said.

···❧ *Fourteen* ❧···

and one clear call for me

CASTLE GRODZIK FELL to Alf and his men without a struggle. No one, it appeared, had ever really been on Grodz's side. The enthusiasm with which his jailers had jailed, his torturers had tortured, and his executioners had executed had all been a sham. Actually, they had carried out their work with the deepest loathing and reluctance, compelled to cruelty by fear of the greater cruelty of Grodz toward anyone who displeased him.

Or so they claimed. And after thumping a few heads and kicking a few posteriors, Alf and the others decided to accept the lugubrious protestations of innocence and settle down to enjoy the fruits of victory. It was, they agreed, much nicer and far less messy to be heroic liberators than agents of vengeance.

Though he felt no ill effects whatsoever, Kedrigern—at the adamant insistence of Princess—spent the next two days lolling about their chambers in a warm robe, sleeping late, being tucked in, and sung to, and fed tidbits, and generally cosseted and coddled, like a sick child. It was not unpleasant, but two days of it was quite enough for him. On the third morning of the post-Grodz era he was up early, dressing in his customary clothes, eager for something to do.

"Keddie, are you sure you're all right?" Princess inquired earnestly as he tugged his boots on. "Don't you think it would be wise to rest, repose, and recuperate for one more day?"

"I feel fine, my dear. Bubbling with health. Bursting with energy."

"Maybe so, but remember, you were poisoned."

"I wasn't poisoned, I was drugged. It's a different thing altogether."

"I still think you ought to take care of yourself," said Princess.

"What I need most right now is something to do. And I'm sure there's plenty to be done in Castle Grodzik. There are always a lot of loose ends dangling about when a tyrant is deposed."

"Things seem to be going smoothly so far."

"I'm glad to hear it," said the wizard. Rising, he reached for his tunic. "I'll just look around. If everything is going well, we can start for home all the sooner."

"Must we rush home? I thought we might stay here for a few weeks."

He looked at her in horror. "A few *weeks?*"

"It's nice here, now that Grodz is out of power. Everyone's grateful to us. Let's enjoy it, Keddie."

"A few weeks?" he repeated, making it sound like a death knell. "What about my work? And Spot? Think of poor Spot, all alone, worrying. . . . And my clients! What about my clients?"

"We never go anywhere. I want to enjoy it while I can."

"But a few *weeks . . .*"

"All right, then, a week. We'll stay a week. It's just so nice to get away. We really needed a vacation, Keddie."

"What vacation? Is this your idea of a vacation? Did we need betrayal? Dungeons? Assaults on your virtue?" Kedrigern demanded, his voice rising with each phrase. "Did I need poison?"

"You weren't poisoned, you were drugged," she said calmly. "Besides, think how nicely things worked out. Think of the good we did."

"Think of the strain. The anxiety. This is what happens when you travel, my dear. I've said it all along, but you never listen. Now you know. Travel is deadening."

"A week, Keddie."

He flung up his hand in despairing surrender. "All right, a week."

Things were indeed going smoothly at Castle Grodzik, as Kedrigern learned during his stay. Alf and his companions, though they lacked experience in running a principality, were honest workmen, accustomed to getting things done in an orderly fashion and repairing structures that had fallen into dilapidation. These were precisely the skills most needed at Castle Grodzik. During his brief sway, Grodz had directed all his efforts toward his machinations to the neglect of everything else, and now there was a good deal that required fixing. Alf and his men went to work, and everyone at the castle pitched in willingly.

The household staff, no longer working under the constant threat of flaying, flogging, or mutilation, were a tad slower but much more cheerful. They could not do enough for their liberators. The master cook, when he recovered from the shock of learning how Grodz had tampered with his work, insisted upon serving Kedrigern generous portions of superbly prepared, and unadulterated, sautéed morels each day for lunch. The court calligrapher, a man who had spent the reign of Grodz doing his best to remain anonymous and unobtrusive, emerged from the scriptorium to present Princess with an elaborate scroll proclaiming her Grand Enchantress and Deliverer of the People of Castle Grodzik. It was on fine vellum, with illuminated capitals and at its top a charming depiction of a very angry toad glaring out of a boot. She was quite touched by the citation, and showed it to everyone.

In the early afternoon of the day before they were to depart, a dusty and bedraggled stranger arrived on foot at the castle. He stumbled through the gate, into the courtyard, as Kedrigern was walking off a huge platter of sautéed morels. Kedrigern nodded to him, and the newcomer addressed him in a weak, despairing voice.

"There is thirsty I am, good sir. May I have a drink from yon well? I will then crawl off somewhere to die," he said feebly.

"Are you sick, my boy?"

"Look you, now, if I were sick I could hope to get well. But I am Red Gruffydd, and there is no help for that."

The name rang a bell. Kedrigern stared hard into the dim

blue eyes, scratched his chin, concentrated, and at last said, "Red Gruffydd, of course! But what are you doing here, in such a grim mood? Last I heard, you were household bard to a great lord."

"If I may have a sip of water to wash away the dust of the road, I will relate the whole dismal tale. Otherwise, I will die of thirst altogether."

"Have all the water you want, my boy," said Kedrigern, taking the mournful youth's arm and leading him to the well. He drew up a bucket of cold, clear water and handed it to Red Gruffydd, who drank off nearly half of it without a pause, poured a bit over his head, and then noisily drank the rest. Gasping with relief and repletion, Red then sat down in the shade of the well.

With the dirt washed away, he was very pale. His eyes were light blue rimmed in red, his brows almost invisible. Kedrigern recalled Rhys's description of him as "whining, whey-faced Red Gruffydd," and judged it unkind, but accurate.

"You have heard of me then, have you?" Red asked.

"Yes. Someone . . . a person I met mentioned your name," Kedrigern said.

"Ah, there is famous I was, sir. *Bardd teulu* to Llewellyn Da when I was a mere boy, so I was, and a favorite of the king himself. The king would visit the castle of Llewellyn Da regularly for no reason but to hear me tell a tale. But that is all over now, and I am *bardd teulu* no more. It is the life of a wandering minstrel for me, or begging along the high road," said Red with a sigh. "Maybe I will even have to work."

"What happened?"

The ex-bard shrugged listlessly. "That is something we would both like to know, sir. One night I had the court on its feet, cheering and throwing gold pieces. The very next day, look you, I told Llewellyn Da a story, and he said it was the worst thing he ever heard in his life, and threw me out."

"Some people don't have a very good sense of humor."

"It was not a funny story at all, it was a tale of mystery. Would you like to hear it, and judge for yourself?"

"Why not?" said Kedrigern. He settled into the shade, stretching out his legs, and relaxed. A good lunch, a sunny afternoon, and now a mystery tale told by a first-rate bard: a pleasant way to pass the time, he thought comfortably.

"There was a pretty young milkmaid, and she married a

great king," Red Gruffydd began. "Now, you may not believe that, and I cannot make much sense of such a match myself, but there you are, there is no telling with some people . . . a milkmaid and a king. Hard to say what things are coming to, when milkmaids and kings forget their proper places. But there is not much you and I can do about these things. It was a great wedding, and when the feasting and the dancing were done, they went to live at the king's castle. Now, this king—I think I should have told you this at first—this king had been married eight times before, and each of his wives—no, *nine* times, it was *nine* wives he had and the milkmaid number ten—each of his wives had disappeared shortly after coming to the castle, and no one knew how or why. The milkmaid, Betty—yes, her name was Betty—she was completely in the dark about the disappearing wives. That should not surprise anyone, though. What should a milkmaid know about the goings-on at the castle, I ask you?"

"Not a thing."

"Right you are. And she did not. But the very night they came to the castle, the king said to her, 'Lottie, there is one . . .' Of course, *that* was her name, Lottie was her name. Am I confusing you?"

"No. Please go on," said Kedrigern.

"'Lottie,' he said, 'there is one thing you must never do, if we are to be happy together. You must never look behind the green door at the end of the hall.' And Lottie said, 'I will not.' And the next day the chamberlain of the castle took her aside and said, 'My lady, there is one thing you must never do, if you and my lord are to be happy together. You must never look behind the green door at the end of the hall.' And Lottie said, 'I will not.' And after dinner the chief steward whispered to her, 'My lady, there is one thing you must never do, if you and my lord are to be happy together. You must never look behind the green door at the end of the hall.' And Lottie said, 'I will not.' And that night, as she was preparing for bed, her maid, Betty—ah, *that* is what confused me, look you, the *maid's* name was Betty, and the milkmaid's was Lottie— Betty, the maid, said, 'My lady, there is one thing you must never do, if you and my lord are to be happy together. You must never look behind the green door at the end of the hall.' And Lottie said, 'I will not.' Are you following the story so far?"

Kedrigern, caught in the middle of a wrenching yawn, nodded vigorously. Red cleared his throat and went on.

"That night, Lottie woke up and noticed immediately that her husband was not in the bed. She called his name four times, but he—no *three* times, it was—she called his name three times, but he did not answer. She slipped from the bed, quiet as a mouse, look you, and went to the door, and peeked out, and she saw her husband the king coming out of the green door at the end of the hall. In a great panic, she ran to the bed and jumped in and pulled the covers—he was carrying a candle, you understand, and that is how she could see him in the dark in the middle of the night—she pulled the covers over her head and pretended to be asleep. And the king entered the room, and took a little golden key from around his neck on a string, and he put it into a little silver box and put the box in the bottom of a great wooden chest at the foot of the bed. Then he climbed into bed and went to sleep, and in a little while, Lottie went to sleep, too."

And so will I, if this goes on much longer, thought the wizard. For politeness' sake, he tried to look interested.

"So Lottie never looked behind the green door, and they lived happily ever after. They had their little quarrels now and then, you understand, but nothing serious," Red concluded, turning to Kedrigern with a satisfied smile.

"Is that the end?"

"It is."

"What about the green door?"

Red looked hurt and puzzled. "How am I supposed to know about that? I was never in the bloody castle! And if I had been there, do you think I am silly? If everyone says, 'You must never look behind the green door at the end of the hall,' you will not catch this fellow taking a peek. Do you think I am not as smart as a milkmaid?"

"But people might want to know what's behind the green door."

"Well, I cannot help them there, and I would not even if I could. This is a tale of mystery, and if I tell everyone what is behind the green door, the mystery is all spoiled."

"I hadn't thought of it that way. So that's the story you told Llewellyn Da, and he threw you out."

"Look you, sir, he barely gave me time to tell the ending where they get to live happily ever after."

Kedrigern was pensive for a time, rubbing his chin and looking off into the distance. Finally, he asked, "How did you get to be a household bard in the first place, Red?"

"It was not easy," said the youth. He sounded uncomfortable.

"I'm sure it must have been very challenging, but how does one go about it? Are there auditions?"

Red looked around cautiously, then leaned closer to Kedrigern and in a soft voice asked, "Do you believe in charms and spells, now?"

"I've known such things to be very effective."

"They are indeed. My brother Ivor and I studied all sorts of spells and charms as part of our training, and one of our favorites was the charm for getting ahead. Ivor was very good at it, look you, but he could never get it to work for himself. He could get jobs for his brothers and cousins and even for total strangers, but not for himself."

"Rather embarrassing for Ivor, I should think."

"He did well enough on commissions that it did not bother him overmuch. It was Ivor who worked the charm that got me the place with Llewellyn Da. There was a young fellow who looked to have it all sewed up—a nasty surly type he was, too, named Rhys ap Gwallter, but with a voice ten times better than mine and more good spells and charms at his command than our whole family together—and Ivor worked a charm on Llewellyn Da that made the young man's voice sound in his ear like the creaking of an outhouse door, while I was made to sound like a nightingale. So I was made *bardd teulu*, and Rhys ap Gwallter went off to work the roads as a minstrel."

"He must have been angry."

"He uttered threats that would shrivel the guts of a stone troll," Red Gruffydd said darkly.

Rhys had been very close about his plans, and left the cottage on Silent Thunder Mountain without giving any indication of his destination. Kedrigern was certain that he was seeing evidence of Rhys's handiwork, and thought it best to keep his surmises to himself. He did not like to get involved in artistic controversies.

"Well, now that you're at liberty, Red, what will you do?" he asked.

"I will starve for a while, and eventually I will die a miserable death," the youth said gloomily.

"Not much to look forward to. Is there no alternative?"

"Look you, sir, I am a trained and practiced bard, and it has dawned on me that without the help of powerful charms I am not a very good one. That limits my options."

"Listen, Red . . . there's been a big change here at Castle Grodzik. New management, new ideas. It could mean opportunity for a bright young man. You look for Alf, and tell him Kedrigern sent you. He may have something for you," said the wizard.

"A good meal, do you think?" Red asked, his eyes lighting up.

"A job, maybe."

Red's face fell. He sighed and hauled himself to his feet. "Afraid I was that it might come to this. Tell me, good sir, does this Alf like stories?"

"I think he prefers good work."

Shaking his head fatalistically, Red walked off, toward the castle. Kedrigern watched him go, then dusted himself off and went to his chambers to complete the packing. Tomorrow was the day of departure.

Much of that evening and a good part of the following morning was given over to hearty embraces, warm hand-clasps, protestations of undying friendship, and promises to get together for dinner very soon. Princess had a dozen offers of assistance in mounting her horse. When she was safely astride, Kedrigern mounted his great black steed, for which he still had not settled on a name. Alf, Dan, and Fred gathered around him for a last leave-taking.

"That's a fine horse, Master Kedrigern. I've never seen the like of him," Alf said.

Kedrigern patted the beast's shaggy neck. "He used to belong to a giant barbarian swordsman. A chap named Buroc."

Fred said, "I thought so. It looks like the kind of horse a giant barbarian swordsman would ride."

"Those giant barbarian swordsmen, they be hard men," Dan observed solemnly.

Kedrigern smiled. "Buroc is harder than most. Before I go, I'd like to ask you something."

"Anything you want, Master Kedrigern," Alf said, and the others nodded in agreement.

"You mentioned a wizard—the one who turned you into rats, and was later flung down into the pit. Do you recall his name? It's not really important, just professional curiosity, but I'd appreciate it if you could tell me."

"Funny name, it were," Dan said. "Like 'Chatterax,' I think."

Fred, grimacing with the effort to remember, said, "It was something like that. Maybe 'Spatterax.' That sounds right to me."

"No, 'Scadderall.' That was it," said Alf confidently.

"Could it have been 'Jaderal'?" Kedrigern suggested. They looked at one another and then at him, their expressions showing great uncertainty.

"We only had dealings with him twice, you see. The first time we were confused, suddenly finding ourselves rats, and the second time we were angry and starving," Alf explained, looking rather embarrassed.

"He weren't much of a wizard, Master Kedrigern," Dan volunteered. "Down in pit, he tried to work a spell against us, but he mixed it all up."

"He wasn't much of a meal, either. Tasted like dogmeat," said Fred with a wry face.

"That sounds like Jaderal."

"Not a friend of yours, I hope, Master Kedrigern," Alf said.

"A bitter enemy, Alf. Jaderal got exactly what was coming to him. And speaking of just deserts, did a young minstrel with red hair come to see you yesterday?"

"He did. I agreed to give him food and lodging for a week while he composes a ballad about the liberation of Castle Grodzik, with special verses about your lovely wife and yourself, if it pleases you."

"It likes us well," said Princess, smiling radiantly upon them all.

"If he makes us a good ballad, we can keep him on as our bard. If he does not..." Alf shrugged, and concluded, "There's always room for another hand in the scullery."

"Couldn't ask for fairer treatment," said the wizard.

Princess and Kedrigern rode out the gateway of Castle Grodzik waving to well-wishers on all sides, clasping the eager hands thrust up at them by the liberated subjects of Prince Grodz, smiling and nodding and feeling very much the celebrities of the moment. Again and again on the long straight road to the mountain pass they were stopped by little knots of cheering peasants who gathered around to press gifts of food upon them and wish them well. Whenever they looked back, they saw diminutive figures eagerly waving, and heard distant voices raised in tribute. It was all very pleasant.

A short way beyond the pass they stopped to eat and rest. Kedrigern spread a blanket on a knoll overlooking a pleasant pond, and they reclined in comfort to a lunch of fresh fruit and cheese. At intervals during their lunch, Kedrigern noticed Princess gazing gloomily into the water. Her good mood had passed, and she seemed preoccupied. She frowned, and several times she turned to him as if she were about to speak, but it was only as they were rising and making ready to go on that she blurted, "Keddie, I wish I hadn't done it!"

"My dear, whatever do you mean? I thought you were enjoying yourself."

"I turned Grodz into a *toad!* What a terrible thing to do! Even Grodz doesn't deserve to be a toad."

"There are a lot of people around Castle Grodzik who'd say he deserves something much worse."

"They've never been toads. I have. I should have shown compassion and sympathy, but instead . . ." She covered her face with her hands, and in a muffled voice, said, "Sitting in a bog, or a swamp, or a pond day after day . . . losing all track of time . . . forgetting one's past . . . one's own family . . . It's awful, Keddie," she said, looking at him and shuddering.

"For a man like Grodz to forget his past and his family might be all to the good, my dear," Kedrigern said, putting his arm around Princess's shoulders to comfort her. "You mustn't dwell on Grodz. It will only upset you."

"It already has. Oh, Keddie, I do so wish I could remember who my parents are, and where I come from—can't you do something?"

Kedrigern scratched his head thoughtfully. "Amos is no longer available . . . and it's difficult to work an effective spell with so little basic information to go on. . . ." He lapsed into silence, and spoke no more until he had helped Princess onto her horse and was himself mounted, then he drew up beside her and said in a reluctant, tentative way, avoiding her eyes as he spoke, "There's a chance . . . a remote chance . . . *very* remote. . . ."

"There is!?" she cried.

"About a day's ride to the north is the valley of the

Harkeners to the Unseen Enlightened Ones."

"I've never heard you speak of them. Who are they?"

"A bunch of lunatics. There's nothing to fear from them; they're completely harmless. Very kind and gentle people, actually. They listen for voices in the air."

She looked at him narrowly. "There are no voices in the air."

"You know that, my dear, and I know it. I daresay a great many people know it. But the Harkeners to the Unseen Enlightened Ones listen for voices in the air."

"Do they ever hear them?" she asked, fascinated.

"Not so far. But they're firmly convinced that somewhere out there, on another plane of existence, are Enlightened Ones who are trying their best to get through to us with good advice and consoling messages. The trouble is, we don't know how to listen properly. So they've taken it upon themselves to listen in every possible way."

Princess shook her head. "They sound very odd."

"They are. On the other hand, nobody else has been able to tell us anything about your family. I know it's unlikely, but it's the only chance left."

They rode on for a time, both thinking over the possibilities, and at last Princess turned to the wizard and said, "A day's ride?"

"An easy day's ride. A leisurely side trip, no more."

She nodded and said nothing. After a while, she said, "And they're really kind and gentle people?"

"They are kindness itself, my dear. If they've heard anything that might help you, they'll feel bound to tell you. That's the whole point of their listening."

"Only a day each way? We could spare that."

"We certainly could," Kedrigern agreed.

And so they went north, to the valley of the Harkeners to the Unseen Enlightened Ones. Kedrigern's loathing for travel, and his reluctance to be away from his work for more than a few hours, was offset somewhat by his curiosity and by the infinitesimally tiny and utterly irrational possibility that this band of eccentrics might actually be on to something. If one could discover the proper way to listen, and listened long enough and hard enough, perhaps there *was* something to be heard. It seemed worth a slight detour to find out. At best, it could make Princess very happy; at worst, it would cost them

two days' additional travel; and even then, it would provide a
subject for conversation in years to come.

The Harkeners had set up no signs or markers, built no
barriers, posted no guards or watchmen. Kedrigern and Princess had no indication that they were among them until they
came upon a man in a very dirty greenish robe clasping a birch
tree, his ear pressed against the trunk. Kedrigern waved to
him. The man smiled back at him vacantly, but did not move.

"Do you hear anything?" the wizard asked.

"Not yet," the man replied.

"We're here," Kedrigern said to Princess. "Where will I
find the other Harkeners?" he called to the man at the tree.

Without speaking or moving his head, the Harkener indi-
cated by a gesture of his thumb where his fellows were to be
seen. The travelers rode in the direction given. In a very short
time they came to a clearing where about a score of people
sat, stood, or lay about listening, in various postures, to various objects. One man reclined on his side with his ear in a
bowl of cold oatmeal. A woman listened attentively to a large
glove. Others had their ears pressed to items of furniture,
food, and clothing, or stones of assorted sizes; several were
clustered around a large pile of sand. They all appeared to be
quite absorbed in their work. A young lady who had been
listening to a thick slice of buttered rye bread approached the
travelers and greeted them cheerfully.

"Good listening, strangers! Have you heard enlightenment?"

"No. We were hoping you had," Kedrigern replied.

"'It is better to hope than to fall down the well,' as Versel
has heard," she replied cheerfully.

"Very true. Would it be possible to get a drink of water?"

"Of course it is. As Versel hears, 'Fire is only fire, but
water is wet,'" she said.

Princess and Kedrigern silently exchanged a glance. Dis-
mounting, they followed the girl to a well. It was roofed over,
providing cool shade from the afternoon sun. Kedrigern drew
up water for them and their horses, and as he drank, he looked
out at the unmoving Harkeners.

"Has anyone heard anything at all from the Unseen Enlightened Ones?" he asked the girl with the rye bread.

"Only Versel has achieved momentary contact with them.
He has been told many things, but the messages are couched

in a mysterious language, difficult to decipher. Even when deciphered, their meaning is obscure."

"Would it be possible to speak to Versel? I don't want to disturb him if he's busy listening, but I might be able to help in some way. I'm Kedrigern of Silent Thunder Mountain. I'm a wizard. And my wife, Princess, is Grand Enchantress and Deliverer of the People of Castle Grodzik."

"Would you like to see my scroll?" Princess asked.

"That will not be necessary," the girl assured her. "Versel is always glad to hear visitors. You will find him in the building just behind those trees. Forgive me if I do not take you there personally. I must get back to my duties," she said, clapping the slice of bread to her ear.

When they were a safe distance away, Princess asked, "What can that poor girl hope to hear with a piece of buttered bread stuck to her ear?"

Kedrigern shrugged. "Flies?"

"Not much else. I can hardly wait to see what Versel is listening to."

"I hope you're not too disappointed, my dear."

"I didn't expect much, Keddie. And there's always a chance that Versel is hearing something helpful," said Princess, smiling hopefully.

As it turned out, Versel was not listening to anything at the moment. He had a basket of fresh blackberries before him, and a big bowl of clotted cream, and he was dipping the blackberries, one by one, into the cream and eating them, with obvious delight. At sight of Princess and Kedrigern, he waved and gestured to a pair of empty stools standing near his.

"You're eating those berries. I thought you'd be listening to them," Princess said when they were seated.

"I don't listen to fruit anymore. I listen to the gleam," Versel said. "Help yourselves, please. They're delicious," he added, holding out basket and bowl.

They were. When he had consumed his tenth sweet fat juicy berry, Kedrigern wiped his lips and said, "Thank you very much, Versel. What gleam?"

"It isn't here yet. Every evening, when the sun reaches that crack on the floor," Versel said, pointing, "it reflects off a piece of glass stuck in there and sends up a gleam of light. That's what I listen to. It will be coming soon, and you're welcome to listen, if you'd like."

"Can *anyone* hear it?" Princess asked.

"Oh, yes. It doesn't last long, and it doesn't make much sense, but at least we're finally hearing something. It's a real breakthrough for us. And I found it completely by accident one evening when I was listening to some raisins," Versel said, beaming at them.

"You must be very pleased. And proud," Princess said, patting his hand in a fond maternal gesture. Kedrigern studied the crack in the floor and said nothing. He looked somber.

"Just lucky, I guess," said Versel, blushing.

"It comes from the gleam of light, you say? And only when the sun strikes it at a certain angle?" Kedrigern asked.

"That's right. It will be along soon, and you can hear it for yourselves. There's just time to finish these blackberries and settle down for a good listen."

Kedrigern grunted and looked thoughtful.

"Don't expect much," Versel went on, taking a blackberry. "It's mostly gibberish. We *think* we've been interpreting it correctly, but it's hard to be certain. Yesterday, for example, the voice said, 'A puddle, a gooseberry bush, a wooden spoon—these are three things.' At least that's the interpretation that makes the most sense."

Princess, looking uneasy, asked, "Do you know what it means?"

"I'm not a philosopher, I just listen."

"Do you know, Keddie?"

"No," said the wizard distractedly. "That's probably not what he said, anyway."

There was no more talk, as they worked their way through the remaining berries and cream. When they were done, Versel methodically licked the bowl clean, then licked his fingers and wiped them on his plain brown robe. He studied the borderline of light and shadow moving slowly across the floor and warned them, "It's nearly time. Quiet, please."

They drew their stools together and watched the line, now a fingernail's breadth from the crack, inch ever closer. It crept to a straw's width away; then to a hairbreadth; and then a beam of reflected light shot from the floor and a wild yammer of sound filled the air. Shrill, grating, cacophonous, unmistakably a human voice, it was impossible to determine what language it spoke or what its precise mood might be. It could equally well have been in transports of ecstasy or paroxysms of murderous rage; childishly happy or steeped in despair. For several seconds it was everywhere, and then the light moved on, and all was still.

"Did you understand it?" Princess asked, her voice hushed.

"I think it said, 'Bravely paint shoe, living windmill of the pudding,'" said Versel cautiously.

"It didn't sound like that to me," Princess replied. "I couldn't catch everything, but I think it said, 'Drum, drum the paper lake.' Did you understand it, Keddie?" she asked.

"I didn't hear anything like that," said the wizard, looking grim.

Versel rose, stretched, and took up his stool. "Well, that's it for today," he announced. "Sorry it wasn't clearer. It never is. You can stay here if you like. I'm going to sit under a tree until dinnertime."

"We'll be moving on, too. Thanks for the chance to listen, Versel. And for the blackberries and cream."

"Drop in anytime. Good listening," said Versel with a wave of farewell.

There were no other parting words. The rest of the Harkeners were too busy harkening to notice the departure of their visitors; most of them had not even been aware of anyone's arrival. Kedrigern helped Princess to her horse, and they rode for a long time without either one speaking. The wizard seemed lost in thought. Now and then he shook his head, but he did not speak until they had stopped for the night in a clearing by a brook, and then only in response to Princess's glum observation that their trip to the valley of the Harkeners to the Unseen Enlightened Ones had been a complete waste of time, and that they knew no more now than they had when they left Castle Grodzik.

"Not about your family, no," he said, staring into the fire.

"Not about anything! What a lot of nonsense! Listening to fruit and furniture and rye bread, and when they finally hear something, it's 'Drum, drum the paper lake.' Really, Keddie . . . what a shocking fraud!" she said angrily.

"That's not what he said."

"Who?"

"Quintrindus, my dear. I recognized his voice at once."

"What *did* he say?"

"Things I would never repeat in the presence of a lady. He's very angry. And very frustrated." Kedrigern turned to her, smiling faintly. "In a sense, the Harkeners have found what they're looking for. I wouldn't call Quintrindus enlightened, exactly, but he's certainly unseen. And he's definitely on another plane, where Jaderal sent him."

"How can we possibly hear him?"

"There are all sorts of leaks in the spell. Jaderal was always a poor speller. At certain times, under certain conditions of light and shadow, Quintrindus's voice breaks through. Fortunately, he's using one of the old tongues, and it's so distorted that scarcely anyone will be able to understand a thing he says, no matter how closely they listen. He's swearing like a drunken necromancer." With a sigh, the wizard rose and rubbed the small of his back. "Shall we turn in, my dear? We'll get an early start tomorrow."

"Good idea. Will we need protection?"

"A small warning spell should suffice," he said, assisting her to her feet.

"Allow me. I need the practice."

Kedrigern bowed graciously. "I leave everything in the hands of the Grand Enchantress and Deliverer. Choose your spell, my dear."

They completed the trip without further incident, making good time on firm, dry roads. As Silent Thunder Mountain rose before them, Kedrigern's spirits improved. He became more talkative, and his talk was more cheerful than it had been for the past few weeks. Princess took advantage of what she saw as a rare opportunity.

"Well, it wasn't so terrible after all, was it?" she asked.

"What wasn't?"

"The trip to Castle Grodzik. You're always complaining about how awful travel is. I thought this was a very nice trip."

"It was better than some, I must admit. But not every trip gains one praise and gratitude. Far too many trips end in narrow escapes and headlong flight."

"Well, let's try to avoid those," said Princess.

A bit farther on, Kedrigern paused and drew out his medallion. He peered through the Aperture of True Vision, sighting in on their little cottage. All was well: the windows were clean, the dooryard had been swept, the garden was still flourishing, and Spot was busy weeding the flower beds. Kedrigern smiled and sighed with relief.

"It wasn't a bad trip at all," he conceded. "It's nice to have the loose ends tied up. I feel better knowing what's become of Quintrindus and Jaderal."

"And Grodz," Princess said pointedly.

"And Grodz, of course. Very nice work, my dear."

"Thank you. But we still don't know anything about my parents, or my old kingdom."

"Still no memories?"

"Not one," she said with a wistful sigh. "If only the Harkeners really could hear wisdom and good advice from outside, instead of just hearing an unfortunate wizard—"

"Alchemist," Kedrigern corrected her.

"Alchemist, to be sure. Sorry. In any event, they still hear him swear once a day, and that's all. And they can only hear it on sunny days."

"It's probably best that they don't find what they're after," Kedrigern said.

"Why ever do you say that?"

"Success would ruin them. People would flock to their valley. You can't sit and listen to a plate of stewed figs when there are hundreds of people milling around."

"That's true. There'd be huge crowds," said Princess.

"People camping everywhere."

"Building fires."

"Selling food and souvenirs."

"Long lines on the roads."

"Oh, my, yes. They'd be lined up . . ." He paused, groping for the proper phrase. Princess turned to him with a sly smile.

"Three deep?" she said.

Stories
~ of ~
Swords and Sorcery

Prices may be slightly higher in Canada

Available at your local bookstore or return this form to:

ACE
THE BERKLEY PUBLISHING GROUP, Dept. B
390 Murray Hill Parkway, East Rutherford, NJ 07073

Please send me the titles checked above. I enclose _____. Include $1.00 for postage
and handling if one book is ordered; add 25¢ per book for two or more not to exceed
$1.75. CA, IL, NJ, NY, PA, and TN residents please add sales tax. Prices subject to change
without notice and may be higher in Canada.

NAME_____

ADDRESS_____

CITY_____ STATE/ZIP_____

(Allow six weeks for delivery.)